THE WOARD LIFTED ITSELF UP on one arm and turned. The two combatants came face to face. Teyla was a little shaky, but she held the blade out and stood her ground. The Woard saw her. It tried another roar, but the sound was feeble — a shadow of its former strength and rage. It half rose, and it seemed the effort would be too much for it. Teyla looked ready to drop the blade and walk away, but in that second of hesitation the Woard lunged.

Every bit of its remaining life went into that final attack. Teyla staggered back. She held the blade high, and the Woard's weight drove it down over the cold, hard steel. The creature's momentum took it forward, and it fell heavily atop Teyla, who was lost from sight.

"No!" Rodney cried out.

In that moment, the image on the screen dimmed, and grew dark. The panel in the wall closed, and the team were left to stare at one another in shock as the crowd's cheer erupted in the arena above.

STARGATE ATLANTIS™

BRIMSTONE

DAVID NIALL WILSON & PATRICIA LEE MACOMBER

FANDEMONIUM BOOKS

An original publication of Fandemonium Ltd, produced under license from MGM Consumer Products.

Fandemonium Books
PO Box 795A
Surbiton
Surrey KT5 8YB
United Kingdom
Visit our website: www.stargatenovels.com

S T A R G A T E
A T L A N T I S

METRO-GOLDWYN-MAYER Presents
STARGATE ATLANTIS™
JOE FLANIGAN TORRI HIGGINSON RACHEL LUTTRELL JASON MOMOA
with PAUL McGILLION as Dr. Carson Beckett and DAVID HEWLETT as Dr. McKay
Executive Producers BRAD WRIGHT & ROBERT C. COOPER
Created by BRAD WRIGHT & ROBERT C. COOPER

WWW.MGM.COM

ISBN: 978-1-905586-20-2
Printed in the United States of America

CHAPTER ONE

THE AUDIENCE MURMURED in anticipation as a tall, gray-haired man with thick spectacles and a cloud of puffy hair stepped to the podium. There was a tinkle of crystal and a scuffle of chairs as the night reached its climactic moment. The speaker cleared his throat, and the crowd grew silent. He shuffled some note cards and glanced up at the audience.

"I believe you all know why we are here." His voice was dry and brittle, but it carried well. "Tonight we will honor our best and our brightest. I venture to say that if we tried to calculate the combined IQ of this room, we'd need a very powerful computer — but even in such company, one stands out clearly. We here at The Academy of Science bestow this honor annually, and I'm pleased to report that for the first time in our history, the voting is unanimous. Few have distinguished themselves so clearly, and in so many varied fields. I could go on, as many of you know…"

He paused and there was a ripple of laughter.

"But I will not. Without further ado, I'd like to introduce our keynote speaker, a woman we all know and admire, Dr. Elizabeth Weir."

There was an enthusiastic burst of applause. From behind the old man, a slender dark haired woman in a shimmering low-cut evening gown stepped forward. In stark contrast to the first speaker, she was tall, vibrant and attractive, catching the eye of each of those seated below her. She smiled brightly and waved to a few acquaintances in the front rows. She held no notes, but placed her hands almost provocatively on the podium and leaned down to the microphone.

"I am pleased," she said, "and honored, to have been chosen to introduce one of Earth's finest minds — possibly the most brilliant physicist we've known — certainly the most brilliant in my lifetime. This is a man I have served with proudly, who has saved my life on countless occasions, and who I consider to be the foremost human expert on Ancient technologies. I'd like to tell you all a few things you might not already know about this amazing man…"

As she spoke, Dr. Rodney McKay rose slowly from his seat in the back of the room. He knew she would go on for a while, praising his mind, but it was her smile he was really interested in. He was certain she was looking directly at him as she spoke. He thought, maybe, there was something more than usual in that smile — something inviting. It was the most important night of his life, and he intended to milk it for everything it was worth.

He worked his way down the row of seats toward the center aisle, apologizing graciously to those he passed and shaking a few hands. They all knew him. Many of them owed their own careers and research to his work. It was the culmination of a lifetime of research and experimentation.

Suddenly, Dr. Weir's speech was interrupted by a sharp buzzing tone. Rodney spun, confused, searching the room for the source of the sound, but he could find nothing. He shook his head, and as he did, the room faded. His darkened quarters came into focus, and the blaring sound resolved itself into the buzzer on his door.

He rolled over, checked the time — 0300, then rolled back and closed his eyes. It wasn't until the third buzz that he rolled off his bunk, wrapped up in his blanket, and stepped to the door. He pressed the Intercom button.

"Who is it?"

"It's Cumby, sir." The voice was bright, cheerful, and irritated Rodney through to the bone.

"Cumby, do you know what time it is? There's a device in the lab — you'll know it from the digital readout with all the numbers and pretty colors? It's called a clock, and we use it to decide when is, and when is not, a good time to wake people up."

"Colonel Sheppard has something on the long range scan that he thinks you ought to see."

Rodney glanced back at his rumpled pillow longingly, and then sighed. "This had better be good."

He dressed quickly, ran his hand through his hair in place of a comb and blearily rubbed sleep from his eyes. A moment later, he stepped into the hall and turned toward the lab. Not many others were up and about, a fact Rodney considered the one positive thing about three o'clock in the morning.

When he reached the lab, he saw Cumby, who was one of his newest lab technicians, bent over a monitor screen. The young man was tall and thin, completely bald, and at that moment the most irritating thing in Dr. McKay's universe — next to the slender, dark haired officer standing *beside* Cumby. Rodney stepped up beside Sheppard and glanced down at the monitor.

"What is it that's so fascinating you dragged me out of

a sound sleep?"

"Look for yourself."

Rodney was already looking. He pushed Cumby out of the way and scanned the image on the screen. He frowned, twisted a number of knobs in quick succession, and stared again.

"I've recalibrated the scan three times," Cumby said. "No matter what I do, the readings on MC4-502 are still way off."

Rodney glanced up at the young man and scowled.

"You think?" he said. "I don't know why you recalibrated. Wait…I know. You looked at the screen, applied all the second-rate scientific wit you could muster, and concluded that maybe the scanner was exactly accurate on 99.99 percent of the objects it's reading, but a glitch in the system caused it to be inaccurate just for that one moon. Brilliant."

Cumby started to answer, but Rodney ignored him. He seated himself in front of the scanner and zeroed in on MC4-502, the fourth moon around a distant planet.

"What do you think?" Sheppard said, leaning in over Rodney's shoulder.

Rodney stiffened, tilted his head, and said, "What do I think? I think, in the thirty seconds I've had to think about it, that MC4-502 has left its orbit. I think it's very early in the morning, it's difficult to concentrate with you leaning over my shoulder, and that as far as I can tell, you've wasted my night's sleep — and a perfectly wonderful dream, I might add — for a simple astral anomaly I could have studied over coffee in about three hours."

Colonel Sheppard, who was grinning widely, took a sip of coffee from the mug he held and waited.

"I think, in fact," Rodney continued, "that—"

He stopped. His hands returned to the controls, and flew from keyboard to knobs with uncanny speed and precision.

"Oh," he said, pushing back and away, nearly causing Sheppard to spill his coffee, "this is *not* good."

"I knew you were gonna say that," Sheppard said.

Rodney paid no attention. He'd changed screens, brought up a tracking grid and was plotting MC4-502's course through its solar system. He punched in some numbers, cleared the screen, punched them in again, and spun back to face the Colonel with a frown. "It's headed straight into the sun."

"That happens, right?"

"No," Rodney said, "it doesn't. Not that quickly. Sure, over time orbits can erode and break down. Things can shift—a really big meteor could strike the moon's surface and knock it off course, but this?" He waved his hand toward the screen. "I've never seen anything like this. If I didn't know better, I'd say the thing had been flown off course on purpose."

"Is there any danger to Atlantis?"

"Not per se," Rodney said. "It's thousands of light years away. But," he frowned and punched more keys, "I guess it depends on who's flying it, doesn't it?"

He turned back to the computer screen and began typing furiously. After a few moments, he glanced up. Colonel Sheppard was gone and Cumby stood off to one side looking very uncomfortable, clearly uncertain whether he should try to regain his seat at the console, or even speak.

"What?" Rodney snapped. "Don't you have something

to calibrate?"

Cumby turned and left, and Rodney returned to the console, everything else forgotten as he lost himself in the data on the screen.

CHAPTER TWO

RICHARD WOOLSEY SAT AT HIS desk, drinking a cup of hot tea and scanning reports on his tablet PC. He smiled, because scanning reports was something he enjoyed — the regularity and security of continuity appealed to him. Since taking over command of Atlantis from Colonel Carter, his life had been a string of almost out-of-control adventures and crazed life or death situations. They were not activities he was comfortable with, because they rarely came with ready solutions or simple answers. He cherished the times when things ran smoothly and his post was largely a bureaucratic one. When the door opened without warning and Dr. McKay charged in, nose buried in the laptop he carried, Woolsey heaved a heavy sigh. In his experience, such an incident rarely ended well. He closed the document he'd been working on and sat back. In his late forties, slender and balding, at first glance the commander gave the impression of being a timid bookkeeper. He'd proven, over time, that he was made of much sterner stuff than he appeared, but certain characteristics stuck with him.

"Dr. McKay," he said. "I understand that you are very often caught up in your work, and that it muddies your otherwise impeccable judgment, but my door was closed for a reason. The least you could do…"

Rodney held up a finger, still staring at the screen in his hands.

"Rodney!" Woolsey raised his voice and glared.

Rodney looked up, startled.

"Did you hear a word I said?"

"I...no."

Woolsey sighed again and rolled his eyes. "What is it, Doctor? I have a lot of work to get through this afternoon."

"It's something we found last night — well — I didn't find it, but..." Rodney stepped up to the desk and placed his computer on the surface. He turned it so that the commander could see the information he'd been scanning.

"What is it?"

"I've been digging through the data we've managed to translate in Atlantis' memory banks. Last night we — Airman Cumby, I mean — noticed an anomaly in the moon's around one of the planets we've charted. One moon, designated MC4-502, broke orbit and changed course very suddenly."

"That's odd."

"Of course it's odd," Rodney said. "Why else would we be talking about it?"

Before the commander could comment, Rodney continued.

"It's possible for a moon's orbit to erode over time, or for some unforeseen occurrence, like a strike from a very large meteorite knocking it off course, but this is different. From the trajectory it looks as if the planet propelled itself out of orbit."

"Is that possible?"

"Of course it's possible." Rodney said, annoyed. "We can do it ourselves with our city, and a sufficiently strong tractor beam could do the trick. There are a number of ways the moon could shift from its orbit, but that's not what I came here to tell you. Look."

Woolsey saw that Rodney was irritated with him for not immediately grasping whatever it was that bothered him about the data on the screen. He counted to three, very slowly and very quietly, and waited.

"Here," Rodney said. He traced his finger along a colored line superimposed over the chart. "This is the new path. If there is no other significant push to change that eroding orbit…"

"It will plunge into the sun." Woolsey concluded.

"And soon."

"I assume there is a reason you believe this is significant?"

Rodney turned and glared at him, and again the commander was forced to calm himself. Dr. McKay was possibly the most brilliant man the commander had ever encountered, but he was also very likely the most arrogant and the one graced with the least ability to interact properly with his fellow human beings. The doctor had little or no patience for the inability of others to keep up with his overly agile mind, and was fond of pointing it out when they failed.

"I found references to that moon," Rodney said. "None of what I have is clear yet, but there was definitely a gate there at one time, a well traveled one. I believe it is possible that there was a great deal more than that, as well. I haven't had time yet to work through it. I have a couple of people digging deeper right now."

"A gate?" Woolsey said. He sat up straighter. "Do you think there might still be people on there? Surely if there are, and there's a gate, they will…"

"Someone is on there," Rodney said. "When I found the references, I started some long range scans. I picked up a power signature — a powerful one. It was just a spike, like some sort of power surge, and then it all went dead."

Woolsey stared at the screen in front of him. He'd already seen all there was to see, but the moment of scrutiny bought him a few moments to order his thoughts.

"I don't know what we can do, maybe nothing," Rodney admitted. "Whoever was there has probably evacuated through the gate already. But I was able to pick up traces from the burst that knocked it out of orbit and the energy signature was consistent with that of a ZPM. I can't be certain, but if there's any chance, and if that gate is still operational…"

"Yes, I understand," Woolsey said. "We could use the ZPM, and if there are other artifacts, or if there's a civilization there in need of rescue…"

"Exactly."

"There's one problem," Woolsey said.

Rodney glanced up, momentarily distracted. "What?"

"Do you have a gate address?"

Rodney stood very still. "Well, no, not yet, obviously. We're working on that. I'm sure it's in the database. There are records indicating others have traveled there."

Woolsey picked up his reports and turned away. "Let me know if you find a way to reach that gate," he said. "If you do, we'll discuss our options. I also want to know how long you believe it will be before that moon is too close to the sun for human habitation."

Rodney stared at Woolsey a moment longer, then smiled and turned away. No doubt he was already deep into his calculations and research as the door slid closed behind him.

CHAPTER THREE

WHEN RODNEY RETURNED TO his lab, he found Cumby hunkered over a console with Radek Zelenka and Colonel Sheppard. They were so intent on whatever it was they were studying they didn't even notice his approach.

"What is it?" he said.

"These two found something about your moon," Sheppard said, stepping back.

Rodney started to ask a question, thought better of it, and pushed Cumby out of the way so he could see what was on the screen. The top half of the monitor was filled with a series of Ancient hieroglyphic characters. The lower half was a text screen containing a partial translation. The Atlantis databases were filled with information that they'd not had the time, nor the facilities to unravel. When they had a particular object or subject in mind, they could narrow their efforts and often came up with amazing bits and pieces of the puzzle that had once been a city of the Ancients.

"We found a reference to the moon," Zelenka said. "When we cross-referenced it with data we've translated from the city's database, we found a name. It's not the name of the moon…"

"I can read," Rodney snapped. He scanned the screen rapidly, and then stepped back in surprise. "My God. It's not just a moon."

"It's a city," Cumby said. "Very much like this one."

"Admah," Zelenka added. "The city of Admah."

"It's not the only reference to the name Admah," Cumby said helpfully. "On Earth, the city of Admah was one of those destroyed in Biblical times, along with Sodom and Gomorrah."

Sheppard turned to Cumby. "My Biblical history isn't too strong, but weren't those cities destroyed by…"

"Fire," Cumby said. "They were consumed in flames."

"Very appropriate," Rodney muttered. He barely paid any attention to the others. He was busy staring at the Ancient symbols and working out their meaning.

"You said you found a power signature over there," Sheppard said. "You think there might be an active ZPM?"

Rodney glanced up and nodded distractedly. Then he turned away from the screen and began to pace. "A ZPM, yes. But that's not all. This isn't just another planet with a gate, it's a city. A flying city. If there's anything more left of it than ruins, we could be looking at a goldmine of Ancient technology. Computer banks — drones — it could be another Atlantis! My God — do you have any idea what this means?"

All three of the others stared at him.

Rodney stared back, and then said "What? Okay, so you do know, but…"

"Let's forget that you're the only one in the room for a minute," Sheppard said. "How long before that city, or moon, or whatever it is takes a nose dive into that star?"

Rodney turned back to the monitor and brought up an image showing a steadily declining orbit that wound closer and closer to the flickering red image of the system's sun.

"Taking into account the steepness of the orbit's decline, the size and mass of the city and the sun, and the draw of gravity...less than a week," Rodney said.

"If the city is like Atlantis," Zelenka said thoughtfully, "the way it broke orbit makes sense. It could be moving under its own power. Maybe there's a malfunction."

"You mean they might have tried to break orbit and sent themselves straight at the sun instead?" Sheppard turned to Rodney. "If that's true, they might need our help. If there was something wrong with the star drive, but it was still functional enough to move the city, could you fix it?"

Rodney turned to Sheppard in irritation. "We don't even know if there's anything to fix. We don't know if it's a star drive, we don't know if there's a city still standing, and we have no idea — given both of those things — what could have gone wrong."

"But if there was, you could?" Sheppard prodded.

"Given enough time, of course."

"We need to get a team over there before it's too late to get a look at the city," Sheppard said. "If there are people still living there, we need to see if we can help them, and if not, I can't imagine leaving an Ancient city to burn and be destroyed without at least taking a look around."

"There's one problem," Rodney said. "We don't have an address."

"Sir?" Cumby said.

"Not now," Rodney said, waving a hand. "I think it's possible that if we run a new search and cross reference everything we can find on the city, we can come up with —"

"Sir," Cumby said again.

"Not now," Rodney snapped. "Can't you see we're in the middle of something important here? Or do you come from some part of Earth where people all talk at once? Maybe the reason you know so much about the history of the Bible is because you come from Babel?"

"I think you should take a look, sir," Cumby said, unruffled.

Irritated, Rodney turned. "What? What is it that you think is so important that..."

He fell silent when he saw the sequence of symbols displayed on the screen.

"I ran a new search," Cumby explained. "I input all the terms I could find associated with Admah that were unique. I found this address, but..."

Sheppard peered at the screen. "But what?"

"I'm not sure, sir," Cumby replied. "There's some kind of block. The final two symbols of the address are obscured."

"Let me see that," Rodney pushed forward.

"There's a warning message," Cumby said as he stepped aside. "Maybe..."

Rodney paid no attention. He typed furiously, frowned, grumbled, typed again, and then slapped his finger down on a key decisively. "Huh," he said, then started typing again, frowning.

"What is it?" said Zelenka.

"It's safeguarded. I'm trying to override it."

The warning message on the screen blinked once, twice, and then disappeared. Rodney stopped typing and stared. "Great," he said. "Just great. Now I not only can't get in, but I don't have the warning message that would have told us why I shouldn't."

Cumby was scribbling furiously. Rodney turned to him, trying to shift the focus of the moment. "What are you doing?"

"I think I got it," he said.

"Got what?"

"The warning," Cumby held out a piece of paper with a series of hastily scrawled symbols drawn across it.

Rodney stared at it, and then passed it back. "You must have gotten it wrong," he said. "I can't translate any of that."

Zelenka reached out and plucked the paper from Cumby's hand. "I'll see what I can do with it."

Cumby looked as though he couldn't quite decide whether to be grateful to Zelenka or irritated with Rodney. Colonel Sheppard watched the entire exchange with a grin curling the edge of his lip. "There's not a lot of time."

"I'll let you know what I find," Zelenka said. He left the room with the paper clutched in his hand.

"He won't find anything," Rodney muttered. Sheppard laughed and turned away while Cumby continued to work at the controls of the computer console.

"How could you draw that?" Rodney asked him, turning back around. "You don't have a background in Ancient and it was only on the screen for a couple of moments."

"I don't know what it says," Cumby replied. "I have no idea how to translate any Ancient symbols."

"Then how…?"

"Photographic memory," he said, turning back to Rodney. "My IQ isn't as high as yours, but I can keep things straight. It's come in handy in research work; I'm not the best person to explain results, but I don't forget them. I thought it was in my personnel record. Didn't you review it?"

"Well, yes, obviously, but…" Rodney trailed off as Cumby turned away.

The younger man left the room, following Sheppard and Zelenka into the hall. Rodney stared after him for a moment, then turned back to the screen and shook his head. In silence he continued hitting keys, searching for a way past the security protocol on the address file for Admah.

CHAPTER FOUR

MR. WOOLSEY SAT AT THE HEAD of the conference table. Gathered around it, Colonel Sheppard, Ronon Dex, Teyla Emmagan, Rodney and Zelenka sat quietly, waiting for the commander to scan the documents they'd placed before him. To one side, Airman Cumby sat alone, looking uncomfortable.

"You've managed to piece together quite a story," Woolsey said at last. "There's more here than just a simple moon leaving its orbit but," he smoothed the papers on the table and gathered his thoughts before looking up to meet their collective gaze, "it's not exactly definitive, is it? There are a lot of random facts here, a lot of bits and pieces of stories, but not much concrete information. What exactly do you propose?"

"Rodney says we have about a week before Admah crashes into its sun," Sheppard said, getting right to the point. "It's not a lot of time, but it's more than enough for an exploratory mission to the city. I want to take a team over there. If there are refugees to be evacuated, that would be our first priority. If there's a city — a ZPM — Ancient technology..."

"It's very tempting," Woolsey said. "But I'm concerned by this gate address. You say there was a warning, but that you've been unable to translate its message?"

"We're still working on that," Rodney cut in. "Someone didn't want us to retrieve that address. There's something dangerous about it, but we have no idea what."

"You've seen a message like it before then?" Woolsey raised one eyebrow and waited. "It seems to me that if this much effort has been made to warn us of something, we should take heed."

Rodney looked down at the table, but kept talking. "I agree. We haven't seen all the possible error codes in the system — it could take decades to decipher them — but I'm certain that ignoring the warning would be foolish. The Ancients weren't timid by nature — if there's something dangerous on that planet, we need to figure out what it is."

"What about sending a MALP?" Woolsey said.

"Of course we'll send a MALP," Rodney snapped. "We have to check there's a breathable atmosphere, acceptable surface temperature, and so on. But the warning might not be about anything the MALP can detect."

"So we don't know whether the message came from the computer system, or if it was associated with the gate address?"

"No, but — "

"Mr. Woolsey," Teyla cut in, "if there is a power signature then it is possible that there are survivors. Do we not have an obligation to at least investigate?"

Woolsey raised his hand. "I'm not saying no," he said. "I'm saying I'm concerned. I want people working on translating that message around the clock."

"We can't wait long if we're going," Sheppard said. "It's going to start getting hotter over there pretty soon."

"Understood," Woolsey said. "Go ahead and prepare your team Colonel, but first I want your thoughts on... this."

He shuffled through the papers in front of him and brought out several copies of a report. He handed one to each of them.

Rodney started to speak, then stopped and turned to Airman Cumby. "Go ahead," he said.

Cumby smiled and scanned his own copy of the report. He started to read.

"By all indications," he said, "the city of Admah and the city of Atlantis were in close communication at one point. What we've uncovered is more like a story book, or a legend, than a real record. There appear to have been more complete records at one point, but they are either corrupt, or inaccessible. This is all we could put together.

"Admah was one of the great cities of the Ancients. They developed an advanced civilization with strong trade. Admah was a preferred destination for travelers on leave, or visiting dignitaries. They developed a taste for entertainment and games. Apparently they became one of the foremost vacation spots in the galaxy."

"That doesn't sound much like the Ancients we've encountered," Woolsey commented. "In fact, I can't imagine a description of a city that sounded less like their civilization."

"The records aren't clear on exactly what happened," Cumby continued, "but over time they appear to have grown somewhat decadent. The games became more than simple tournaments, and the citizens began seeking greater and greater excess. Travel to and from Admah slowed to a trickle, and over time stopped almost completely.

"Then the Wraith rose, and communications were cut off. Though there are several later mentions of the city, they are cryptic and vague. Attempts were made to renew communications between the cities, but all records of those attempts have been hidden, encrypted, or deleted. It seems as if the city was either destroyed by the Wraith, or withdrew into itself and cut off access to the rest of the galaxy."

"That's not promising," Woolsey said.

"The address that we found is active," Zelenka said. "We didn't open the gate, but it's there."

"And you are sure it's Admah?"

"Yes," Zelenka replied. "It's Admah alright."

"Keep working on that warning," Woolsey said. "Colonel Sheppard, when can you have your team ready?"

"We're ready," Sheppard replied. "Just waiting for you to give the word, sir."

"Very well," Woolsey said. "I want extra caution on this one, Colonel. We have no idea what we're getting into, and if the Ancients didn't want to travel there we can assume they had their reasons. We're hardly in a position to protect ourselves from something they had enough sense to avoid."

Sheppard nodded. "There is one problem, sir."

"Just the one?"

"For now…" He nodded toward Rodney. "We can't take a jumper."

"Why not?"

"Because," Rodney said, "I noticed a number of coronal loops on the sun's surface. Naturally I examined the Zeemen effect lines — coronal loops are a direct consequence of a twisted solar magnetic flux — and quite frankly, it's off the scale."

Woolsely blinked at him. "Very nice, Dr. McKay, but

what does it mean?"

"It means," Rodney said with a sigh, "that the stellar magnetic field is enormous."

Tight lipped, Woolsey turned to Sheppard. "Colonel...?"

"Puddle Jumpers are susceptible to electromagnetic fields, sir. A field of that scale would disrupt all the systems as soon as we got through the gate."

"And?"

"And we'd crash. Just like we did on M7G-677."

"Oh much worse than that," Rodney said. "In comparative terms, the electromagnetic field on '677 was like a AAA battery compared with 240V of mains power."

Woolsey held up his hand. "Okay, I get it. I don't like it, but I get it." He turned to Sheppard. "If you don't have a jumper as a backup, then I want a more regular reporting schedule, Colonel. And I want you out of there long before things start to warm up."

"Suits me, sir."

Turning back to McKay, he said, "Could the magnetic field be the subject of the warning message?"

"It's possible," Rodney admitted. "Although it wouldn't have been such an issue if the moon was still orbiting its planet." He looked at Zelenka. "What exactly is the holdup in translating that message, anyway?"

Zelenka shook his head and frowned. "There are a number of symbols that we have seen before, but still it does not make sense. I have developed an algorithm to compare it with other warnings we have found, but so far there have been no hits. If it is a warning, it is very specific."

"Rodney," Sheppard called across the table.

Rodney glanced up, startled, as if he was afraid he'd missed some comment or question directed at him.

"We're going to need you on this one. Will you be ready?"

He stared at Sheppard for a moment, opened his mouth, closed it, and then nodded, though he looked anything but enthusiastic. "I have a couple of things I need to wrap up, and I'll be ready."

"Good," Sheppard said. "We're counting on you. If that city is a ship, and it can be flown…"

"I know, I know," Rodney said. "Fix it."

"I'd like to accompany the team as well," Airman Cumby said.

"I think that's a great idea," Sheppard replied. "I want you on that team in case we run into any more warnings that Rodney can't resist deleting. We'll be in contact with Atlantis, if we run across anything maybe you can recreate it—like you did before. I kind of like the idea that there's a guy with a perfect memory checking over the details."

Cumby smiled. He obviously enjoyed the compliment. "It's not perfect," he said. "But it would be nice, for once, to put it to some good use. Most people just want me to use it to perform, like parlor tricks. What was on page two-fifteen, second paragraph, of *A Brave New World*."

There was a pause, then Sheppard said, "So, what was it?"

"I never read it," Cumby replied with a grin.

"Fair enough," Sheppard laid a hand on the younger man's shoulder. "We're counting on you."

Cumby nodded. "I'd better get ready then."

The rest of the group dispersed slowly. When the room

had emptied, Woolsey gathered the papers in front of him, tapped them on the table to straighten them, and stood slowly. He was the last to leave the room and his expression was grim. He hated sending a team into something so tenuous, and since there appeared to be no other course of action, he fell back on his paperwork. It didn't help, but it kept his hands busy.

CHAPTER FIVE

THE TEAM GATHERED EARLY in the morning. Sheppard checked his gear twice, and then helped Cumby with his. He was a little nervous about taking someone he hadn't personally worked with into the field on a potentially dangerous mission, but he kept his smile in place. Ronon and Teyla had been ready for at least half an hour, and the only missing team member was Rodney.

"Figures he'd be late," Sheppard said. "He's probably filling his pack with sunscreen, insect repellant and food."

"I could go to his quarters and see if he's ready," Cumby said.

"I've already been by there," Sheppard said. "Rodney is up. He's just late."

Cumby nodded. They waited in silence for a moment longer, and then they all turned at the sound of approaching footsteps.

Rodney burst into view, moving very quickly. He had his gear slung over his shoulder and his laptop tucked under his arm. He was grinning from ear to ear. It was the kind of grin you'd expect if a kid was running away from a school bathroom just before the firecracker took out a toilet.

Ronon frowned. "What's wrong with you?"

Rodney cocked his head and his grin widened. "Absolutely nothing," he said. "Why would there be anything wrong? Shall we get this show on the road?" But everyone just stared at him. "What?"

"We were supposed to leave ten minutes ago," Teyla said.

"Sorry. I had to get a few things. We don't want to be unprepared."

"What things?" Sheppard said, expecting more of an answer than he really needed.

But Rodney surprised him. "Technical things. Aren't we late already?"

Sheppard shook his head and let it go. "Okay," he said. "So we're all clear, we're going through to look for the city. If we find it, we have priorities. First priority is to look for survivors and see if there's anything we can do to help. If there are working ZPMs we'll try to bring them back. If there is anything we can do to keep the city from crashing into the sun, we'll give it a shot, but if it starts to get too hot — we get out. We'll be heroes if opportunity knocks, but we aren't going to put ourselves in any unnecessary danger. Understood?"

Everyone nodded.

"I did a little more research last night," Cumby said as the gate began to spin.

"Yeah?" Sheppard said. "What did you find?"

"It wasn't anything about the planet," he said. "I researched more about the name of the city — Admah. It really *was* a city, not just a Biblical myth. It was in the Valley of Siddim, southeast of the Dead Sea, and was inhabited by the Canaanites. Historical records indicate that the city really was destroyed by fire."

"Destroyed by whom?" Ronon said.

Cumby shrugged. "If you believe the Bible, then God," he said. "It was destroyed by God. The historical records aren't clear on what started the fire only that the city was absolutely consumed."

"Nice story," Ronon grunted.

The last chevron locked and they all watched as the gate came to life. The air within the circular portal shimmered. There was a strange sound like a heavy breath of air, and the center of the shimmering light bulged inward. It surged out from the center forming a swelling cylinder of light and then snapped back flat. The room seemed charged with energy when the gate opened, and every time it happened, it gave Sheppard a thrill.

"Receiving MALP telemetry," Woolsey called down from Stargate Operations. "Atmosphere is acceptable, temperature... I hope you packed your sun block, Colonel, it's going to be hot."

From his position at the gate, Sheppard glanced up. "Tell me something I don't know." Then he turned and gave his team the nod, watching as one after the other, they stepped into the wormhole and disappeared. Woolsey watched until they had all passed through and the gate had shut down. He stood still for a few moments after they were gone, then turned to the technician on duty.

"Dial again in two hours for a SITREP — I want to keep a close eye on this one."

He didn't tell the man why he felt uneasy, but ignoring a warning of any type rubbed against the grain and now that the deed was done he couldn't get it out of his head. His time in Atlantis had worked subtle changes in the way he viewed things and, though he still had to bite his lip at times to keep from speaking up, he'd learned to trust the instincts of those who served under him. Sheppard in particular. Still, it was one thing to trust Sheppard to do the right thing, but changing the cautious, careful nature of his personal world to accept that trust was a different thing entirely. He was working on it, but old habits died hard. He had to let one or the other rule his mind, and now that he'd made his decision, he had to find his own ways to deal with the mental fallout.

The gate stood silent and empty and he stared at it, wondering what was happening on the other side, but its giant eye stared back at him and held no answers. After a few moments, he turned away. He trusted his team, but there was nothing he could do to prevent his own fear. And he didn't really want to prevent it, he realized — it kept him alert.

CHAPTER SIX

THE TEAM STEPPED INTO A dusty clearing, the MALP parked off to one side. They were surrounded by trees, but most of the branches were bare. There was a breeze, but it was hot and dry. The gate stood in a small valley between rolling hills and there was a stone tiled circle surrounding them, creating a perimeter that had once kept off encroaching plant life. But the trees and shrubbery were brown now — desolate and forgotten. The clearing was surrounded by the remnant of what seemed to be a terraced garden, the gate set into the stone at the lowest level, and several more flat, open levels rising like huge steps up to the right and left. Directly ahead, a trail wound off into the distance. It didn't look as if anyone had traveled that way in a very long time.

"Cheery place," Rodney said.

The team fanned out. Sheppard, Ronon and Teyla circled to either side, weapons leveled. They scanned to the right, left, and behind, watching for any sign of movement. Rodney switched on his scanner and began running sweeps of the area. Airman Cumby hovered close by and watched over his shoulder.

Rodney glanced up. "What are you doing?"

"I'm watching," Cumby said. "I thought maybe I could help."

"You thought that maybe by blocking sunlight or

shielding me from deadly radiation with your body I might think more clearly? Or maybe you think you'll see something I'd miss?"

"Let it go, Rodney," Sheppard said. "Which way is it to the city? Have you got a lock on that power signature?"

Rodney eyed his screen, and then glanced up. "Straight ahead, down that trail," he said. "I'm picking up several signatures, but they are weak, and not exactly like anything I've seen before. Something is out there."

"Then let's go find out what it is," Sheppard said.

Ronon took point and moved out ahead of the others, Teyla crossing over to the opposite side of the trail. Rodney and Cumby followed behind, the former lost in some signal on his scanner, and the latter glancing about nervously.

"Any signs of life?" Sheppard asked.

Rodney was studying the scanner as he walked. "Nothing so far," he said. "I...wait." He tapped at the device and then glanced up.

"What is it?" Sheppard peered over his shoulder.

"There's something alive," Rodney said. "I'm getting a variety of readings, but they're even weaker than the power signatures. I'm not sure, but they look as if they might be coming from behind some sort of shield."

"You can't tell what it is?"

Rodney shook his head.

"Alright," Sheppard said. "Keep your eyes peeled. We don't seem to be alone here, so let's not have any surprises."

Ronon glanced back over his shoulder and raised an eyebrow. It was obvious from his expression that he'd like nothing better than a few surprises, but he kept his silence.

They headed up the trail slowly. Nothing moved. There were signs that others had traveled the trail before them, but they were aged and faded. They walked in silence, not wanting to give away their position, in case whoever else was nearby wasn't friendly, and not wanting to accidentally muffle the sound of a potential enemy approaching. The trail wound up the hill before them and curved off to the left. Ronon disappeared around the bend, and then Teyla. Moments later, Sheppard reached the turn. He spun, scanned the trail ahead, and then gestured for Rodney and Cumby to follow.

"Look!" Teyla called out.

As they rounded the bend they caught sight of her and followed her gaze. In the distance the spires and towers of a city had come into view. They were so tall they speared the clouds overhead. The walls of the city rolled out to the right and left and curled in behind more hills. It was a magnificent sight.

Between where they stood and the city walls, a series of gardens and parks formed a trail of death and decay. Nothing had lived in any of them for a very long time, and the layout of the trees and the way the dead vines trailed up and over stone decorations and abandoned resting places was macabre.

"Those walls look familiar," Ronon commented.

Sheppard shook his head in amazement. "Looks like you were right, Rodney," he said. "If I didn't know we'd just left it behind, and that we'd have to be standing in an ocean for it to be true, I'd swear that was Atlantis. The walls are different, but I suppose that's because there's no sea surrounding them. The gardens are…were…a nice touch."

Cumby stared up at the rising spires. He didn't smile, but his face was transformed. It was an awe-inspiring sight, and the implications of it were even more far-reaching.

"You could stand there gaping," Rodney said, "or we can move on and see what's over there. I'm guessing that the computer systems and artifacts will be even more intriguing than the picturesque skyline."

Cumby shook his head to clear it, grinning ruefully. "Sorry but — "

"Let's move out," Sheppard said, cutting them off. "We don't have much time here."

They all glanced up at that point toward the sun overhead. Normally sunlight was comforting, but given the circumstances it felt like the ball of fire and death might fall and crush them at any moment.

They hurried down the trail toward the city, moving as quickly as they could without compromising their safety. It was easy to believe, studying the desolate landscape they passed through, that nothing else could be alive nearby. Surely if there was a civilization here, there would be some sign? If people lived in or around the city, there had to be signs.

"There's a gate ahead," Ronon called back. "It's open. Looks like the door is broken."

"Broken?" Sheppard said. It wasn't really a question.

Ronon was right. The gates leading into the city hung at odd angles. The one on the left was cracked at the hinges, as if it had been blasted by a high powered projectile. The right was still attached to its hinges, but the outer bottom corner had dug into the dirt. Debris was piled around it, holding it in place.

"That can't be good," Sheppard said. "No one I've ever met uses rubble for a doorstop."

Teyla reached out to touch the gate. "Whatever did this, it happened a long time ago."

"Yeah," Sheppard said. "But you'd think if the 'good guys' won, they'd have fixed it eventually, wouldn't you? Let's get in there. We don't want to spend any more time here than we have to."

They moved ahead again, Ronon and Teyla disappearing inside the city. The gates were massive and loomed over them menacingly.

"What could have broken these?" Cumby wondered as he passed through, running his hand down the frame of the door.

"Let's hope we don't find out," Rodney said. "The life signs are stronger now, and the power signatures are definitely from multiple ZPMs. I don't know if anything still works in there, but there's still power, and if there's power, we should be able to use it to do *something* useful."

Once they'd stepped over the gate's threshold and could see beyond the still formidable walls of the city, they noted that the trail of ruined gardens and outbuildings continued on toward a large, central structure. The main entrance to the city was overgrown with plants and there were signs of damage, but it was in much better repair than the gates. Dusty marble stairs led up and into a huge main hall that was obscured in shadow.

"Whoever is in there," Cumby said, "they aren't much on yard work."

"It looks pretty familiar," Sheppard said. "Remind you of anything, Rodney?"

"Of course it does. It's almost a duplicate of Atlantis, but on land. This is what the city might have been if it weren't floating like an island."

They climbed up the stone steps and entered the main hall, Ronon and Teyla moving ahead of the others. Inside the entrance they fanned out, Ronon to the left, Teyla on the right. They swept the huge chamber quickly. Nothing moved, but they didn't relax their guard.

"Keep your eyes open," Sheppard said. He stood aside and let Rodney and Cumby enter ahead of him, then brought up the rear, turning now and again to check the entrance behind them.

They moved in slowly. Rodney kept his eyes on his computer. Now and then he punched a button. Now and then Cumby gently urged him onward, reminding him to walk.

"If this was Atlantis," Teyla said, pointing to the right, "The control room would be that way."

They turned down a corridor that ended in another set of stairs. Their steps echoed eerily. The stairs were strewn with dust and small bits of rubble, as if they'd been abandoned and overrun by animals for decades. There were no footprints, or any other sign that anyone had passed that way for many years.

"Look at this," Ronon called out.

They climbed up to stand beside him. He pointed to the wall beside the stairs. Cumby stepped closer and brushed his hand over the wall, removing a coating of dust. Beneath it was a colorful image. It had what was obviously a lighted frame, but the lights weren't lit.

Teyla cocked her head, studying the image. "What is that thing?"

"It looks like a dragon," Cumby offered, turning to Teyla and Ronon. "On Earth, we have legends of giant lizards that breathed fire — they never existed, but we have stories about warriors fighting them. Ancient legends are full of them."

"I wouldn't want to fight that," Sheppard said.

In the picture, an alien with long dark hair and rippling muscles lunged at a giant scaled lizard. The man wielded an impossibly heavy broadsword that seemed to shimmer with some form of energy. The creature reared back, long neck rippling and jaws open wide enough to swallow the warrior whole. Cumby brushed the dust away from more of the image, revealing writing at the bottom.

"It's a poster," Sheppard said.

"Advertising what?"

"If I'm translating this correctly," Rodney said, "it's an 'entertainment'. That's all it says. No indication if it's some sort of movie, or…"

"There's another one up here," Teyla called.

She'd moved up the stairs and they joined her. The second poster showed a creature that seemed to be part human and part Wraith. It stood twice as tall as either and brandished its feeding-hand, ready to suck the life from a pair of very human warriors. They held spears, and appeared to be taunting the creature. Its expression of rage and hunger radiated from the poster.

"Not sure what that means," Rodney said. "I can catch a couple of words. One is undefeated. This one," he reached out and tapped an odd symbol, "Is something like 'Woard' — but that doesn't mean anything to me."

"What kind of place was this?" Cumby muttered.

"Fun?" Ronon raised an eyebrow and grinned. Teyla shook her head.

"Let's keep moving," Sheppard said. "We don't have much time."

They continued up the stairs. Along the way they saw a series of the odd posters, each more fantastic than the last. All of them appeared to advertise some sort of event, but none was any clearer what the event might be. There were huge creatures, aliens pitted against one another with an array of strange weapons, and always the lifeless lighted frames that indicated the images had once had significance. Rodney took pictures for later translation, but they didn't slow down to ponder them further.

At the top of the stairs they found another corridor. They took the large double doors to their right, and stepped into a large room. The room resembled the control room in Atlantis, with the noted exclusion of the gate.

"I wonder why they built their gate so far outside the city?" Teyla said. "It would have made more sense to place it here, within the walls. Like in Atlantis."

"The walls don't seem to have made much difference to whoever, or whatever, took this place out," Sheppard said.

"It makes more tactical sense to have the gate outside the walls for a land-based city," Rodney said. "They could launch ships or teams and still keep their shields in place to protect the city. If something came back through the gate, or managed to open it without their knowledge, it would still be beyond the city's defenses."

"Makes sense," Sheppard agreed. "What about this

place? You said there were power signatures..."

Rodney had already stepped up to one of the control consoles. As Sheppard's words trailed away, he pressed a sequence of buttons on the panel in front of him. There was a deep hum that vibrated through the floor and the walls. The panels to either side of him flickered, and then came to life. Within moments, the room was powered up. Lights in the hallway came on as well, and music filled the air.

"What's that sound?" Ronon stepped back to the door, his gun raised.

"It started when the power came back," Cumby cut in. "It's got to be a broadcast of some sort."

They fell silent to listen.

"Tonight, one night only," a voice called out. "In the main arena — undefeated in twelve confrontations — he's half man, half wraith, and ALL battle. The Woard! Arrange your seating now, and get your bets in early. We have a new warrior just in from off world. You won't want to miss his first — and possibly last — appearance."

In the corridor beyond, the posters lining the wall had come to life. Lights ran and flickered around their edges and the voice they'd heard moved along the passageway, first emanating from one speaker, and then the next, singing the praises of whatever event was heralded by each display.

The music playing in the background was intricate, beautiful and haunting, yet at the same time oddly repellent. It was like something you'd expect to hear at a carnival.

"Rodney," Sheppard said quietly. "Can you locate the ZPMs?"

"I just turned on a city that's been sitting dormant for, what, a thousand years? And now you want to know if I can find the battery?"

"Well?"

"I'm working on it," Rodney said, turning back to the computer.

As he worked, Teyla and Ronon stepped up to two of the other consoles and began checking systems and maps. "It's very similar to Atlantis," Teyla said. "There are a number of lower levels. Power is active on all of them. There's a shield in place that is causing some interference."

"Of course they're active," Rodney snapped irritably. "I just turned everything on."

"No," Teyla said. "If these logs are correct, the power on the lower levels has been on for many years."

Rodney flipped through some screens and looked up. "She's right," he told Sheppard. "The computers have been active all along. All we did was activate the main level. There has been access to the system regularly. We are very definitely not alone here."

Sheppard's hands tightened on his weapon. "Who's down there?"

"I might be able to answer that." The voice rose from down the corridor and Teyla and Ronon spun into the hall, weapons raised. A man stood at the far end of the corridor, dressed in very fine clothing — long robes festooned with gold ornamentation, and brightly polished black boots. His hair was thick and flowed down over his shoulders.

"That would be appreciated," Sheppard said, stepping forward and reaching out to press the barrel of Ronon's gun down gently. "Maybe you could tell us why the surface of this planet looks like it's been through a war, why the lights are off, and who you are?"

"No need for weapons," the man said. "I'll be happy to answer any and all of your questions. First, I would like to welcome you all to the city of Admah. I am Saul."

CHAPTER SEVEN

SAUL LED THEM DOWN THE wide main stairway into another hall on the level directly below. It was equally run down. He stopped at the end of the corridor, pressed his hand into an intricately carved bit of masonry, and a crack opened in the wall. It widened slowly and they all waited to see what it would reveal.

"If you don't mind my saying so," Sheppard said, glancing up and down the hall, "you guys could use a good housekeeper."

Saul smiled. "You'll find the lower levels better tended," he said. "When the Wraith threatened, we managed to fight them off — but we found it simpler to allow them to believe we'd been wiped out than to make ourselves a target for repeat attacks. We retreated to the lower levels and we left the main floors and the outer grounds untouched. We had sufficient shielding to prevent detection from long range scans, and the appearance of the planet's surface acted as a shield against visual searches. A very simple ploy, I know, but it has served us well."

"Oh really?" Rodney said. "That's interesting, because I had no trouble detecting your power signatures, or your life signs. If I can tell you're here, what's to prevent the Wraith?"

"We've turned the shields off," Saul said with a smile. "We no longer fear the Wraith, or any other form of attack."

"Why not?" Ronon said. "Wraith are active again. Didn't you know that?"

"Yes, of course we do, and I'll be happy to explain what has changed for us in good time," Saul replied. "But first, please, allow me to offer a proper welcome. You are our guests. There will be plenty of time for talk."

He stepped through the opening in the wall into a lift beyond. Sheppard looked at the others, shrugged, and followed. One by one, they stepped in, and when the last of them had crossed the threshold, the opening in the wall closed cleanly behind them, cutting them off from the dead, vacant halls beyond.

Rodney wasn't willing to give up on his inquiries so soon, or to be distracted by a welcome to the city. He was still studying readouts on his computer screen, and he pushed forward so that he walked closely beside Saul.

"The city," Rodney said. "It has a star drive?"

"It does," Saul agreed. "How did you know that? Were you able to detect it as well?"

"We've come from the city of Atlantis," Sheppard replied. "Admah is very… similar."

"Almost identical," Saul said. "Two cities with incredibly similar architecture and technology, but so different in other ways. Some used to call them the light and the dark. But I'd heard Atlantis was abandoned, sunken beneath the waves and forgotten?"

"The rumors of her demise were, exaggerated," Sheppard said. "Atlantis is very much active and inhabited."

"I'm glad to hear it," Saul said. "I never expected anyone from that city to visit us again. It is an honor."

Teyla eyed him speculatively, eyes slightly narrowed. "Which were you?"

"What do you mean?"

"You said they referred to Admah and Atlantis as 'the dark and the light.' Which were you?"

"That would depend on who you asked, I suppose," Saul smiled.

When the lift doors opened, they stepped into another corridor. This one was clean and cheerful. There were colorful lights running along the ceiling and the floor was polished stone. The walls were lined with tapestries and, in stark contrast to the corridors of Atlantis, each doorway was ornate.

"Welcome to the real Admah," Saul said.

The team stood in the center of the corridor, turned in a circle, and stared. Ronon walked over to one wall and examined something more closely.

Sheppard followed him, and then turned back to Saul. "We saw a lot of these on the upper floor. This one seems newer, though. They're advertisements?"

The poster showed a beast with the head of a great cat and the body of something similar to a horse. Its fangs dripped saliva and its eyes gleamed as if lit from within. It was squared off against a tall, slender warrior with long blonde hair and a spear twice his own height. The spear had some sort of sphere midway down its shaft. The sphere glowed, and the man's hand disappeared into its center.

"We've been here in this city for a very long time," Saul said. "We've found ways to amuse ourselves. Entertainments, we call them. The problem with entertainment in any form is that they are limited unless you change either the milieu, or the stakes. Variety is the key. We have become quite adept at changing things up and avoiding boredom."

"But what is this thing?" Cumby said, stepping up beside Ronon. "This creature? It can't be real? I mean, I've never seen anything like it."

"You never will," Saul replied cryptically. "It was one of a kind. If you like, I'll tell you about it later on, but for now, if you will all follow me, I'd like to introduce you to some of the other citizens of Admah."

"I'd like to get back out to the gate and get a report through to Atlantis," Sheppard said.

"First, I must insist that you come with me," Saul said. "I'll arrange to have one of your people taken to the surface later — they can establish contact and set your people's mind at ease. Will that be acceptable?"

He smiled at Sheppard, but there was something odd in the expression. They all caught it, but managed not to react, though Ronon glared at him openly. Teyla looked perplexed, Rodney turned from Saul, to Sheppard, and back to Saul.

"Alright," Sheppard said at last. "Let's go. It will have to be soon, though," he added. "Commander Woolsey directed us to report in every three to four hours. If we don't make contact, he won't wait long before sending another team."

Saul smiled and led them on down the hall. Ronon dropped back beside Sheppard. "I don't like this," he said.

"I don't either, but we don't have much time to find out what we need to know. If we return to the surface now…"

Ronon met Sheppard's gaze and held it, then nodded. They passed by a number of the colorful posters. There were more warriors and more creatures, some familiar, others incredible, and still others that appeared to be amalgams of creatures they knew — sometimes mixed with those they didn't. Rodney studied the images, scanning a few as he passed, and then hurrying to catch up.

"What do you think they are?" Cumby asked Rodney, his voice low. "Surely they aren't images of actual creatures."

"I don't know," Rodney admitted. "I've tried to scan farther out to see if I can locate any other life signs, but the signal seems to be dampened. The range of what I can reach is limited."

"Have you analyzed the signal dampeners?"

Rodney turned, irritated. "How would you suggest I go about that? Let's see, I use a signal to analyze it, but…oh! It's dampened. Of course I'm trying to analyze it."

Cumby frowned. It wasn't an expression of irritation, he was thinking.

"What?" Rodney snapped.

"I'm remembering something. Almost everything I've learned as an adult is crystal clear…eerily so, I suppose. Things I saw and read when I was younger are still there, but it's like the data is running in the background."

Ahead, Saul had opened a door on the right side of the hallway. Light and sound spilled out of it. Cumby looked almost frantic and Rodney hung back, waiting.

"What's *not* there!" Cumby said, snapping his fingers in relief. "Instead of trying to find what *is* available and what *is* there — scan for signals and think about what *should be* there. It's an old game I learned as a boy. To find something that *is* there, you remove all of the things you expect to be there first. Whatever is left, that's what's different. I don't know if it will help, but…"

Rodney was already walking, following Saul, Sheppard, and the others. Cumby followed after quickly. "Rodney," he called. "Dr. McKay?"

The group disappeared through the doorway and Cumby scuttled to catch up. He entered the room just as the door closed behind them.

CHAPTER EIGHT

"MR. WOOLSEY?"

Woolsey glanced up from his desk to find Zelenka standing in the doorway, a tablet computer in one hand.

"Yes," Woolsey said. "What is it?"

"It's the gate, sir," Zelenka replied. "We've been trying to open it to receive Colonel Sheppard's SITREP as you requested. It won't open. We've tried everything, and we've been unable to reopen it, despite the fact we know the proper address. We haven't heard from the team since their departure, and now we're completely cut off. We had one short message from Colonel Sheppard right after they passed through the gate, but since then, nothing."

"If they attempt to report in, and that attempt fails, they should return to the gate, open it, and re-establish communications."

"I know sir. It's not like the Colonel to miss a report—but he's already half an hour late."

Woolsey sat and forced himself to count to ten as he thought. His first instinct was to try and force the gate open and send another team through to be certain nothing had gone wrong. It wasn't the first time that Colonel Sheppard or the members of his team had failed to act in strict accordance with regulations, and he didn't want to appear to have a knee-jerk reaction every time it happened. He also didn't want to fail to act if they were in trouble, and the irony of the moment wasn't lost on him.

His own philosophy was one of strict adherence to protocol. He'd come to Atlantis with a very straight-forward, no nonsense attitude toward command, but over time he'd learned that there could be more than one set of rules. Time and again, when strict adherence to regulations would have ended in disaster, death, or worse, his people had come through in startling and spectacular ways that he himself could never have conceived. It wasn't easy, but he'd brought himself, and them, to a sort of compromise.

"We'll give them a couple more hours before we panic," he said. "But I want a full crew working on getting that gate opened again, and I want a second team on alert to be ready at a moment's notice. Get Major Lorne to handle it." He paused, then added, "And see if we can dig up anything else on Admah. I'm beginning to dislike this situation."

He turned back to his work. Zelenka stood in the doorway a moment longer, as if he might say something further, such as reminding the Commander that he wasn't an errand boy. Woolsey kept his gaze firmly fixed on the paperwork he was processing, and eventually Zelenka took the hint.

When the doorway was empty, he glanced up and stared thoughtfully into the blank space for a few moments, then returned to his reports.

Major Lorne gathered a second team in a ready room just off the main control area. They spent their time inventorying equipment cases, checking their weapons, and chatting quietly. No one showed any particular concern, but the tension in the air was thick. The longer they went without word from Colonel Sheppard, the thicker it grew.

Zelenka had his own team gathered around a group of computer consoles. They had several screens open at once. One scanned for any type of radio or communication signal from the gate, concentrating primarily on weeding out static from the last moments the gate had been open to see if something had been missed. The rest of the personnel were divided between those running a variety of searches on the exhaustive data in Atlantis' databases, seeking any mention of Admah — good or bad — and a frantic team trying to open the gate back to the city. Very little had surfaced, and what they'd found was open in yet another window being translated.

"Here's something," said a young woman, Doctor Quint, tapping the screen.

Zelenka leaned closer. "What is it?"

"It's another of the same sort of isolated reports we've been finding," Quint replied. "Travelers visited Admah, and they never returned. The translation isn't complete, but in this report it says that there was a malfunction with the gate itself. They were unable to send anyone through to search. It's just like now, isn't it? They continued to try for some time, but they never managed to reopen the gate to Admah. Their people were never heard from again."

"I think we just discovered the meaning of that warning we ignored," Zelenka said, feeling his heart sink. "Keep searching. There has to be someone who took the time to study this. I can't believe they lost an entire group of their own people and all it received was a simple warning label."

Quint went back to her computer screen and Zelenka turned toward the gate. He thought about Rodney, on the other side of that portal. The two men were at each other's throats constantly, Rodney going on about how much smarter he was than the rest of the universe, and Zelenka trying to ignore him. He never argued the exact point, because it was very likely true. Arrogant, socially inept, and rude, Rodney was possibly the most brilliant man Zelenka had ever encountered. Still, no amount of intelligence granted the right to lord it over others, and there was a certain lack of common sense that accompanied Rodney's brilliance — evidenced in actions like the one that had erased the warning about the Admah Gate — that grated on Zelenka's nerves.

The missions rarely fell to Zelenka. Rodney had more experience, but that came in many cases from greater courage. Zelenka had signed on as a scientist, not an adventurer. He preferred to remain in the lab and provide support. Rodney plowed into things at full speed and, more often than not, his presence was crucial to a mission's success. Zelenka felt a certain amount of personal guilt connected with the role he'd chosen, and with his reluctance to take the plunge into adventure. At times like this, he felt that guilt most strongly.

"Where are you Rodney?"

The gate, and the radios, held their silence.

CHAPTER NINE

THE ROOM THEY ENTERED was chaotic. Rather than the bright even lighting they were used to in Atlantis, lanterns and strings of track lighting broke the huge room into smaller areas, making it look like some sort of weird alien bazaar. They stopped in a foyer, separated from the main room by beaded curtains that glittered like droplets of water in the low, flickering light. There was something overwhelming about the sights, scents, and sounds that assaulted them, and none of them was in a hurry to cross the threshold.

Saul smiled at them as they took it all in — or attempted to. "What do you think?" he said. "Am I correct in guessing it is somewhat different to Atlantis?"

Rodney glanced down at his scanner, frowned, and then turned to Saul. "You do know that your moon — uh, *city* — has jumped out of orbit?" he said. "Unless my calculations are wrong, in fact, and they never are — or almost never — you have less than a week before the sun is too close to allow for any means of escape, even assuming the city has an operational star drive."

"You don't waste any time on pleasantries, do you?" Saul said with a chuckle. "If it eases your mind in any way, we are well aware. We've had a lot of time to work on the star drives. If memory serves, your city sank beneath the waves…many years ago. We have been here all along, and though we choose to spend a great deal of our time entertaining ourselves, we have not been completely idle in scientific advance. Some might say we've been here a bit too long. You seem to forget, Dr. McKay, that while you have a working knowledge of the star drive, my people built it. And we have made modifications. By embedding anchors into the bedrock of the planet's surface, we've merged the city and the moon. Modifications to the star drive have enabled us to —"

"Fly the entire thing as if it was a starship," Cumby cut in.

Rodney glared at him, but Saul nodded and smiled. "Exactly. We are able to change the orbit of the planet itself—even to fly it to a new location, or remove it from orbit completely. We could explore the galaxy."

"Yes, very *Space 1999*." When Saul looked perplexed, he added, "So you decided to test it by driving into the sun?" He made no attempt to hide the sarcasm or the frustration in his voice. "Of all the possible uses for such technology, you chose mass suicide?"

"There is nothing to be concerned about," Saul said, waving the comment aside. "You'll have to trust me when I tell you that we know exactly what we're doing. Now, come. I want to introduce you to some of the others. It's been a long time since we had any company and you, Dr. McKay, are putting a damper on the party."

Saul stepped forward and swept the curtains aside.

The room beyond was much larger than Rodney had first imagined. In fact, it was more a long string of small rooms, segmented off by low walls, architectural constructions of every sort, shape, and variation of light. There were fountains that bubbled with liquid of varying hue, flickering in the corners and along the walls.

There were acoustically divided alcoves, and a variety of music floated out from within them, soft and muted so that each melody and harmony blended subtly with those from the other rooms.

To the right, on a slightly raised platform, a woman danced. There was a man seated on a stool beside her, bent over an odd stringed instrument. It vaguely resembled a guitar, but it had three necks. The musician's hand flowed from one to the next, and by some trick of electronics, or acoustics, the notes from whichever strings he left lingered as he plucked the next into life. The woman wore only the sheerest of gowns, and she danced seductively, her eyes closed and her lips provocatively parted. Those gathered nearby watched, but the musician never looked up.

Straight across from them a group of tables was arranged in a semi-circle. The people gathered around them wore a startling diversity of color and style. One man lounged back in his chair, dressed head to foot in black leather. His hair was a bright, shocking white, and his shoulders were almost as wide as Ronon's. At his table sat a very slender woman in a long green dress that shimmered in the dim light, a squat, burly man with a beard, and a blond woman dressed in brilliant blue. Her hair was piled on top of her head and tied in place with strings of crystal. None of them seemed quite…natural. It was as if their personas had been donned like clothing, or a disguise — a caricature of decadence.

"They don't seem to be part of one race at all," Sheppard commented, nodding across the room. "I thought you were all Ancients?"

"Indeed," Saul said. "Most of us still bear the appearance with which we began our lives, but some have chosen to find their pleasure in… reconstruction. There are many ways to amuse one's self and, believe me, we have traveled all of those roads from end to end.

"You are welcome to take part in any of our entertainments. There are games of chance, refreshments, musicians — if you delve deeper into the city you'll find theater and comedy, battles and anything else you could possibly desire as… diversion.

"In fact," he said, turning to sweep his arm out in a gesture encompassing the room and the city beyond, "I think you'll find yourselves very popular. As I said before, it's been a very long time since we had any visitors here. We have been too long without variety, and it has not been good for us. Please, make yourselves at home."

"You said that we'd be able to send someone to the surface to make contact with Atlantis," Sheppard said. "I'd like to take you up on that. Now. We have a scheduled report to make and we're already overdue. They're going to be opening the gate and expecting to contact us and if we don't report in…"

"Of course," Saul said.

He turned and gestured to a thin, dark man standing along one wall. The man was not dressed in the same level of finery as the others and his expression was devoid of emotion. He wore what appeared to be a military uniform, or that of some sort of security guard, and there was a weapon holstered on his belt. He stopped a few feet away from Saul.

"Henrik, I need you to take Colonel Sheppard, or one of his people, to the surface and out to the gate," Saul said. "They will need to get close enough to the gate to get their signal past the dampeners. When they have established contact with Atlantis, you will escort them back down into the city. I don't have to tell you to be discreet."

"I'm very sorry, but it can't be done, sir," the man said.

Saul grew very still. He controlled his voice with an obvious effort. "I gave you an order, citizen," he said softly. "These are our guests, and we owe them this courtesy. What prevents it?"

"The storms have blown in, sir," the man said, still emotionless. "There is no way to make it to the surface without raising shields over the outer walls of the city. That would prevent communications and might draw… unwanted attention."

"How long?"

"The storm is expected to last through the night," the man replied. "There is no way anything can pass on the surface, but it should blow over by morning. I will post a watch on the monitors…the moment it is clear, I will send word."

"Very well." Saul turned away, and the uniformed man melted back against the wall, becoming part of the shadows. "I'm afraid we have a problem," Saul said. "I can offer you accommodations until morning, and the hospitality of the city, but you will be unable to leave before dawn. Admah has long borne the brunt of such storms. Sand blows across the surface of the planet with such velocity it would flay any man who stepped into it, and I'm afraid that even if we could get you safely to the surface you would not be able to send or receive a radio signal. We have had to raise our shields once more, to protect the lower city; you may have noted the effect the storms have had on the gardens and the outer walls. Our scientists tell me they're caused by the occasional shifts orchestrated by the star drive you are so concerned about, Dr. McKay. Do you have an opinion?"

Rodney was torn between the chance to show off and the desire not to be drawn in. Saul's eyes twinkled, and it was obvious he didn't really care what the answer would be.

"It makes sense," Rodney said. "Even small axis and orbital shifts can cause cataclysmic changes in planetary systems. I'd have to do more research, of course, but…"

"Perhaps another time," Saul said. "Eventually I'm sure you'll find your way into the company of like minds. We have some truly brilliant men in the city. I am sure they would find you…amusing."

Rodney felt himself flush, but he managed, for once, to keep his mouth shut.

Sheppard's eyebrow lifted, and he studied Saul's face carefully. There was an edge to Saul's conversation. Despite all the welcomes and well wishes, there was something the man wasn't sharing.

"It looks like we're here for the night," Sheppard told his team. "We'll get someone with a radio up to the surface as soon as possible. If Atlantis doesn't have the gate open for our report, we'll dial it ourselves."

"We've had guest quarters prepared in the delta wing," Saul said. Then, turning to Henrick, he said, "Show our guests to their rooms, and see to it that they are provided with refreshments. I want them to be as comfortable as possible."

"Follow me, please." Henrick started off without speaking another word and without waiting to see if they followed. There was obviously no love lost between the guard and Saul.

Ronon and Sheppard exchanged a glance, and then followed.

Though none of the activities around them ceased, every pair of eyes in the room turned as the group passed. Women sized them up, men took their measure. There were smiles and whispered comments. More than once fits of giggles broke out. Then the team was out of the room and moving deeper into the city, leaving the huge chamber to return to its revelry.

CHAPTER TEN

THE TEAM WAS LED TO A SERIES of rooms that were lavish by any standards, although their guide strode down the hall without acknowledging any of it. It was hard to tell whether he was annoyed at the task of escorting them, or simply bored. He opened one door after another along a lushly carpeted passageway until he had settled them all in, two to a room. Teyla had a room to herself. He spent a bit longer at her doorway, and when he asked if there was anything she needed, anything he could do for her, his eyes lingered on her face. She cast a glance at Sheppard, and then shook her head. There was little humor in her polite smile.

She pulled back into her room and closed the door. Henrick stared at the doorway a moment longer, and then led the rest of them to their quarters.

As with most of the other rooms in Admah, the floors were of polished tile, or possibly stone. They were covered with thick rugs and heavy carpet in bright reds, purples, and yellows. Tapestries hung on the walls and the beds were covered in soft velvet. It looked more like the accommodations at a palace than guest quarters for travelers. It was, in fact, the most decadent lodging that Sheppard or any of the others had ever seen, but they kept their silence until their guide bowed low and left them alone.

Then Sheppard glanced around. "Is it just me or is anybody else reminded of Caesar's Palace on steroids?"

"I was thinking a medieval Disneyland," Cumby agreed.

"I like it," Ronon said. "They appreciate a good fight."

Teyla smiled, but said nothing.

"We have to find a way to contact Atlantis," Sheppard said. "There's something going on here, and I don't like it. The hospitality seems genuine enough, but that storm sure rolled in conveniently."

He glanced across at Rodney.

"We need you to find us a spot—any spot—where we can get a signal through when Atlantis opens the gate for a SITREP. Can you do that?"

"Of course," Rodney replied. "I can tell you where that spot is right now."

"Really? Well suppose you pry yourself away from the scanner for a minute and tell me."

Rodney glanced up and glared. "It's on the surface. In fact, it's on the surface, outside the shield protecting the city, probably in that stone circle surrounding the gate."

Sheppard folded his arms over his chest and scowled.

"What did you want me to say?" Rodney protested. "Maybe I could run around the city, broadcasting randomly in all directions and looking for a gap in their shield? 'Can you hear me now?' 'Can you hear me now?' I'm working on it. I'm sure we'll find something—but there's one thing holding me back."

"What's that?"

"People interrupting me to see if I've discovered something, when I should be working."

"Just get us a link to Atlantis," Sheppard snapped.

"What do you make of all those posters?" Cumby said, changing the subject. "Do you think any of those creatures could possibly be real?"

"Probably not." Ronon's hand dropped to the butt of his gun, and he sighed.

"Don't sound so disappointed," Sheppard grinned.

Ronon shrugged. "I've seen a lot of things, but nothing like any of those."

"I guess it could be some sort of a movie," Cumby suggested, "or a staged computer generated entertainment. Then again, until I came to Atlantis, I'd never seen anything like a Wraith either. And what was it Saul said when I asked about the creature on the poster? 'It was one of a kind.'"

"Good point." Ronon smiled, a feral baring of teeth. It was obvious that he wouldn't be disappointed if one of the creatures turned out to be real, or for that matter if all of them did.

"This doesn't make any sense," Rodney muttered. He turned the scanner one way, and then another, frowning.

Sheppard drew closer, peering over McKay's shoulder. "What doesn't make any sense?"

"If there are storms up there like the ones Saul described, I'd be able to find some trace of them. I can't. I can't find a single anomaly in the pressure or weather patterns."

"What if your signal isn't reaching the surface?" Cumby suggested. "I mean, to scan for weather patterns, you'd have to be able to reach beyond the city…"

"I don't know if it is or not, do I?"

"Wait a minute," Sheppard cut in. "Are you telling me that you think Saul is lying about the storm?"

"Yes, I think they're lying. That's exactly what I think. I think they don't want us getting to the surface, opening the gate, or contacting Atlantis. I think they don't want us knowing why they knocked a moon onto a collision course with the sun. I think being here is a very bad idea, and I think we should be on our way back to the gate right this moment."

"Okay then," Sheppard said. "We need to find a way to get someone to the surface."

"I'll go," Ronon offered. His hand had already dropped to the butt of his gun.

"Hold on," Sheppard said. "I don't want anyone roaring around, weapons drawn. They're acting suspiciously, but so far they've offered no direct threat. I want to get in contact with Atlantis, but I don't want to tip our hand until we're absolutely certain we have no choice."

"Oh, sure, they're the perfect hosts so far," Rodney said. "Other than the whole driving us into a sun thing, I can't see any reason for complaint."

Sheppard ignored him. "Our best bet is to go back into the city and mingle. They invited us to sample their hospitality and we're going to do that. I want all of you to keep your eyes and ears open and find us a way back to the upper levels. We also need to see if we can get a feel for their motives. If there isn't a storm, what reason could they possibly have for keeping us here? We need to find out why they've changed the city's orbit, and how, or if, they intend to stop it."

"Of course they intend to stop it," Rodney cut in. "Or change it again. Why would anybody in their right mind launch themselves toward the sun if they couldn't stop it?"

"Can *you* stop it, Rodney?" Sheppard leaned closer, trying to get a feel for what the man was studying so intently.

"The planet, I mean. If you got into the system, could you change the course?"

"That would depend."

"Depend on what?"

"Do you really want me to go into it? Whether the guidance system is intact. How much power they have diverted to the star drive. The age of the parts. How long they've been inactive. How much power is available. There are multiple ZPMs, and they seem to have plenty of power, but I don't really know that until I get a chance to measure their charge. There are too many variables." He scrubbed a hand across his face. "Right now I can't even get into their system."

"On Atlantis," Teyla said, "there is access to the main computer system in almost every room."

"Yes, yes," Rodney said, rolling his hand impatiently. "We aren't on Atlantis."

"Dark, and light," Teyla replied. "The cities are twins. I believe we will find the control panels here."

Sheppard nodded. "Rodney, stay put and do what you can to get into their system, everyone else with me. Let's see if we can't find out a little more about these people — and whatever it is they're up to here."

CHAPTER ELEVEN

AS SHEPPARD RETRACED THEIR tracks, the sounds of the inner city floated back to him. The halls of the huge building spun off in all directions, but the heartbeat of the city pulsed in that single chamber. Voices and music echoed down the hall. The sound confused their ears, reverberating off the walls and polished floor. It seemed as if it were a part of the walls, its essence powering the people rather than the people creating the sound. The city had a presence all its own.

Eventually he caught the glitter of lights ahead and stepped out into the huge, pavilion-like chamber they had visited before. Coming into it from the opposite side, they had a view around the corners to the right and left that had not been afforded by the main entrance. The place was a labyrinth of sights and sounds. The young woman still danced on her raised platform and her eyes turned toward them briefly before she spun away and quickened her rhythm. As before, the musician did not look up, paid no notice to anything around him, least of all the dancer. His fingers sped on the strings of his instrument, matching her tempo. The two of them seemed to be joined in some way that went beyond the physical, two parts of one performance.

"Okay, we'll find a central spot to use as a base of operations, and then spread out and see what you can see, learn, or figure out. Do your best to play along with whatever they have in mind; try to blend," Sheppard said. "Anything you can find out might make a difference."

The group wandered over to a long and sinuous bar behind which a small man shuffled bottles, bored and purposeless. He looked like he was killing time. Sheppard stepped up to the bar and leaned on it as he scanned the room. It was a quiet spot, for the moment, and seemed as good as any to take in the layout of the place.

When the bartender turned toward them his face transformed. He beamed as he spread his hands flat on the bar's surface. "Welcome! Welcome, my friends. My name is Damien, Damien Walz, and I am at your service."

"Damien..." Sheppard flung a glance at Teyla. It was impossible to tell if the barman was simply happy they'd chosen to speak with him first, or putting on an act for their benefit. In the end, he supposed, it didn't matter — if they were going to mingle they had to start somewhere. "Good to meet you, Damien Walz."

Still beaming, he said, "What would be your pleasure tonight? If I don't have it in a bottle, describe it, and I'll see what I can do to recreate it for you."

"That sounds great," Sheppard said. "I'll take you up on that in a little bit, but for the moment I'm looking for Saul. Any idea where I might find him?"

"He'll be here soon enough," Walz said. "He's not going to give up the chance to show you all off. So, while you're waiting, you must have a drink! I insist!"

Sheppard started to frown, caught himself, and smiled. He set his elbows on the bar and leaned forward as casually as he could manage. "Okay, since you insist, what do you recommend?"

"You must try the house wine." The voice was melodic,

provocative, and it came from very close to his left ear. "The grapes are organic, pressed between the soft pale thighs of virgins and lovingly bottled in crystal decanters."

Sheppard's eyebrow rose. He turned slowly to find himself face to face with a tall, slender woman in a very sheer evening gown. Her hair was dark with highlights that caught in the flickering glow of the room and trailed lazily back over her shoulders. Her eyes were wide and deep, glinting somewhere between blue and gray. She sipped from a graceful goblet and smiled at him over the rim.

"Are you one of the virgins?" Sheppard said. "Because if you are, I'll take two bottles."

She laughed and shook her head. "Oh my, no. I treasure my entertainment far too much to have missed out on that. Damien, let's have a decanter of your wine for our guests. On me."

Damien, the bartender, moved to gather the decanter and glasses. He set them out before the team and filled each glass.

"Watch her," he said, winking at Sheppard. "When she says the wine is going to be on her, you never know just what she might mean…"

Sheppard lifted his glass to the bartender, and then to the woman. "Thank you for the wine. My name is John Sheppard."

She placed a hand on his wrist and smiled. "Well, then, hello John Sheppard. It is a good thing that it was I, and not Damien, who first suggested the wine."

"Why is that?"

"Because," she said, "we have a custom here in Adamah.

No traveler should taste our wine for the first time but from a woman's lips. Failure to comply can... sour the experience." She leaned in closer.

"But I don't even know your name," Sheppard said.

"Mara."

Her voice had grown husky and deep. She lifted the glass and took a long sip, her chin tilting upward as she offered her lips to Sheppard. Her eyes never left his.

"When in Rome," Sheppard whispered. Leaning in he brushed his lips across hers, very lightly, and drank. Their lips touched for mere seconds but it was enough to stop his breath. When they parted, Sheppard was grinning from ear to ear.

"Me next!" Ronon offered, pressing forward.

Teyla struck him in the chest hard enough that the sound of the blow echoed through the room. "Sit down!"

Everyone at the bar roared with laughter at this. Ronon frowned, but he was smiling. He did as he was told and dropped onto the nearest seat, lingering over the glass of wine he was served and staring out at the room as if he was searching for a woman to help him with the first sip.

"This place makes me nervous," he said to Teyla, his voice low but loud enough for Sheppard to catch. "They're all staring at me."

"Well, they've probably just never seen such a fine physical specimen."

"You think? Because it's only the old men who are staring."

"You know, I believe you may be right."

Sheppard was about to comment when Mara gripped his arm possessively, her fingers caressing him through the fabric of his uniform with disturbing persistence. Her eyes sparkled and she sipped her wine slowly as he studied her face and tried to work out what the hell was going on. Suddenly, she put down her glass and stood.

"You know, John Sheppard, we really are wasting too much time here. You are visitors, and you've seen so little. You and your people are the talk of the city…why not let me introduce you?"

He glanced over at Teyla, and she gave him a subtle nod. "All right," he said then, "as long as I don't have to drink from all their lips before they tell me their names."

Mara laughed. "I like you, John Sheppard," she said. "I like you very much."

She linked her arm with his and pulled him away with a smile. "Come with me. You will find that you already have many friends here. They've been watching you and talking about you since Saul brought you through the door."

Teyla watched from her table as Sheppard was led — almost literally by the nose — into the crowd. Soon, he was lost from sight.

"I am not comfortable here," she murmured to Ronon. "These people are…unnatural."

"Jealous?"

"No, of course not. But I do not trust her. For all her good will, she was quick to separate us from Colonel Sheppard. He is the ranking officer — if I was planning something, this is exactly how I would proceed. I am going to follow them and watch for trouble."

"You do that," Ronon said. "I'll stay here and keep my eyes open. I'm hoping to meet one of those dragons."

He saluted her with his glass and turned his warrior's gaze upon the pulsing room. She knew him too well to be deceived; he was as uneasy as herself.

As always, Sheppard demanded the impossible.

Just get us a link to Atlantis, McKay. Just find a hole in their shield in the next ten minutes. Just figure out how this ten thousand year old computer system works — I'm sure it's compatible with Vista!

Well, this time it was a no go. There was nothing in their Disney Princess quarters to help, no handy docking station and animated paperclip. His scanner only told him so much, and today the headline news was that the alleged storm was a lie and there was only one thing to do — get out of the city and hike back to the gate, dial up Atlantis and go home.

End of story.

Stuffing the scanner into his jacket, Rodney left their quarters and headed back toward the hive of scum and inequity that was Admah's meat market. He needed to find Saul and he needed to find out exactly what was going on with Moon Base Alpha.

He could hear the thump of music and smell the alien aromas of food and people before he stepped through the doors, pausing to let his eyes adjust to the dark. He saw Saul right away, standing beside the dancer on the small stage. The woman continued to sway and move as Saul spoke to her, and the musician never hesitated. But Saul's gaze wasn't fixed on the dancer — strange — and as he spoke, Rodney realized he was watching Sheppard cross the floor arm in arm with a beautiful woman.

Typical.

Stuffing his hands into his pockets, he made his way across the room.

"It's beautiful, isn't it?" Saul smiled, stepping down from the platform as Rodney drew closer, careful not to disturb either dancer or musician. "He rarely repeats a song, or a sequence of notes. I've been listening to him for a very long time and I can't remember the last time I noted a repetition."

"Fascinating, I'm sure," Rodney said. "There must be literally millions of variances possible, depending on the range of the instrument. But I didn't come over to ask about the music — I need to ask you some questions. If you have time, that is."

"There's nothing but time here," Saul said, his expression serene.

"Yes, that's what has me confused. Tell me why it is, with all the time in the world at your fingertips, you launched yourself directly at the heart of the sun?"

"I did not say that we had," Saul replied. "You jumped to that conclusion from your limited observations."

"Well, if you didn't do it," Rodney said, confused, "then who did?"

"All will be made clear in due time Dr. McKay. Are you always so impatient?"

"No, usually I'm incredibly patient. It's just when I'm trapped on a moon on a collision course with the sun that I get a little tense."

Saul's smile was less friendly. "I would have thought a man of science such as yourself would appreciate coming slowly and carefully to new knowledge."

"So tell me, slowly and carefully, that you *do* intend to steer away from the sun," Rodney said. "I mean, you're not really going to fry yourselves are you? I say this because I've given some thought to the best and worst ways of dying—believe me, I've had reason to worry about it—and I have to say that self-immolation is a spectacularly insane way to go."

"As I said, all will be made clear in time."

"Really. Could you *be* any more cryptic?" Rodney sighed and attempted to swallow his irritation. "So, the star drive is under control of a command computer, yes? And the computer is still functional?"

"All systems of the city are functional except those which we have purposely shut down."

"Then you must have control over the field that's preventing any signals from reaching the surface. You could shut it down and allow me to contact—"

"I'm afraid I can't do that." He glanced around the room, obviously distracted; he was still watching Sheppard and the woman, barely paying any attention to Rodney's questions. "I've told you the dampeners are physical in nature. They aren't controlled by an electronic console, or a computer program. It was never our intention to remove them."

"Then take me to the surface and let me walk back to the gate," Rodney insisted. "I only need a few moments up there to open a wormhole and…"

"Did you forget about the storm?"

"Ah yes, the 'storm'. How could I forget?"

Saul turned toward him suddenly, his eyes dark and his back board-straight. "You're wasting your time, Dr. McKay. No direct communication is allowed out of this city. I believe I explained fairly clearly how we have prevented detection by the Wraith, and I'm not about to break that successful silence now." He took a breath, forcing a smile. "Why don't you relax and enjoy yourself? I'm sure even *you* can find a suitable distraction here. There are so very many." He swept his hand in an arc across the room and smiled as he turned and walked away.

"If you're still worried about the Wraith," Rodney called after his retreating back, "then why lower your shields? Why allow us to detect you?"

Saul either didn't hear him or ignored him completely and continued walking.

Just at that moment Teyla passed by, focused on something ahead of her. He called out, but just like Saul she didn't answer.

"Right," he grumbled, "Rodney McKay being ignored in a nightclub. How novel."

He pulled the scanner out of his pocket, but it still held no answers.

As Teyla crossed the huge hall, she kept Sheppard and Mara in her sites, their path winding in and out of small alcoves. Here and there, Mara grabbed someone else by the arm, or called out to a friend and introduced them to her guest. Despite the detours, Teyla noted that the woman was working herself steadily toward a particular set of doors along the far wall. Just as she was about to follow and see if she could get close enough to hear what they were talking about, Teyla felt a hand on her shoulder. She spun around and found herself face to face with Saul.

"I trust you're finding everything to your liking?" The man's features were a mask of serenity and peace, but something danced just beneath the surface of his eyes that made her nervous. He kept his hand on her shoulder, and she fought the urge to brush it off like a bug.

"Yes, everything is well, thank you. Perhaps we may speak later, but right now I need to have a word with Colonel—"

"Excellent." Saul cut her off, but did not release her. "Somehow, I knew you'd enjoy it here. I sensed it about you."

Teyla forced a smile, aware of the need to maintain good will. "Your hospitality is admirable. But, excuse me, I need to catch up with Colonel Sheppard." She glanced over her shoulder, but Sheppard and the woman were gone.

"Your Colonel Sheppard seems to be well taken care of at the moment. Why don't we sit and share some wine?" His smile widened. "You can tell me all about your home world and I can introduce you to a few of our citizens. The more people you know, the easier it will be to fit in here. Perhaps we have some common ground. If Atlantis is inhabited again there should be opportunities for trade."

Teyla shot a sideways glance at the point where she had lost sight of Sheppard, but the two had not returned. "Very well," she said. "Perhaps you can tell me more about your people. Specifically the one they call Mara."

Saul nodded as he pulled her toward the bar and eased her into a seat. She saw Ronon, watching her out of the corner of his eye as he pretended to watch the dancer. She smiled, but it was an uncomfortable attempt and she doubted Saul was convinced.

"Suppose you go first," he said, sipping his wine. "Tell me about Atlantis. I've been there you know, a very long time ago. For you, it would be lifetimes."

"I'm afraid that the current inhabitants of the city would be very unfamiliar to you," she said. "Your people — who we call the Ancestors — have been gone for a long time."

"Fascinating," Saul said. "And your people rule the city now?"

Teyla shook her head. "No, that is a long story."

CHAPTER TWELVE

MARA HELD SHEPPARD'S HAND as she pulled him through the door and into the darkened passageway beyond. They stood together in the cool darkness, until she passed her hand over a small panel. A series of lamps illuminated a long, winding staircase that passed up into more darkness. Sheppard stopped for a moment, disoriented by the sudden change in light, but Mara tugged insistently at his hand, urging him forward.

"Come on, John Sheppard," she said. "I have something to show you — something important. You're going to love the view from up here. It's extraordinary."

"I'll bet."

He followed her up the stone steps, trying not to watch her too closely as she climbed ahead of him. He scanned the walls as they went, looking for anything that might help him understand what was going on, or give him insight into the city's systems. They climbed for a very long time, until finally stepping out into some sort of observatory. The ceiling was domed and appeared to be made of crystal, or heavy glass. He stared up through it into the night sky. From that vantage point he felt like he could see every star in the universe.

"We're not supposed to come up here," Mara said. "Saul says that it's too close to the surface, and that if there were scans in progress we might be detected, but I've been here many times over the years. I've watched Wraith craft fly directly over the city, and they never suspected a thing. I think he just doesn't want us away from his entertainments. It's very beautiful, don't you think? I wanted to share it with you."

Sheppard felt her press against his back, felt her breath against his neck. "It is beautiful," he replied. "It feels like we're standing right in the middle of all those stars. I can see why you come here."

She wrapped her arms around his waist and pulled him closer. "Exactly."

Carefully, Sheppard disentangled himself from her grasp. "Listen, I know this is probably not what you expected from me just now, but let me ask you a few questions, okay?"

The corners of her lips drooped. "I suppose."

She drew nearer once more, playing with the buttons on his shirt. "You ask your questions, and I'll try not to get…distracted."

"We're staring out at the night sky, right?"

She frowned. "Of course, you can see it…"

"Where's the storm?" Sheppard said. "Saul told us that we couldn't go to the surface to contact our people because of horrible storms sweeping across the surface."

She looked down in silence.

"What's really going on here?" he pressed. "Is there any way that I can get a message back to my people? I need to be able to contact them next time they open the gate."

Mara bit her lip and turned away. Then, as if making up her mind about something important, she turned back.

"I'm afraid that isn't possible." She drew closer, her lips brushing his neck as she sighed deeply. "Saul isn't going to take you to the surface, and there aren't any storms.

There never have been any storms. I'm sorry, but you can't contact your people."

Sheppard stepped closer and reached out a hand, laying his palm on her cheek. He smiled and said, "That's a shame. I have dozens of friends back in Atlantis who would love this place."

He leaned in, close enough to breathe his words softly into her ear. She shivered, and he knew that his moment had come. It was a cruel trick to play, but he had no choice.

"But they can't come if they don't know. There must be a way I can get word to them, to tell them about the wonders and the entertainment — the hospitality. How can I reach them? How can I let them know?"

She glanced up at him, as if checking his sincerity, then dropped her eyes. "I'm sorry, it's impossible. You can't dial out and they can't dial in — there are protocols in place that prevent any gate from connecting with Admah more than once."

"Protocols?" He drew back with a sick feeling, eyes narrowing. "What sort of protocols?"

"Once a connection has been established with another gate, it can never be dialed again. That's how we've kept our secrets all these years. We've had our problems, and our small invasions, but they were cut off from their people and eventually they were forgotten. No one who comes here can ever leave and their home world can never send a search party."

"What?" He stepped back in horror. "No one can leave…?"

"You think us cruel?" She sighed. "I understand, but you must try to understand too — our people fled this galaxy, abandoned us alone here. What choice did we have? How else could we survive? Saul believed —"

"Saul." And how come that wasn't a surprise?

"Saul created the protocol," Mara confessed. "Long ago, he was head of our science counsel. It was his plan to seal us off, to install the dampeners and separate us from those who meant us harm. I'm not familiar with the technology used to create it, I only know that it has been in place and has protected us for a very long time."

Sheppard pushed her out to arm's length. "Protected you? By trapping your enemies here? If the Wraith ever dialed your gate, they'd come through and be trapped—but they'd still be *here*."

"I told you," she said, "the Wraith *have* come through. We aren't without defenses, and they thought they were trapped on a lifeless world. We picked them off a few at a time. The protocols limit the numbers and assets of any attackers. Saul and his men have handled the rest."

"And what about travelers who aren't your enemies? What about those who only came here to explore or offer trade? Where are they?"

"The protocols are in place to keep us safe," she repeated.

He stepped back, disgusted. "Do you know what's funny?" he said. "When we came here, our first priority was to search for survivors. We saw that your city was plunging into the sun and we thought 'Hey, there might be people in trouble over there.' Some gratitude."

"We did not ask for your help."

He glared at her. "Fine. Well, if Saul created the protocols, then Saul can reverse them. We're just going to have to get them switched off."

"There is no way to reverse them. They have been engineered into the system itself. Saul says — "

"I don't care what Saul says. I'm getting my team the hell out of this city and you can either help me or get out of my way." He pushed past her. "Maybe you're happy to be a prisoner for the rest of your life, but that doesn't work for me."

She looked stung, like he had just slapped her in the face. "I thought you liked me, John Sheppard."

"Are you kidding me? You just told us we're trapped here." He took a breath. "Look, I do like you. Why wouldn't I? You're a beautiful woman and you're the first person in this city to tell me the truth, but this changes everything. You have to see we can't just stay here."

She nodded and bit her lip. The corners of her eyes welled with tears, but she managed to keep them under control.

Sheppard watched her for a moment longer and then turned away. He hurried down the stairs and back toward the main room where he'd left the others. After a moment he heard Mara's footsteps echoing on the stairs as she followed.

CHAPTER THIRTEEN

SHEPPARD PLOUGHED BACK INTO the main room, blinking to accustom his eyes to the semi-darkness and flickering lights. The giant party that was the heartbeat of Admah continued unabated. If anything, there were more dancers and musicians, more laughing revelers and passionate couples than before. It took a moment to orient himself, but as soon as he spotted it he returned to the bar where he'd met Mara. The rest of the team — including McKay — had gathered around a single table, where Saul sat talking to Teyla. A couple of the local women hovered near Cumby, full of smiles and seduction.

"Returning to us so soon?" Saul raised an eyebrow. "I'd assumed that Mara would be giving you an… extended tour."

"You have a beautiful city," Sheppard said, struggling to keep his anger in check. "She took me to the observatory — the view was…overwhelming."

Saul's jaw stiffened, and then his smile returned. Clearly caught by surprise, he didn't seem perturbed. "Startling view isn't it?"

"Eye opening," Sheppard agreed.

Ronon, Teyla, and the others stared at him but Sheppard kept his expression neutral. He was about to speak again, when Saul stood and clapped his hands. The crowd grew silent, chairs shuffled, and a whispered murmur fluttered across the room.

The chamber grew lighter gradually as lamps were lit along its walls, and a group of men emerged from the shadows and began to slide tables together near the center of the room. It all took place in a matter of moments — obviously a well-practiced ritual. Sheppard and his team stood, watching in silence and waiting to see what new surprise Saul had in store.

"As it turns out," Saul said, "you've returned just in time for dinner, Colonel."

He turned to Teyla and offered his arm. She stared at it as if it might be poisonous and glanced at Sheppard. Though he longed to throttle the truth from Saul's lips now was hardly the time, so he nodded to Teyla and she reached out and took Saul's arm.

Turning away from the bar, Saul smiled and made his way down the dinner tables.

The rest of the team followed and Sheppard dropped back, falling in step beside Rodney.

"Listen up," he whispered, keeping his eye on Saul. "You're going to love this."

Rodney cocked his head, clearly trying to appear inconspicuous, but only succeeding in looking supremely suspicious and uncomfortable. Stealth was not among his talents.

"There is no storm, you were right. Mara says there's a protocol in place that prevents the gate from connecting to the same address twice. Once someone comes through from one gate, they can't return to where they came from and no one else can come through from there."

"But—"

"Just listen. I need you to figure out how they could do that — and then disable the protocol. Otherwise we're not getting home before we're all deep fried."

"There's a surprise," Rodney said through gritted teeth. "Whatever we do let's *not* get into a situation where Rodney has plenty of time to save the day. In fact, let's see if we can't complicate it hopelessly, encrypt it using Ancient code, and — oh, yeah — why not make sure it only involves equipment we've never seen?"

Sheppard looked at him. "Just do it Rodney."

Saul seated Teyla near the head of the dining table. He leaned close to one of the men hovering nearby — it was hard to tell if they were servants, or guards, or just used to doing what Saul told them. The man asked something, Saul answered, and the other nodded. He broke off from the group he'd been conversing with and approached Sheppard.

"We have taken the liberty of assigning you seating," the man said. "Many of our people have voiced an interest in meeting you, so we've done what we can to spread you out and give everyone the chance to entertain you. I hope you don't mind."

"That's fine," Sheppard said.

"If you will follow me then?"

Before Sheppard could do so, a hand fell on his shoulder. Mara was standing beside him, smiling tentatively. Teyla wondered what had occurred between them during their absence, but could not read the truth on Colonel Sheppard's face.

"If you don't mind," Mara said, "you could sit with me?"

"Of course," Sheppard said smoothly, breaking free of the pack and taking her arm. "I was hoping you'd catch up."

The man who was guiding them seemed irritated by the interruption, but he shrugged it off as Sheppard turned to follow Mara down the table and away. He led the rest on down the table and, within a few moments, Rodney had been deposited between two women who eyed him with interest, and Cumby had been escorted down to an oddly dressed group of diners near the far end of the table.

Ronon was the last to be seated. He found himself placed between a pair of elderly men who didn't speak to him at all. They studied him up and down, and cast glances back and forth. When one of them winked, he leaned forward, very close, and scowled. The man scuttled back and Ronon turned away to hide his grin.

As soon as everyone was seated, a round of appetizers was served. There were small platters stacked with warm, fresh bread, fried vegetables and fish of some sort, and more of the wine they'd been served in the bar. Next they brought out the main course, which was a smorgasbord of scent, color, and style. There were roasts of various types, large bowls of vegetables, exotic fruit, soups and breads and cheese. No matter how many times the wine glasses were filled more appeared as if by magic. It was the sort of feast that Sheppard imagined was usually reserved for royalty, but the citizens of Admah seemed unimpressed.

"You've gone to a lot of trouble," he said, leaning closer to Mara. "Or do you eat this way all the time?"

"We always dine at this time," Mara said simply. "Remember, we are a people who have dedicated ourselves to excess. Saul goes to a lot of trouble to keep us happy and we have become accustomed to our pleasures. It's the curse of living too long in isolation. When your options are limited, you spice them up."

"There's a question for you," Sheppard said. "You live in this place, the surface of the moon you've attached your city to is barren, and yet you can provide a meal like this? Where does it all come from? Does Saul send teams through the gate to forage? Does he have a way to override the protocols that lock gates out after one dial-in?"

"I'm afraid not," Mara replied. "I know what that would mean to you, but we have extensive gardens in the lower levels of the city. We raise the animals, grow the vegetables and fruits. It's become an art form, much like everything else remotely associated with pleasure and entertainment."

She reached out and trailed her fingers down his arm. "I have to admit though, that while the meal is nothing special, you make a rather pleasant spice."

Sheppard forced a smile and glanced down the table toward McKay. Rodney had magicked his computer out of nowhere and it was open on the table in front of him. A woman with long platinum blonde hair and green eyeliner leaned over his shoulder on his left, trying to whisper in his ear as he worked. Whatever it was she was saying, he did his best to ignore her, but she was persistent. She ran her index finger up and down his throat, teasing his earlobe and laughing softly. Eventually, Rodney drew back, exasperated.

Across the table and farther down, Teyla had engaged Saul in conversation. He was smiling and speaking expansively while she pretended to sip at her wine and nibbled the food. Sheppard saw that she kept a close eye on those near her, and he smiled. He didn't have to worry about Teyla letting her guard down, and if anyone could get something useful out of Saul, it was her.

Cumby was talking to a thin woman with so much hair piled on her head that it stretched a foot above her head. He kept glancing up at it, as if afraid it might topple into his food, or fall across his face and smother him. Under different circumstances, it would have been funny.

When Sheppard turned to Ronon he caught the big man's eyes. Ronon was eating. Of them all, he probably had the most common sense in situations like these. His plate was piled high with a little bit of everything available. He leaned over the table, his elbows planted firmly on either side of his plate, creating as threatening a countenance as possible. He shoveled the food in quickly, using his fingers when possible, and from time to time he glanced in irritation, or distrust, at one or other of the old men beside him. When he saw Sheppard looking at him he nodded toward the hallway leading to their rooms. His eyes were desperate.

At that moment, one of the old men reached out and squeezed Ronon's bicep. The big man shied away, turning toward the offender and scooping up another bite of the stew he was gulping down.

"I don't like being separated from my people," Sheppard said, turning back to Mara. "It makes me nervous."

"Please," Mara said, her voice low. "Eat. Later there will be an entertainment. I will see to it that you and your friends are seated together and, when there is more noise to cover our words, we will talk."

Sheppard met her gaze for a moment and then nodded. He had no choice but to trust her — she was the only one who had told them the truth, and that had to count for something. He turned to his plate and began to eat, keeping one eye on what happened up and down the table as he did so.

CHAPTER FOURTEEN

WHEN THE MEAL WAS OVER the lights were dimmed. Chairs slid back from the tables and the murmur of voices rose, then stilled. Near one end of the room another set of lights grew brighter. Saul stood, and those up and down the length of the table did likewise. They moved in a ripple of sound and shadow until everyone was standing, and then there was silence.

"What is it?" Sheppard whispered. "What's happening?"

He glanced up and down the table, but with the lights dimmed he couldn't be certain he was seeing the others. He saw silhouettes and shadows. He was pretty certain he saw Ronon, towering over everyone near him.

"It's time for the entertainment," Mara replied. "This is the moment Saul has been working up to all day. I'll be right back. I'm going to make certain Saul seats you in a group. I did promise."

She slipped away down the length of the table. Sheppard watched her go, and then studied the dimly lit group moving slowly toward the lighted exit. He was determined not to let the citizens of Admah make off with any of his team in the confusion. Mara had said to wait, but after only a few moments, he started off toward where Saul and Teyla had been seated. When he reached them he found Mara there ahead of him.

Saul turned, saw him approaching, and smiled, though

there was little humor in the expression.

"Mara has volunteered to escort you and your team to your seats," Saul said. "She will be your guide for the evening. If you have any further questions, she'll answer them to the best of her ability. The entertainments are self-explanatory, but there may be aspects that will confuse you. I will walk with you as far as I can, but there are details to which I must attend. I have my own part to play in what is to come and there are preparations that must be made. I will rejoin you, if I can, before the finale."

Teyla folded her arms in a gesture Shepard knew well. "What sort of 'entertainment' are we in for?"

"All things in their time, my dear," Saul said. "Are all the people in Atlantis so impatient? There is no reason to hurry—and all will be answered very soon. I can tell you this…you will not be bored."

Just then, a commotion arose off to one side and Sheppard turned to see Rodney and the others pushing their way through the crowd. They seemed relieved to see him and he smiled, though he didn't have much to put behind it.

"Speaking of answers," Rodney said, stepping up beside Saul, "I want some."

Sheppard tried to wave him to silence, but Rodney cocked his head, set his jaw, and plowed on. He had something to say and nothing on the planet was going to prevent him. Sheppard sighed.

"I want to know why you've prevented communication in and out of this city," Rodney said. "I want to know what possible reason you could have for sabotaging the DHD and the gate. I want to know why we're headed straight into the sun, and I want to know what you plan to do about it. All of this," he waved his arms to encompass the huge hall, "is ridiculous! You all go on eating and drinking and dancing and singing as if nothing has changed, but you know it's not true — right? You all know?" He turned to stare out into the crowd. "You all know he's aimed you into the heart of a sun, that death by fire is neither noble nor pleasant?"

Saul stood very still. His expression was grim. A man behind him stepped forward and moved toward Rodney, but Saul held out a hand and prevented him. Ronon stepped up beside Rodney, hand on the butt of his gun.

"You are a very difficult and persistent man, Dr. McKay. I owe you no explanation. The affairs of my city and my people are not yours to question. No one invited you or your team through that gate, but I'm afraid it was the last such trip you are likely to take. Long ago, before you were born, and likely before your parents, or even their parents were born, we made a decision.

"Our ways were not the ways of others of our kind. Those in cities like Atlantis concerned themselves with spiritual growth and ascension. We chose a different path. When it became clear that the differences between our cultures had become irreconcilable, we devised a plan. We sat on that plan for a very long time, working it out and refining it. We waited for the right moment and when the Wraith arose — we acted.

"Our city is protected. The gate is still active, but there have been modifications. It is possible to dial the coordinates to or from this gate one time from any other active gate. Once that has happened, a sequence of signals is initiated. Any further attempts by that particular gate to reach this one pass through a series of phase shifts that change the coordinates presented and prevent connection. There is no way to detect the frequency of this shift; it appears only as a failed address. Eventually, whoever is at the far end of that gate realizes that they are never going to make the connection again, and they give up."

"And you keep whoever came through here as prisoners?"

"Guests," Saul said. "They become our long term guests. We are not monsters here, Dr. McKay, but we have our laws and we have our security protocols, much as I suppose your own people do. We do not bend or break those laws — they have kept us safe for many, many years. There are those who would say too many."

"You have already broken those laws," Rodney said. "You turned off the shields. You opened up this world to long range scans and invited us here. If you'd left them in place, we would never have detected you, and we wouldn't be here, plunging to our deaths. There has to be a way to reverse —"

Sheppard grabbed Rodney by the arm and propelled him toward the lights and the door at the rear of the hall.

"What are you doing?" Rodney spluttered. "You heard him. He's holding us prisoner here, preventing us from reaching Atlantis, preventing Atlantis from reaching us. We have to —"

"What, Rodney?" Sheppard said softly. "Yell him into submission? You might have noticed that we're outnumbered and surrounded. We can keep arguing with the man, and end up locked away in some cell, or we can go along for the moment and find a way to get you logged into their system. Saul created the protocol, Mara told me as much up in the observatory, and he doesn't strike me as an insurmountable genius. How about you?"

"Of course not, but this can't be our plan?" Rodney said. "We just go along with them, eat drink and be merry, and hope we find a way to break into their system and escape?"

"You have a better one?"

Rodney glanced down at the floor and closed his eyes.

"John Sheppard," Mara said, stepping up beside them, "the entertainment is about to begin. I don't mean to interrupt, but we need to get to our seats. If you'll follow me?"

Rodney started to speak, thought better of it, and turned away. Sheppard held out his arm and Mara took it, smiling up at him. Ronon stared at the two of them and then fell in behind Cumby. Teyla started after them, but Saul grabbed her arm.

"I would be honored if you would sit with me. I'll be busy much of the time, but I do have a spectacular view."

"I would prefer to stay with my team."

"Of course." Saul let her go, reluctantly. "I will try to join you before the finale."

Teyla smiled thinly and turned away. She had no illusions about the man's intentions. He was attracted to her, and he was used to getting what he wanted. There was a confrontation in her future, but for the moment she'd avoided it. She hurried her steps and caught up with the others just as they reached a well lit exit, leading into a passageway beyond. This hall was only dimly lit, lined with more of the colorful posters, but these were newer. They were framed in brilliant moving tubes of multicolored light.

"It's like walking into a casino," Sheppard commented.

At the far end of the passageway they entered a large, round room. There were sealed doors all around it with keypad locks. Sheppard stared at them, started to ask what their purpose was, and then thought better of it. On the far side of the chamber, a large set of double doors stood open. Mara led Sheppard ahead of the others, and they walked through into much brighter light and a dull roar of sound.

Sheppard stopped, and the others were forced to wait as he took in the scene before him. They stood on a ledge that led off to the right and to the left, circling around and rising up and back in tiered seating. At intervals around the huge circular chamber there were blocks of more private seating, sealed off from the larger areas by clear walls.

"Come," Mara said. She tugged on Sheppard's arm, and he followed her around the circle.

The others followed slowly, taking in the glass-walled chamber. Below them was a large space that resembled a stone bowl. The walls were painted in bright colors, murals circling the room, and thick barred doors were scattered around the perimeter. It was dark on that lower level, and it was difficult to make out what might be down there.

"What is it?" Rodney said uneasily. "Some sort of theater?"

"Not exactly."

Mara led them around the first group of open seats and into the terrace below. Inside were two rows of more comfortable seats fronted by low-slung acrylic tables. "This is where we will sit," she said. "The entertainment will start soon."

"But what *is* it?" Rodney persisted. "What is this place?"

"Looks like some sort of arena," Cumby said. "Like a coliseum, maybe?"

Mara stared down into the silent, empty space. "You are closer to the truth than you know. In other times and places that is exactly what this would have been called — a coliseum. We only call it 'The Entertainment.'"

They took their seats and as the citizens of Admah filled in on either side, whispering under their breath, the lights began to dim.

"Here we go," Sheppard said.

Mara squeezed his arm and he glanced at her. She was staring into the darkness below, eyes sparkling and lips parted.

He turned back, just as spotlights lit a raised platform that emerged from the darkness near the center of the room.

CHAPTER FIFTEEN

SAUL STOOD ALONE ON the raised platform. He wore a jacket of a sparkling material that caught the spotlights perfectly. If he'd had a top hat he'd have looked like an Ringmaster — as it was, Sheppard thought of Vegas again. He expected trained animals, or jugglers, or maybe some steroid enhanced wrestlers to appear. Saul smiled, and the platform slowly turned, rising even higher above the open expanse of the arena. Rings of lights circled the space. At first, only the very lowest ring of lights illuminated, then they grew brighter, and the next row followed suit. The process slowly gained momentum until the lights rippled up the walls and brought the floor of the arena to life.

By some trick of projection, the brightly lighted walls shifted color and reformed, creating the image of large blocks of hewn stone. The doors, which had already seemed large, now appeared arched and their surfaces had the aspect of thick, carved wooden planks. Wrought iron rings were set in the surface that had not been there moments before. It was a grand illusion, and its effect wasn't lost on Sheppard or his team

"Welcome," Saul cried. "Welcome one and all to the latest and the greatest, the finest entertainment Admah can offer. Ready your bets and prepare to be amazed. Most of you know me so well you could stand here and speak the words for me, steal my very soul and breath. Tonight, though, is different. Can you feel it? Tonight there are strangers among us. Tonight there is new blood in the audience, and I — for one — can almost taste it."

The words flowed with practiced ease. Sheppard glanced around him and saw that the citizens of Admah leaned forward in their seats. Their eyes were open wide, their lips parted. They appeared fascinated, though the fascination held an edge of desperation. Whispered comments rustled through the air, and more than once Sheppard caught money changing hands as bets were laid. Whatever they expected to see tonight, on some level, they also expected to be let down and disappointed. For Sheppard and the others, the entertainment was new. For the people in the stands, it seemed to be a shot at something new — something unique and interesting. Something to talk about.

Then the lights brightened another level, and all his attention was focused on the floor far below.

"Without further ado, I bring you the first of the night's contests. From the far off world of Celzin, with five wins under his belt, the challenger — Alden Zane!"

Saul's voice echoed through the speakers and reverberated from the walls. A loud grinding sound arose and one of the huge sets of wooden doors rolled slowly open, splitting in the center and widening to reveal a darkened tunnel stretching off into the lower levels of the city. There was a low murmur and a smattering of applause. The audience knew what was coming, but they savored it. They waited. Finally, a figure emerged from those shadows, and the applause grew from a hum into a roar.

Alden Zane was tall. He had blond hair and he wore it swept back over his shoulders, which were bare except for the leather straps holding a breastplate over his torso. His arms and legs were encased in leather and he wore a huge, gleaming sword on his belt. He looked for all the world like a warrior stepping out into an ancient Roman gladiatorial battlefield. He didn't seem frightened. He seemed eager. He turned and waved to the crowd, fanning their applause into serious flames.

"What is this?" Sheppard whispered, leaning closer to Mara. "Who is he?"

"Didn't you hear?" Mara said, confused by the question. "He is Alden Zane. He is one of the favorites of the entertainment. He has fought many times, worked his way up through the ranks of the contestants. His last five battles have been amazing victories. The betting on him will be heavy."

"But who *is* he?" Sheppard said. "What...?"

Mara shushed him as the crowd grew silent once more.

"Despite a most impressive string of victories," Saul's voice boomed, "tonight our champion must take his game to a new level. Tonight he will face a challenge that ten men before him have attempted — and failed. Tonight he will do battle with a servant of darkness, born of the hunger of the Wraith and the miracle of science. Stronger than any ten ordinary men — and very hungry. Wonder, or abomination? It is not for us to decide. A creature undefeated in mortal combat since his creation — could this be the night that it all comes to an end?"

"His creation?" Rodney said, looking right and left as if to see if the others had heard. "Did he say — ?"

"Shhh," Mara interjected.

"The Woard," Saul concluded with a flourish.

Across the arena from Alden Zane, who stood his ground bravely, another set of doors slid slowly open. The creaking and groaning sounds piped through the speakers were campy, but effective. The opening portal revealed yet another tunnel. Within that tunnel, something growled. The sound was deep and resonant. The room actually shook, and though the effect was caused by speakers and amplification, it sent a thrill of fear rippling through the audience all the same. The growl was very real, and in an entertainment thus far built on showmanship and glitter, that bit of realism lent tension to the moment and brought the crowd to the edge of their seats.

The Woard was slower in exiting the shadows than its opponent had been. It moved with deliberation, one powerful, reverberating step at a time. Rather than staring at its opponent it swung its huge head in a semi-circle, taking in the crowd far above, and the walls surrounding it, with blank indifference. The creature's eyes were huge and pale; there was no hint of emotion reflected in their depths. The head and shoulders were those of a Wraith, with the blue skin and a forked, silver beard, but they were much larger than any Wraith had a right to be and were perched on a grotesquely huge body — it was a giant. A giant mutant Wraith!

The creature was so large that Alden Zane, who was himself a large man, had to crane his neck to gaze up at it. The two were so mismatched in size that it seemed a foregone conclusion the huge creature would prevail without much of a fight. It roared again and the room shook, and this time, despite its seeming indifference, it moved more quickly.

The Woard lunged and struck out at Alden with one

fist, hoping to swipe him against the wall. Its attempt at stealth failed. The smaller man was too quick, and had anticipated the attack. He leaped back, avoided the blow, and swung his blade in a lightning swift arc that opened a deep slice behind the Woard's huge, pale knuckles.

"Nice," Ronon said.

Sheppard turned on him, eyes wide.

He shrugged. "What?"

Against all apparent odds, Alden Zane took the fight to his adversary. He was fast, much faster and a good deal more agile than the Woard. His blade, though he wielded it with strength and skill, seemed to bite deeper than his blows should have driven it. Light, Shepherd noticed, flickered up and down the length of the blade.

"It's more than just a sword," Rodney said. He almost sounded excited. "There's something more — some sort of technology. Look at the energy rippling along the blade."

"Of course." Mara smiled at Rodney. "Alden would have no chance at all against the Woard if all he had was a blade of steel. He's strong and graceful — very quick — but the Woard is genetically designed for battle. Its only purpose is to fight and to kill. Hardly a fair contest, under normal circumstances. We've worked a very long time to carefully even the odds in the entertainment. If we knew for certain that the Woard would win, or that Alden Zane would win, there would be nothing to bet on."

"You call this fair?" Sheppard scoffed. "You throw them into an arena together, force them to fight to the death, and you talk about how it's fair? Tell me, what does the winner get?"

"He lives to fight again," Mara said. "He receives adulation, food, drink — whatever he desires — unless of course the Woard wins. I'm afraid there's not much of a mind there to work with. His one desire is to feed. He lacks the organs to drain victims, as the Wraith would, but his hunger is — intense."

"And the loser?" Sheppard pressed. "He goes home to his own room at night, eats with his family, listens to music or hangs out at the card tables back in your big game room?"

"Of course not," Mara replied. "It is, as you said, a fight to the death. But the warriors are not citizens. We could not produce a warrior strong enough, or an opponent dangerous enough, to be interesting by simple genetic selection."

Sheppard recoiled, disgusted. "So what do you do? Make the visitors trapped here fight your monsters? Take them apart too, like the Wraith, and play God with their genetic codes? Is that how you make them strong enough to fight?"

"We don't — "

"Yes," a voice cut in from behind them. "I'm afraid that's exactly what we do, my dear."

Sheppard turned to find Saul standing in the doorway. He held a drink in one hand, sipping from it as he watched them all carefully.

"It's a voluntary service," he said. "We don't force visitors to our city into the arena. Everyone who comes here is given the chance to choose citizenship, join us in our revelries, and share in the good life we've managed to create for ourselves. We can't offer them a way home to their own people, but we can make them comfortable. Over time, most make that choice. There are others, though — those who are more difficult — who never come around. These find their way, eventually, into the arena. Some of them have donated their genetics to the creation of the 'adversaries,' as we like to call them — others can't get the desire to fight out of their minds. Men like Alden."

"So you let them fight, for your entertainment?" Sheppard rose to his feet, struggling to keep a lid on his revulsion. "You watch men die for fun?"

Saul smiled. "Not only men." His gaze slid across them all, lingering briefly on Teyla, then returned to Sheppard. "Our warriors are given many years of training — both martial and psychological. We are not barbarians, Colonel Sheppard, we don't send them straight into the arena with an adversary like the Woard. In fact, most never earn such an honor. It's one thing to defeat another human warrior, or a wild animal, it's quite another thing to face off against something like that." He tilted his chin toward the arena and took a sip of his drink. "We use the entertainments themselves to weed out those who can, and cannot, sufficiently entertain us."

"And what about the ones who don't make the grade?"

"They either change their minds and join us as citizens, as consumers of the entertainments, or…"

"Or they die fighting one another in your arena," Teyla guessed. Her eyes flashed and she started to stand. Ronon put a hand on her arm and held her in place.

"That is their choice," Saul said. "We give them every opportunity to join us. It's very simple, really, and none are allowed to choose the arena until they have witnessed several entertainments for themselves." He took another sip of his drink. "But this is wearisome. I trust you are enjoying the show?"

As if in response, a huge roar of defiance rose from the floor below. The Woard had stalked Alden Zane until it seemed that he had the man trapped. Zane's back was to the wall, blood trickled from a wound on his cheek. The Woard had deep cuts and gouges all over its huge, mis-shapen body, but none of them seemed to have slowed it. It drew back one huge hand and drove it forward with deadly force, intending to squash its opponent into the stone wall.

Zane moved with incredible speed. He narrowly avoided the Woard's strike, slipped between its legs, and as he did so he lifted the huge blade and swung it in a wicked arc across the Woard's ankle. He caught the creature on the back of its Achilles tendon. The blade cut deep and the Woard screamed. It tried to spin, but one ankle no longer supported it. Even as it fell it swung at Alden Zane, who jumped back nimbly. He held his ground and then, when the moment was perfect, he made his move. With a battle cry half rage and half desperation, he launched himself, came down with both boots on the Woard's chest, and slashed the creature's throat with a single swipe of his blade.

Everything grew still in that moment. The crowd was silenced and the air was thick with tension and disbelief. Zane stood for a long moment atop his fallen foe, and then, as if coming out of a trance, he leaped off. He was no fool. As certain as the Woard's death seemed, he hit the ground in a roll and came up in a defensive stance.

The crowd went wild. The roar of applause was stunning. Sheppard turned to Saul, who shrugged. The man leaned in close.

"The Woard has long been considered unbeatable. A lot of money has just changed hands and the stories will be told for some time to come. This is probably the finest moment the entertainment has produced in a decade — and you were here to witness it. It was a great battle; it's what they live for."

"We have to talk," Sheppard said.

"Tomorrow, Colonel. There will be plenty of time for us to discuss whatever is on your mind tomorrow. As exciting as this was, it is only the beginning of the night's festivities. I'm afraid I have to take my leave."

Before he left, he turned and stared at Teyla. She met his gaze with a fierce glare and after a moment he shook his head and left the room.

Mara touched Sheppard's arm. "We should go," she said. "There will be several more battles, but none like this one. They will be drunk and they will celebrate late into the night."

"Yeah," Sheppard said, glancing down at the sweaty, victorious warrior and the huge dead body of the Woard. "I think I've seen more than enough of what passes for entertainment in these parts. Let's get the hell outa here."

CHAPTER SIXTEEN

MARA LED SHEPPARD and the others through the loud, excited mob and out of the area surrounding the arena. Once they reached the passage leading to the team's quarters, it grew much quieter.

"What was that thing?" Cumby blurted out. "I mean, you've fought them, Colonel — that wasn't a Wraith."

"No, that was no Wraith," Sheppard said. "I don't know what the hell it was, but it wasn't a Wraith."

"There was Wraith in it," Ronon said, his voice betraying the disgust Sheppard felt. "It's head was too big, though. Weird."

"It was like a bad science fiction movie monster," Cumby agreed. "The Pegasus answer to Frankenstein's monster."

"Yes," Teyla said, "while it's head appeared Wraith-like I could not sense its mind — I felt no Wraith consciousness."

"Genetics," Rodney said. "That thing was a hybrid — there was some human in it, some Wraith, and something else that, frankly, I find too repellent even to contemplate."

"You got that right," Sheppard growled.

"Who does that?" Teyla cut in. "Who plays with living beings in this way?"

Ronon raised an eyebrow. "That Woard isn't that different from how you all made Michael."

Sheppard looked at him, but as the sting of truth faded

he held his silence; they hadn't done it for sport, but they *had* done it. And for their own self interest too.

Mara had remained quiet since they left the arena behind. Now, tentatively, she spoke. "The creatures are bred in labs beneath the city. That isn't the first of the Woard, but it is the largest that has ever been bred. Each time one has been defeated, they work harder to make the next invincible. This last one was by far the largest and it lasted longer in battle. They have been working to improve the design for a very long time."

"What?" Cumby looked horrified. "Do they have cages full of Wraith and other creatures down there?"

"Oh no. They take genetic samples — tissue and other data — from fallen entertainers. None of the creatures was ever anything other than what is seen in the arena."

"Oh, well, then," Rodney said, "that makes it all better. Instead of a genetic prison, we have crazy Ancient scientists cooking up monsters in the catacombs. I mean, how could that go wrong? How could there possibly be a problem with changing the genetic makeup of natural creatures to create something new? Has anyone considered what happens if these 'adversaries' get loose?"

"That has never happened."

"Yeah, that's what everyone says before the stink hits the fan," Rodney replied. "You want examples? I can give you ten."

They reached Sheppard's room and gathered inside. Mara started to follow, but he stopped her. "I'm going to need some alone time with my people," he said. "You understand?"

Mara was clearly disappointed, but she nodded. "I will see you later?"

"Anything's possible." Sheppard smiled at her and without a word she disappeared back into the hallway. He watched her go, torn between sympathy and contempt, then he turned and closed the door.

The moment they were alone, Cumby crossed over to where Rodney was circling the room, studying the walls. "I've noticed something."

"Oh really?" Rodney replied. He didn't look up. "Did you perhaps notice that I was busy? Did you notice that I was concentrating on something and think to yourself, 'Hey, if I went over and started talking to Dr. McKay, he'd be distracted, and maybe I could keep him from finding a way to get us out of this mess?' Something like that?"

"About the walls," Cumby said, unperturbed. "Have you studied the pattern on the tapestries?"

"Pattern?" Rodney said. "What pattern? I haven't seen two tapestries the same since we got here."

"There are no matches."

Rodney started to question him and then stopped. "Okay, right, photographic memory. So none of them is alike — they bore easily, and diversify their interior design. So what if none of the images repeats itself? In fact, that would seem to indicate that there is no pattern, so what are you talking about?"

Cumby stepped closer to the wall. He ran his finger down a zigzag stitched seam. "Look here."

Rodney looked.

Then Cumby stepped about four feet to the right, and ran his finger down a different seam. This time, rather than the zigzag pattern, the two tapestries were joined by interlocking strips. The image to the right of that seam included a temple, and on the wall of that temple, a four-armed block cross pattern was formed. Closer inspection showed that the same interlocking pattern ran around the cross.

"I've seen this same anomaly in the pattern around various shapes throughout the city," Cumby said. "At first I didn't pay any attention to it — I'm always noticing things like this, and to be honest it usually means nothing at all. This time, though, I started to realize that the shapes I was seeing fell at regular intervals."

"As if they were hiding something," Sheppard said. "But…"

Before Rodney could speak there was a knock on the door. When it opened, Saul stood in the doorway. He held yet another oddly colored drink, and it was obvious that he'd had several in between. His eyes were dark, and the smile that curled his lips was anything but friendly. Before he spoke, he took a sip.

"I suppose by now," he said, "you've managed to put all the pieces together in your minds. The gate you came through is never going to carry you back to Atlantis, or to anywhere else. No one who visits Admah is treated any differently. You could puff out your chests, threaten me with how your people will come for you — all standard arguments, I assure you — but you'd be wasting your time."

"Is that right?" Sheppard stepped forward, hand on his weapon.

"None of you is ever going to leave this city," Saul said, his gaze resting on the gun, unperturbed. "It's a simple fact that you can either accept or not — either way, you have no ability to change it. I am here to offer you the same options that we offer all our visitors. You've sampled our hospitality. You've witnessed our entertainments.

I've explained the choice."

"As choices go," Sheppard said, "it leaves a lot to be desired."

"I'd have expected more cooperation from you, of all people, Colonel," Saul smiled. "Mara has certainly taken an interest in you and there are far worse fates that could befall a man than to catch her attention."

"You just don't get it, do you?" Sheppard said. "There is no choice, Saul. You're holding us prisoner here. Citizen or entertainer, it makes no difference."

"Not to mention," Rodney said from where he stood by the wall, "the fact that we're flying straight into the sun — and you won't tell us what you're going to do about it!"

"In most corners of the universe, that's hardly considered civilized," Sheppard agreed.

"And yet," Saul sipped his drink again and his smile broadened, "this is the only corner of the universe that will ever matter to any of you ever again. Or to me, for that matter. Those are the rules we exist by, so here we are. You have a choice to make and I will bear witness; join us as citizens, or enter the arena."

"I have a question," Ronon cut in.

Everyone turned to the big man.

"I want to know about the sword," he said. "The sword that was used to fight the Woard. That was no ordinary blade."

"Very observant," Saul said. "Very good indeed. No wonder the elders have been sizing you up. I thought it was just your musculature…"

Ronon glared and even Saul seemed somewhat taken aback.

"The weapons differ in every battle, of course," Saul said. "When the adversary is one of the specials—those bred for extreme size or violence—something has to be done to even the odds. We like a good competition, and we like the bets to be worth our while. No one is entertained by a battle with an obvious outcome. Our weapons are enhanced, of course, to ensure maximum entertainment." His gaze moved to Sheppard. "You," he said, "could use one. And you." He flicked a glance at McKay.

Rodney swallowed. "Me? Are you kidding?"

"We can alter those warriors who choose to fight the specials," Saul said, studying Ronon with a speculative air, "but the weapons respond so much better to those who are born to them."

"They wouldn't work for me," Ronon said. "I wouldn't want them."

"Too much honor," Saul chuckled. "Of course, something like the Woard might change your mind. Bravery is all well and good, but it is no substitute for life."

"If you say so."

Saul didn't answer, regarding the rest of the group with his half drunken gaze. "You have until morning to make your decisions. Think carefully, my friends, it is the most important decision you have ever made."

With that he left and Sheppard stood very still until the door had closed behind him tightly.

"We have got to get out of here," he said as soon as the door was shut. "And fast. Rodney—how's it going?"

"Slowly," he replied, as he and Cumby moved back to the tapestry and began running their hands around the seam of the cross pattern they'd been studying. After only a short search, Rodney caught something with his finger, tugged, and the panel of tapestry peeled away. "Or maybe not."

Behind it, the wall was smooth metal, and set into that metal they saw a square panel. Rodney worked quickly. He pulled a hex key from one of his pockets and quickly unfastened the panel. Behind it, circuits gleamed and lights flashed.

He slipped cables from his pocket, plugged them into his laptop. The other ends of the cables fit snugly into jacks in the access. "Yes," he muttered, "just the same as Atlantis."

He tapped some keys, waited, tapped a few more, and then began typing furiously. No one in the room moved, or said a word. Finally, he tapped a final key, and waited. Sheppard found himself holding his breath. Then, suddenly, Rodney raised his hand in a fist, pumped it downward, and said, "Yes!"

"You're in?" Sheppard guessed.

"Of course I'm in."

"Great. Now find us something we can use — I have no intention of dying here."

CHAPTER SEVENTEEN

"WELL?"

Rodney stiffened, but did not turn. "Brilliant as I undoubtedly am, you might give me a full minute in an alien system before you start checking on the status."

"It's been two hours."

"It has?" Rodney glanced at his watch and looked up, blinking. "Hey, where is everyone?"

"Ronon and Teyla went to bed."

His eyebrows rose. "Together?"

"Don't be an idiot."

With a shrug, Rodney got back to work. He moved his connection inside the panel once, then a second time, returned to the keyboard and, finally, with a soft outburst of triumph, he looked up. "It's familiar in concept, but the layout is completely different. I had to trace the power couplings and work backward. Not sure how deep my access is, and if they have any security protocols running they may know we're there, but we're in."

Sheppard sat up. "Can you reach the DHD configuration?"

"Trying that now," Rodney said. He fiddled with his computer, waited, and then nodded. "Yes, I can see it but —"

"No buts," Sheppard warned. "Buts are always bad."

"I can see the circuit that provides the phase shift," Rodney said. "It's not added on or patched in — they've integrated it into the system itself. Without that circuit in place, none of it will work."

"Can you get around it?"

"Given time," Rodney said. "If I go in there and just start trying to bypass things, I'm more likely to break the dialing protocol forever. And I don't have to remind you it's going to start getting hotter around here very soon."

"So there's nothing you can do?"

"I didn't say that," Rodney frowned, keying in a set of commands. "Come to think of it, when was there ever 'nothing' I could do?"

"So what are you doing?" Cumby said, trying to glance over his shoulder.

"I'm trying to work under incredibly cramped and uncomfortable conditions while idiots babble in my ear. When I've done something significant, you'll be the first to know. Or the second, maybe the third. I'll be sure to get you on the list."

Cumby stepped back.

"Don't mind Rodney," Sheppard sighed. "Sometimes he's overwhelmed by his own intellect."

There was an abrupt knock on the door. Sheppard was on his feet in an instant, he and Cumby stepping between Rodney and the open computer access hatch. But when the door opened, it revealed only Ronon and Teyla returning.

"Couldn't sleep," Ronon said with a shrug.

"Rodney was just about to explain whatever it is he just did," Sheppard said. "That might help."

Ronon smiled, but said nothing.

"I've been thinking," Cumby said as the door slid shut again. "What if we don't get the gate working? We're going to have to make some sort of decision by tomorrow. If they just lock us up, we'll never get out of here."

"Oh please," Rodney muttered, not looking up from his work. "As if there's even a choice! Eat, drink, and be merry, or go all Russell Crowe in the arena? It's a no-brainer."

Ronon glanced up and met Sheppard's gaze. "The other choice might work."

Cumby stared. "For you, maybe. How long you think I'd last against something like that Woard?"

"Just hold on," Sheppard said. "Nobody is making any decisions right this second. But whatever we do, we act as a group. If they separate us, we're going to have a harder time getting everyone out when we find a way."

"Yes!" Rodney exclaimed.

Sheppard turned to him, eyebrow raised.

"Sorry," he said. "But I got the signal. I've been able to analyze it and nail down the frequency of the signal that triggers the phase shift. I know what it is that prevents the gate from locking onto an address more than once."

"And can you fix it?"

"It's simple," Rodney said, "and for once I don't mean it's simple for me and impossible to explain."

He placed his computer on a small table and they gathered around. In the center of the screen a modulated sine wave had been captured, numbers and readings surrounding it. Rodney pointed to one.

"This is the frequency of the signal," he said. "When someone dials an address on the DHD that has already been accessed, this circuit is activated. The symbols that are keyed in on the dialer create a precise pattern keyed to the location they are trying to reach. The circuit that Saul designed causes a shift in the phase of the carrier signal for the code — basically, the data itself remains correct, but the manner of its delivery is changed enough that what is dialed, and what reaches the gate, are two different codes."

"And you already told us you can't get past it, recreate it, or predict it," Cumby said, "so…"

"If you'll let me finish?"

Cumby fell silent, and Rodney continued. "The way RF radio signals are sent is by adding your signal to a carrier wave. The receiver at the other end takes the signal, filters out the carrier, and what is left is the message."

Sheppard cocked his head. "We can use this carrier to get a message to Atlantis?"

"In theory. *If* we can get our message attached to that carrier frequency, and *if* Atlantis tries to dial the address into their DHD, and *if* someone on the other end is analyzing the signal to try and figure out why they can't lock onto the gate they are trying to dial. It might open a gate somewhere, if the new code actually coincides with an address, but it breaks the connection to Admah. It's a chance…it might be the only one we have. Zalenka is still back there. If it isn't me working on it, he's my second choice."

"Get that panel closed up," Sheppard said. "If we're going to do this, we're going to have to think it through. We get one message — one chance to try and let them know what has happened, and how to get us out. Right now we don't even know what to tell them."

Rodney disconnected quickly from the access panel. He pocketed the cables he'd used to connect into the system and reattached the panel, tightening the screws as quickly and efficiently as possible. When he was done, he stepped back. Cumby already had the piece of tapestry in his hands and he and Teyla pressed it back into place. They were working on the final seam when there was another knock on the door. This time, there was no hesitation between the knock and the door opening.

Teyla sat down quickly while Cumby stood, gaping at the door. One small corner of the tapestry cover protruded from the design, but there was no way to smooth it out without drawing immediate attention to it. No one moved.

Mara stood in the doorway, staring in at them. The tension caught her by surprise and she glanced first at one of them, then the other, and finally let her gaze alight on Sheppard, where it held.

"What is it? You all look as if you've seen something horrible." She glanced past Cumby at the tapestry, stood very still for a moment, and then turned back to Sheppard. "If you are almost done here, I was hoping you might join me for a drink?"

Sheppard glanced at the others, and then nodded. "Sure, why not?" Like it or not, Mara was their best bet of finding a way out and he wasn't above exploiting her to get his team home. "The rest of you, get some rest. We'll meet back here first thing in the morning."

Mara held out her arm and Sheppard put on his most engaging smile, took the proffered arm and stepped through the door. A moment later it closed behind them and Mara drew closer, a slow smile on her lips.

The things I do for the team.

He wasn't even joking.

CHAPTER EIGHTEEN

MARA LED SHEPPARD down the hall, but turned off before they reached the main room. "I need to talk to you," she said. "I thought maybe we could share a drink and find some privacy. There's a lot that Saul isn't telling you."

"But you will," he said. "Why?"

She looked hurt, but somehow the expression didn't reach her eyes. "Let's just say that not everyone here believes Saul is the end of things. He's made some very serious decisions for the entire city, and he's making others for you and your people. You've been... interesting. The least I can do is even the odds. Without my help, you will not survive long."

"Saul offered us the same choice he's given all other travelers to Admah," he said. "Join your merry band of drunkards and gamblers, or take our chances in the arena. That seems bad enough, but it gets worse?"

Mara bit her lip. "I shouldn't tell you, but under the circumstances there's little he can do about it. I mean, what's he going to do? Kill me? He's already doing that."

"What do you mean?"

"He isn't going to offer you a choice," she said, lowering her voice and glancing down the empty corridor. "He's looking for warriors, and he's short on those with the genes to bring the weapons to life. If you and your team hadn't come through when you did, he'd have culled his entertainers from the citizens. As far as he's concerned, nothing in the universe is more important than the upcoming Entertainment."

"Why?" Sheppard said, feeling a sick kind of inevitability. "Does it have to do with the shift in orbit?"

Mara nodded. "Saul believes we've reached our peak—that there's nothing left in the city amusing enough to be worth our time. A civilization that isn't moving forward begins to decline, and he's convinced that is what will happen to us if we continue as we are. I'm one of those who understand that we've been declining for a very long time already. If we needed any further proof, all we need to do is step back and take a look at what we've become. Saul doesn't see it. He thinks that we are at the pinnacle of our strength, but that we'll devolve into some lower form—some less civilized version of ourselves—if we don't find an end to it now."

"Your people—before you came to this place—they believed in ascending to a higher plane. I've met a few. I have to tell you that I don't see much similarity between them, their lives, or their philosophies, and what you have here. If the games and the decadence have grown stale, why not reverse your track? Why not embrace your history and follow the path you left behind? Sure, it'll take longer, but it's better than just giving up."

Mara shook her head. "We were a part of all of that once. It was so long ago I can hardly believe it happened, but we made our choice. The road back has been lost, we cannot be what we once were or what, perhaps, we were once destined to become. We are the architects of our own demise, and now we must pay the price."

"The price?" Sheppard felt a cold beat of horror. "He's

not going to turn the city away from the sun, is he?"

She didn't answer, for just then they came to a doorway on the right side of the passage. Mara opened it and gestured for him to step inside. Once the door was shut, she said, "I'm not really frightened that he'd try anything with me, but I'll feel better if we talk in here. Admah is very old, and he's had a long time to set up his tricks and traps. Saul is fond of knowing everything that happens in the city."

"Like any tin-pot dictator."

Mara moved straight to a cabinet across the room and pulled out two glasses. Without asking, she dropped ice cubes in each and poured out something dark and golden. She turned back and carried one to Sheppard. "Sit with me?"

There was a small two-seat sofa, and he sat down beside her, not as close as she obviously would have liked, and took the drink. "You didn't answer my question."

"You know the answer already."

"But it's insane!" he protested. "He's going to kill you all."

"Saul decided that we should go out in our prime. He's planning something big, an entertainment grander than any the city has ever seen. There will be dancing, drinking, feasts, and battles. We still have quite a few adversaries and he wants them all to see action. Once it all starts, the plan is to keep the grand party going until we hit the sun, and go out in glory. Something like that."

"You realize he's crazy? Certifiably crazy."

Mara shrugged. "We have been here for a very long time, John Sheppard. It may not even be possible for me to convey the depths of boredom a person can reach.

Under such conditions, who am I to guess at sanity, or insanity? It has been a very long time since anything truly thrilled me — since anything made me feel truly alive. Although…"

She moved closer to him and laid a hand on his leg.

"I don't hold what Saul is doing against him," she continued. "I think, though possibly for different reasons, that it's probably for the best. The difference between Saul and I is that I would not willingly trap you or your team in our fate. There is nothing to be gained by holding you here, other than the possibility of an entertaining battle."

She sipped her drink, and then smiled. "I have to say, your friend Ronon is a very impressive man."

"What's wrong with you?" Sheppard got to his feet. "You're telling me that we're all headed into the center of a sun, and you want to talk about Ronon and what a fine specimen of a man he is? We need to be finding a way off this moon, or a way to break into the Star Drive and turn it around. Don't you even care that you're about to die?"

Her smile was bland. "It would at least be a novel experience."

"This is so twisted…" He backed away a step. "I have to get out of here, I have to — "

"Wait," Mara said. "I can help you."

"How?"

"Saul has convinced most of the citizens that you and your people are great warriors and should be conscripted at once and readied for battle." She gave a wry smile. "It doesn't hurt his cause that the other choice is the citizens themselves going into battle — most of them haven't been more than a few paces from a bed or comfortable seat in years."

"It wouldn't be much of a battle," he growled. "The only two of us who could even use your weapons are me and Rodney, and Rodney wouldn't even know which way up to hold it."

"Then Ronon cannot—"

"He doesn't have the gene, no."

Mara was silent.

Scrubbing a hand through his hair, Sheppard said, "Okay, I'm going to tell Saul we've decided to drink the Cool Aid—that we'll stay and enjoy the city. It might at least buy us some time... I think he expects defiance."

"It won't work," Mara said. "It's already been decided, you have no real choice. I believe that I can keep you out of it—at least at the beginning—but there is nothing I can do for the others. If Saul believes that I want you at my side, he will allow me that. He has allowed me many things over the years, though I never gave him what he truly wanted. I can keep you safe, for a time."

"We need to buy time for everyone," Sheppard said. "How long have we got before Saul starts this grand entertainment of his? It isn't that long before all of Admah starts feeling more like a furnace than a city."

"The first entertainment is set for tomorrow night," Mara said. "Your people will be taken to the arena in the morning to be prepared and scheduled. There is no time to run them through the standard training. There are other warriors—your people may not be called first—but Saul will want to make this as interesting and unique as possible, so I fear he won't wait long."

"I'll talk to him."

"He won't listen," Mara said. She moved still closer.

"But I can remove you from the group. I can keep you free — help you — and perhaps together we can find a way out for your people."

"Why? Why are you helping us?"

She gave an elegant shrug. "If you cannot believe that it is out of compassion, then believe this — the purpose of these last days is to eradicate the terrible tedium of our lives, John Sheppard, and I find that the thrill of finally standing up to the status quo is more intriguing than a final night watching monsters of our own creation destroy men and women — or vice versa."

"And why should I trust you?"

Mara rose to her feet, very close, and leaned in to kiss him on the cheek. "The best reason of all," she said. "Because you have no other choice." She put a hand to his chest, eyes speculative. "I don't suppose I could convince you to spend the night here?"

Sheppard drained his glass and shook his head. "Not a chance. My place is with my people."

Without another word, Mara turned and opened the door. Sheppard followed her into the hall and back toward his quarters, watching the graceful sway of her walk and wishing their visit was something other than it was.

Back in their quarters, everyone was waiting for his return. Their heads jerked up when they heard the door open. Every head, that is, but Rodney's. He sat folded over his laptop, frowning. He paid no heed to Sheppard when he entered the room, nor did he notice the sudden agitation of the others. He simply read the screen and plucked at the keys as though nothing else in the world mattered.

"What did you find out?" Teyla said.

Sheppard clicked the door shut behind him and stepped a bit closer, clearing his throat and lowering his voice. "It seems that we're going to be the grand finale in some bizarre gladiatorial game."

"We have to fight? Those things?" Teyla thrust an angry finger toward the hallway where the walls were lined with posters featuring all manner of mutant combatants.

"That's Saul's plan. But wait, it gets worse."

Rodney glanced up as if startled by Sheppard's voice. "Worse?"

With a sigh, Sheppard sank down onto a bed. He was tired — he'd not slept for at least twenty-four hours — and the insanity of the situation was getting harder to process. "Saul believes that every single one of us is genetically capable of operating their weapons. He plans to put all of us into the battle."

"What?" Rodney was on his feet then, frowning and clutching at his laptop. "Are you kidding?"

"Do I look like I'm kidding?" He gave a bleak smile. "But don't worry, I set Mara straight. I told her that only you and I carry the gene. We'll probably be the only ones to fight."

Rodney stared. "Only ones? But…but…I can't fight those things."

"Well, I told her that too but considering the circumstances, you better learn. And fast. The battles begin tomorrow night. They're coming for us in the morning."

"But," Cumby said, "what about the choice? What if we choose to join them, to become citizens and watch the entertainment with the rest?"

"Yeah, turns out that's not an option" Sheppard said.

"They're not looking for new citizens, they're looking for a grand finale. And we're it."

Rodney sat down hard, staring at some point across the room, his jaw slack. "Even if I can make the weapons work, I can't fight those things. I can fight computer viruses. I can fight a recalcitrant power system. But I can't fight monsters. I'll die."

"We're heading into the sun, Rodney. Unless we can get the hell outa here, we're all going to die."

"Point taken," he said. "I'll get back to work."

"I wish I had the gene," Ronon said. "I'd love to fight one of those monsters. I mean, after fighting the Wraith all these years, how bad could it be?"

There was a knock at the door. It was rapid and strong and made Sheppard think of a process server he'd known on Earth. He stepped across the worn carpet and pulled open the door, stepping back so that everyone else could see. Saul stood in the doorway, flanked by two of his guards. He was smiling his usual humorless smile.

"Ah, Colonel Sheppard! You are well, I trust?"

"As well as you could expect from a group of prisoners on a moon plunging into a star." It was Sheppard's turn to fold his arms over his chest and scowl. It was a fair impression.

"Well, then," Saul said and stepped inside. Behind him the two large guards stood very still. Their expressions might have been chiseled from stone. "I know you spent some time with Mara, so I take it that you've heard about our final entertainment."

"Yeah, I heard. It's a great plan except for one thing—I already told you that only two of us are genetically capable of using your weapons. Those two are myself and

Rodney. If you put the others in that arena with those creatures you'll be sending them to their deaths — and, more importantly for you, it'll be very, very quick and very, very boring."

"Why should I believe you? You have no reason to tell either myself or Mara the truth."

"I see," Sheppard said, looking at his feet and frowning. Either Mara had shared their conversation with Saul, or he had had a bug planted in her quarters. "On the other hand, I have no reason to tell you a lie. If I was going to send one of my men into the arena, do you think I'd choose Rodney? I thought you were after a fight. If you are, you'll have to be starting with me."

Teyla stepped forward, placing herself between Sheppard and Saul. "What you're doing is barbaric! Forcing people to fight and die for your entertainment? Not to mention the creation of those...creatures. Do you think you are gods? Do you care nothing for the sanctity of life?"

"I care very much, young lady. I also care about honor and dignity. That is why I've devised this plan — this final 'Entertainment.' My people deserve a proper farewell...a wake to be remembered."

She tilted her chin in defiance. "Remembered by who?"

There was silence. Sheppard took Teyla's arm and pulled her away from Saul.

"No, I get it," he said. "Go out with a bang. I mean, if I have to go out, I guess fighting a dragon, or a Woard, would be the way to do it. A final battle against all the odds. A last chance at victory and glory."

Saul's gaze moved to him, calculating and suspicious.

"Take me," Sheppard said. "There might even be a time to let me practice with those Ancient weapons of yours."

"I must say, Colonel, you surprise me," Saul's cynical expression belied his mild words. "I marked you as a brave man, but this is not what I expected. Maybe you understand us a little better than I believed that you did. Very well, it will be as you wish."

He turned to Ronon and the others.

"The rest of you can wait here. I'll send someone for each of you when it is your turn."

He nodded curtly and marched out of the room. The guards seized Sheppard's arms and turned him toward the door.

"Colonel Sheppard!" Teyla called, starting toward him.

"Don't," he warned, meeting and holding her gaze. "It's okay. It's better this way."

She subsided, casting a worried look at Ronon. The Runner just gave Sheppard a slight nod. He understood — Ronon always understood how the game was played. "Good luck."

Sheppard winked. "Won't need it."

And then he was through the door and he heard it close behind him with finality.

Now it was time to see whose side Mara was really on.

CHAPTER NINETEEN

WHEN THE DOOR HAD CLOSED and Sheppard was gone, Teyla was unable to contain herself. "Why would he just go with them? He said we should stay together and he didn't even put up a fight." Her fists were clenched and her eyes sparked with anger.

Ronon shook his head. "Something's going on. Sheppard wouldn't just leave us behind."

"He shouldn't have let them separate us," Teyla said. "We need to get off this moon and back to Atlantis, and now before we can do that we must also find John."

Suddenly, Rodney shot up from his seat on the bed. He looked like a parent about to get irritated with bickering children. "I don't see what you're so upset about. I mean, you saw the wink, right? Sheppard winked. And a wink means a plan. That's why he went with them. He has a plan."

"What plan?" Cumby objected. "What plan, Rodney?"

"How should I know? I don't have a little Sheppard decoder tucked in behind my ear. I just know the wink."

"He's right," Ronon said. "It doesn't feel right, because we don't know everything that's going on. But if he let them take him that easy, Sheppard has a plan."

Teyla shot him a doubtful look and sat down. "What do we do in the meantime? Simply sit here and wait for them to take us to our deaths? I do not wish to stay in this room like a sitting duck."

"Sitting duck?" Ronon said. "Not me. They're welcome to try and take me anytime they like."

"Oh swell," Rodney sighed. "I'm stuck on the far side of a broken Stargate holed up with Sitting Duck and Crouching Tiger."

Teyla frowned. "What are you talking about?"

Before he could answer there was another knock at the door. He exchanged a wary glance with Cumby as Teyla and Ronon stood to meet whoever — or whatever — came through it. Ronon pulled the door open with a jerk and Saul stood just outside, flanked by his two burly guards.

"Where is Colonel Sheppard?" Teyla said, chin raised in defiance.

"Colonel Sheppard is fine. No need to worry." Saul stepped forward, into the room and Teyla backed up a step. "It's the rest of you I'd be worried about. Colonel Sheppard has friends."

"No need to worry about us." Rodney cleared his throat. "We're just peachy, thanks."

"Our time here runs short," Saul said.

"Has anyone ever told you that you talk like the villain in a really bad science fiction movie?" Rodney replied. "I suppose by 'Our time here runs short,' you mean that whole crashing into the sun thing? Yes. I can see how that would put a crimp in your plans. Maybe you should postpone your little 'entertainment' and work on your real problem?"

"But crashing into the sun *is* our plan," Saul said. "It's a grand and glorious end to our civilization."

"Really?" Rodney didn't bother to veil his disdain. "And this is everyone's plan? You took a vote? Because I'd be willing to bet that it wasn't something the good citizens of Admah came up with over tea and crumpets. What did you do, threaten to throw everyone who didn't agree with you into your arena?"

"On the contrary, Dr. McKay. My people and I are in complete agreement on this. Boredom is a horrible thing. Its power grows as the centuries pass. When you can no longer grow as a civilization, when you're stagnant, when life offers no more inspiration or challenge, it's time to end the pain."

"Funny, nobody here looks like they're in pain. They all seem exceptionally happy, as a matter of fact. Except for that whole impending doom thing." Rodney stabbed a finger at one of the guards. "He doesn't look like he's in pain. Are you unhappy? Does your job as hired muscle no longer fulfill you? And you — did you vote for this suicide by sunburn plan? I'd bet not."

Saul grew ever redder in the face and the guards, whose sole focus was on the sputtering Rodney, didn't notice as Ronon and Teyla slipped along the wall, toward the door. Suddenly, Rodney wheeled on Saul, his face crimson and his eyes blazing.

"And what you're doing isn't glorious or honorable. It's mass murder! You've been sending innocent people to their deaths for decades and now that you're bored, you've decided to kill them all in one last blaze of glory? How is that honorable? How is that glorious? It's got to be the most idiotic plan I've ever heard."

"Stop them!"

Ronon and Teyla were only a few feet from the door

when Saul cried out his order. The guards spun at his command and sprang to block their way. They grabbed the fugitives by both arms and hauled them backward, away from the door.

Ronon spun and drove back into the wall, crushing the guard who held him into the wall beside the door. Without hesitation he turned and slammed his fist up in a short, hard shot to the guard's jaw. The man was stunned and Ronon pressed his advantage, swinging a second shot from his hip.

Teyla cried out as she was thrown off balance and toppled backward to the floor. The guard — easily twice her size — reached for her, but she swept his legs hard, sending him crashing to the side with a roar of pain. In one swift motion, Teyla rolled onto him, caught him by each wrist as he fell, and flipped him onto his stomach, arms crossed over his chest. She held him there, pulling up on both wrists almost to the point where his arms were ripped from their sockets, one knee crushing his back.

The guard at Ronon's side recovered and delivered a smashing blow to the side of Ronon's jaw. He staggered, just for a second, but the blow had no other appreciable effect on him. Ronon grabbed the man's arm, levered one hand behind his neck and threw him against the wall.

Teyla's guard struggled and shifted beneath her until finally he had his legs curled beneath him. With a loud yell, he threw himself — and thus Teyla — from the floor. The two tumbled backward, arms and legs pin wheeling. The guard landed on top of Teyla, and no matter how she struggled, she could not get out from under him. He had her pinned, one hand to her throat, the other fending off her glancing blows.

Rodney cried out at that and instinctively raised the laptop over his head, ready to deliver a crushing blow to the back of the guard's head. In mid-swing he stopped, eyes locked on the computer. He hesitated, and in that moment, Cumby finally acted.

Grabbing a heavy, decorative vase, he moved with surprising speed and slammed the vase into the back of the guard's head. The man toppled off of Teyla like a broken doll and she rolled to one knee, turning.

Ronon had his guard against the wall now, large body pressed tight against it with one hand as the other continued to bang his head against the stone wall in a steady rhythm.

"Ronon! Look out!" Cumby cried.

Something bit Ronon in the neck. He felt the sharp pain, the sudden near-convulsive shudders rushing through him. The next thing he knew he was on the floor, writhing uncontrollably and staring up at Saul, who held a small electronic device in his hand. It was aimed at Cumby, and he held a second trained on Teyla. Footsteps sounded in the passage beyond the open door.

"That will be enough of that," Saul said. "If you should ever be so stupid as to try and escape again, I'll throw you all into the next combat together. Without weapons."

As Ronon dragged himself to his feet, guards poured into the room, weapons raised. The team stood down, backing together against the far wall. Rodney stepped behind Ronon quickly and tucked the computer under his jacket while he was out of sight.

"Take them all to the arena," Saul said. "Put them in the holding cells for the entertainment. That will keep them out of trouble until we're ready for them." He dusted off his hands and smiled. "Judging by your performance here, you won't offer much entertainment value for the audience — but you might serve as comic relief."

"You're crazy. You know that, right?" Rodney stepped forward quickly and the others followed. He kept the computer clutched under his arm and did his best to be inconspicuous. Cumby pressed in beside him, as if he was in a hurry to turn himself over to the guards.

Teyla stepped out after them, and Ronon brought up the rear. He moved purposefully and slowly, still angry from the shock he'd taken, and ready for another round with any guard foolish enough to press their luck.

Saul trailed after the group, following at a safe pace as the guards led them toward the arena.

CHAPTER TWENTY

THE TEAM WAS LED DOWN several passageways. Each time they turned, the floor slanted down a little more. There were four guards, two in front and two bringing up the rear. Those in back held more of the Taser-style weapons.

Ronon glared at them the entire trip. It was obvious he wanted to make a fight of it, but Teyla kept a hand on his arm.

"We have to get Rodney to an access panel," she said. "We can't afford a fight here that might damage the computer, or get us separated. The time will come."

Ronon glanced at the guards one last time. "You can count on that."

They rounded a last corner and stepped into a larger open area. The room was round with smooth metal walls. A number of doorways were spaced out around that wall, and on the far side of the chamber a frame rose that appeared to be a single huge gate. The guards turned right and opened the third doorway.

"Inside," the first guard said, nodding at the entrance.

Cumby stepped inside first, followed by Ronon, who looked ready to make an issue of it. Teyla hurried Ronon through, forcing Cumby in further, and Rodney brought up the rear.

"You know this is crazy, right?" Rodney told the guard, stepping back toward the door. "You know you—"

The door closed in his face with a snap. He stood, looking at it with his chin tucked and his head cocked to the side.

"Don't think they're interested," Ronon said.

Rodney shook his head and turned to the chamber, skimming his fingers along the wall. "We have to find an access panel."

"Doesn't seem like there'd be one in a holding cell," Cumby said. "Sort of defeats the purpose if you give prisoners access to the computers."

"And how many prisoners do you think could take advantage of that access?" No one answered, and Rodney turned back to the wall.

"I don't think this was always a prison," Cumby said. "The rooms are pretty large and the furnishings are built in. It looks more like some sort of converted guest accommodation. If that's true, then there is probably an access panel here — maybe there used to be a console."

The walls weren't covered with tapestries, as they had been in their quarters, but they *were* decorated. There were posters in frames, just like in the upper city hallways, and there was a sort of brightly patterned wallpaper covering the rest. Rodney studied it, and Cumby moved to another wall, concentrating.

"It's not the same," he said. "None of this has been repeated anywhere that we've been."

"It's here," Rodney said. "We have to find the pattern."

"If you say so," Cumby replied. He sounded anything but convinced, but he kept looking.

Meanwhile, Ronon turned in a circle and studied the posters. One showed the Woard, decimating an opponent. Another showed something closer to a dragon or a dinosaur than anything else. One was a stylized depiction of dancing girls. The next seemed to be two humans fighting, until you looked closer. A tall man with red hair, naked to the waist grappled with a blond barbarian. The difference was, the red haired warrior had a lizard tail, tipped by a barb dripping what looked like green venom.

Ronon stared at it, and then he turned again. Without a word he walked to the poster of the dancing girls, gripped the frame and lifted. It slid up and off the wall easily. Behind it was an access panel.

"Hey Rodney," he said.

"Not now." Rodney waved a hand in irritation. "We have to find an access to the computer."

"Rodney!"

Rodney turned, his irritation boiling to the surface. He pointed at Ronon, caught sight of the access panel, and stopped with his mouth hanging open.

"Like this one?" Ronon said.

Rodney started to say something, then tucked his chin and strode across the room. Ronon set the poster down on the bench, leaning against the wall.

"You'll have to hurry," Teyla said. "If they come back while that panel is open..."

"Yes, yes," Rodney muttered, recovering his composure, "I know. Here you go, Rodney, here's the access panel Rodney, can't you log in and reprogram the planet or something Rodney? Make sure you don't take too long though..."

Cumby sighed. "That's not helping."

Ronon glanced up at the ceiling, then stepped between Rodney and the door.

"What are you doing?" Cumby asked.

"If they have security cameras in this room," Ronon said, "the logical place to aim them is at that panel. If I stand here, it might help buy some time."

Cumby glanced up and squinted, trying to see if he could make out a camera. The walls appeared solid, but the pattern was very intricate. He nodded and stepped closer to Ronon. The two stood as nonchalantly as possible, creating a wall of flesh between Rodney and any hidden surveillance.

"The problem isn't getting in," Rodney said, working quickly at the fasteners on the panel. "The problem is we still don't know what message to send to Atlantis — assuming anyone there is bright enough and quick enough to decipher it."

"Let's think about what Saul told us," Cumby said. "The gate is rigged so that it can only open once to any particular set of coordinates. Obviously we aren't going to get it to open back to Atlantis."

"Obviously," Rodney grunted, pulling the panel off the wall and quickly working his computer cables into place. He snapped the connection together tightly and watched as several lights shifted through a sequential pattern and then pulsed gently. "I'm in."

"If we can't go back to Atlantis," Teyla said thoughtfully, "we have to go somewhere else. But we need to know where."

"Can you check the database for a usable gate?" Cumby suggested. "Can you tell what coordinates have already been locked by their security protocol?"

"Just a minute," Rodney said. He flipped through several pages of data, entered a code, and watched the screen. "Okay, I'm into the DHD control system." He typed another command and watched the screen.

"There are two tables of data," he said after a few moments. He scanned the data on the screen.

Cumby leaned in over his shoulder, then reached out and pointed. "Those are the coordinates for Athos, and that's the Genii home world. That looks like Hoff, and that one —"

"Wait." Rodney eyed him narrowly. "You memorized all the gate addresses?"

"Eidetic memory," Cumby said with a shrug, then pointed again. "Oh, and that's Atlantis."

Rodney batted his hand away. "I know the coordinates to Atlantis," he said. "Give me some room here."

He started going through the data in the other table. "Here's a planet with an active gate," he said. "Cumby, do you recognize it?"

"No," he said with a shake of his head. "We've never been there."

"Well, it's flagged with a symbol I don't recognize but no one has traveled through it. We can dial it, but there's no way to know what's there. It might sustain life, it might be a dead planet, or a Wraith stronghold."

"So…all we have to do is get through to Atlantis and tell them where we're going?" Cumby said. "Maybe they can send a team to meet us there."

Rodney turned on him and rolled his eyes. "Oh, sure, why not? Maybe we could all have a picnic too! *All we have to do* is get a message through to Atlantis giving them the coordinates to a planet none of us knows a thing about — a planet that might not even have a breathable atmosphere! Then we have to escape from this cell, find Sheppard, and make our way back to the gate without the entire population of a city stopping us. Oh, and let's not forget the shield they've put up over the upper city. So, really, no problem at all."

"You finished?" Ronon said.

Rodney started to speak again, rolled his head in a sort of confused circle, and nodded. "I think so."

"Then send the message. We've only got one chance."

"Right." Rodney bent back over the data. He opened the program he'd used to find the carrier frequency of the phase shift and locked onto it. Using the microphone on his computer, he modulated the carrier signal very slightly. The spikes of data were so small they were barely visible on the original signal, but they were there.

"This is Dr. Rodney McKay," he said. "We are trapped in the city of Admah. You cannot reopen the gate to this address, and we can't open it to Atlantis. We're attempting to gate out to the following address and could really use some back up."

He continued the message, speaking slowly and carefully. When he was finished, he played it back, and then nodded.

"I have it recorded," he said. "I'm going to program it to repeat on a loop any time someone in Atlantis tries to dial the Admah gate. There's no way to know if they'll see it, but if they are paying attention and analyzing the signal…"

"Like you would be?" Teyla smiled.

"Exactly. If they're on the ball."

"We won't know if they've picked it up," Cumby said. "All we can do is hope for the best."

Rodney programmed his signal into the system and then closed the access panel. He lifted the poster back into place and then they all sat down to wait.

"We have to find a way to tell Sheppard what we've done," Teyla said. "He's on the outside — maybe he can find a way to get us out in time."

"I gave them a window," Rodney said. "Allowing time for them to get the message, decipher it, and open a gate to that world, we have to be out of here in about eight hours, ten at the most."

"They'll wait for us," Teyla said, with absolute certainty. "They'll be there."

Rodney shrugged. "It's a moot point," he said. "Not much more than ten hours, and we'll all be cooked. Literally."

"The 'entertainment' starts soon," Ronon said. "If we don't get out before then, someone will have a fight on their hands."

They all caught his grin.

"It probably won't be you," Rodney said. "Sheppard and I are the only ones with the gene, as he conveniently *told* them so. I'm sure they'll come for me."

"Well," Ronon said, "at least the weapons will work."

They fell silent again at that. Rodney turned away, his hands on the computer in his lap, staring at the wall. He felt very pale.

CHAPTER TWENTY-ONE

DR. ZELENKA LEANED OVER the console, his hands on the desk, gripping it until his knuckles turned white. With a deep breath he punched in the coordinates for Admah and stared at the readout. Everything seemed fine. The circuits were aligned and calibrated — none of the diagnostics showed any anomaly — but he knew in the pit of his stomach it wasn't going to connect.

There was a hesitation in the system, as if it might actually break through whatever confounded it this time. Then it shifted. The coordinates changed and suddenly they were connected to a different gate on a different planet. There were no symbols in common between the address he'd dialed and the one that connected.

"Damn!" he growled. "I thought I had it that time."

Commander Woolsey, who'd been watching from a few feet away, pushed in closer. "Did it disconnect? Again?"

"Not this time," Radeck sighed. "This time, it shifted to another address completely. I have no idea what world these coordinates lead to, but it has an operational gate."

"Close it down," Woolsey said. "Could it be the DHD? Is it possible that the error is on our end?"

"I've dialed three separate known addresses," Zelenka replied. "All of them connected without errors. Whatever it is that's blocking us, it's only associated with the Admah gate."

"There's nothing else you can try?"

"Let me see." Zelenka turned back to the console. His fingers worked furiously at the keys and he squinted at the console readout. "I keep thinking that maybe with a change in the modulation of the signal I might overcome whatever it is that's preventing the gate from locking on and opening. It's as if the dialer connects, and then something shifts the signal just enough to prevent a lock."

He pushed the symbols for the Admah gate carefully and waited. The wormhole shimmered and began to form. "I've got it!" he cried. "I've…"

The shimmer faded. Just that quickly, it disconnected again. "For the love of all that's holy!" Zelenka exclaimed. He ran his hands back through his hair and stared at the console. Halfway back, he gripped tightly in frustration and pulled the hair taut.

"They're using some sort of phasing signal. When someone dials the coordinates for their gate, it's detected and a phase shift occurs. I don't know how but it redirects the signal, reconfigures the address that's been dialed. The coordinates to the gate change every time somebody tries to access it."

"But," Woolsey said, confused, "why would they do that? And why did it connect the first time and allow our team to pass through?" His brow was deeply creased, and he looked for all the world like he'd just bitten into a lemon. "It doesn't make any sense."

Zelenka shrugged. "Maybe they don't want anyone coming through the gate? Perhaps there is a problem on their end and they don't want to endanger anyone else? I suppose Rodney is capable of creating such a shift…"

"We have to contact them. " Woolsey began to pace, biting into his lip as he went. "Is the *Daedelus* in range, or anyone we could relay a signal through?"

"I have tried. No one is close enough"

"So, our team is stuck there and we can't even contact them? The gate is broken, and as far as we know they can't open it from their side either. Not to mention that the moon they're on is on a collision course with a sun. Wonderful."

"Perhaps we can connect with the phase modulator and disable it?" Radek offered with raised eyebrows. "It's theoretically possible, but I'd have to be very accurate. Trying to reverse the signal might send it into a loop that would prevent the gate from ever working again.

Besides, even if we could get a signal through, we'd have to hack into the system they're using and shut it down before the phase signal closed the gate again."

Woolsey nodded and tapped one finger on his chin. "You're right. There's too much risk."

Radek groaned. "Well, we have to do something. We can't just leave them there."

"Oh, we're not. Believe me." Woolsey sighed and nodded, more to himself than anyone else. "I'll be in my office. If we can't connect to Admah through the gate, we'll have to pay them a little visit in person. I'm going to see if I can contact the *Daedelus*."

"I'm going to stay here and work on this signal phasing a bit more." Zelenka smiled then, but it was a hollow gesture. "There's something here, something I've never seen before, and it's bothering me. If I can isolate it, maybe I can figure a way through the shift."

"Keep me posted." Woolsey said. He turned and strode off down the hall.

Zelenka watched him go, his mind already shifting back

to the problem at hand, running over data he'd been over enough times to give himself a headache, and looking for what he'd missed. He knew he'd missed something, because there was always an answer. His life was science, and next to Rodney he knew more about Ancient technology than any man alive. Somewhere in the signals he'd already recorded, he'd find what he needed. It was just a matter of separating it from what he didn't. His fingers worked at the keys as he thought out loud.

"There are only so many gates to be dialed. Eliminate the ones that have already been contacted, and the number drops significantly. Since almost nothing in the universe is truly random, there is a pattern, and if that pattern can be spotted, even a seemingly random frequency modulation can be predicted."

He pushed off from the table, rolling the chair along its periphery until he reached the second table and an even better equipped console.

"All right, then. If I dial up the gate one hundred times and log the results, then I should be able to write a program that will predict exactly where the signal phasing will connect with a gate, based on those results. Unless of course, against all the odds, the signal *is* random. Then…"

He began dialing Admah, logging his results as the gate randomly disconnected and re-connected with other gates. When these first one hundred attempts yielded nothing in the way of a pattern, he dialed some more. After nearly three hundred attempts to dial up Admah, he felt that he had enough data, so he began feeding it to the computer and compiling a program that would track the signal phasing.

As he worked, he tried several more times to dial through to the planet, mostly to keep his fingers busy and to distract his mind from waiting on results. He was about to call it a night, and let the program search for the pattern while he rested, when he saw something different.

Moving quickly, he recorded the most recent signal. He dialed Admah's gate again, and got the same result. The same phase-shifting signal was present as he'd seen on all his previous attempts, but this time there was something more. Riding on the signal, he detected a small burst of static, or signal — something that had not been present in the signal all the three hundred plus times he'd recorded it before.

"What's this?"

The only way to find out exactly what he had found was to develop a filter that would remove the phase-shifting carrier from the static. If it was static. Somehow, he didn't think so. It was a little too coincidental that the new signal would show up — and repeat — after he'd attempted the same connection more than 300 times without a sign of it. If Rodney had managed to get into the system on the other side, it would be like him to find a way to use the very thing preventing the gate from opening to send a message. If there was a message, no one else but Zelenka himself was likely to decipher it. He leaned in close and focused. There was no way to know how time sensitive the information would be. He wanted to give himself, Woolsey, and the team themselves as much time as possible. It might save lives.

CHAPTER TWENTY-TWO

SHEPPARD STUCK CLOSE TO MARA as she made her way down the passageways back to her quarters. He'd been handed over to her moments after being removed from his quarters. He wasn't happy about the deception, but he knew he'd be of more use to his team if he was free than if he was cooped up with them, waiting to be led off to slaughter.

"They think I've been taken to the arena," he said.

"By now, they know differently," Mara said. "They were all to be taken as soon as we cleared out. I heard Saul talking about it in the passageway."

"What?" Sheppard said, stopping and grabbing her arm. "You didn't say they were all going to be taken so quickly. What if he chooses one of the others, someone who can't even activate the weapons, for the first battle?"

"The entertainment starts tonight," she replied. "They will have to be prepared. There will be no real training, there isn't time."

"You people are out of your minds. This is barbaric. If they take Rodney or Cumby and put them in that ring, they're going to get slaughtered."

"No one will argue with Saul," Mara said. "Most of them are just waiting for the big finale, and the rest hang on his every word. They have long since quit caring whether what we do is wrong, or right. They want to be amused. They want to be entertained. To them, Saul might as well be a prophet."

"I have to get to my people."

"Be patient, John Sheppard," Mara said. She pulled gently free of his grip. "I will take you to where they are being held, but we have to give Saul and his men time to clear out. It's normal for citizens to wander through the holding cells and study the combatants. We can join the others and you'll have a chance to speak to your people. If we go rushing out there, there is no guarantee that Saul won't lock you, and possibly me, up with the others, just to preserve his plan. I will get you down to them. I don't know what good it's going to do, but I can do that for you."

"Thank you," Sheppard said.

Mara stopped and turned, and he all but slammed into her. She wrapped him in her arms. "There are many of my people here," she said, "but I have felt alone for a very long time. No one that I speak with, or drink with, or spend time with captivates me. I have felt as though I were dying inside, very slowly, for many years. When he first suggested it, Saul's plan did not seem a bad one to me because I knew that it would bring an end to this ennui — this horrible, cloying boredom.

"Now there is you. When you and the other members of your team entered the room last night, I felt as if I'd woken from a very long sleep. We have had visitors before, but none of them called to me."

Sheppard held her for a moment, and then pulled back. "It doesn't have to be that way," he said. "This place — this life — doesn't have to be the last thing you experience before you die. Come with us. I don't know how we'll do it, but we are going to get off of this moon — my people will make it happen. Saul's wrong, there's much more to life than what you've experienced here. I think you've all just forgotten."

"You may be right," she said. "But I don't know if I could start over. No matter how bad it has gotten, this is home — has always been home. So long…"

Her words trailed off. She glanced up at him again, wistfully, but she didn't try to hold him again. "I was sort of hoping you'd be my final fling — that good thing to drive me over the edge into oblivion smiling. I know that must make me seem very shallow."

"Yeah…I kind of figured that was what you had in mind," Sheppard said. "The thing is, being held prisoner on a moon hurtling into a sun while my friends are forced to fight monsters against their will kind of drains the romance from me. It's not that I'm not attracted."

Mara dropped her eyes to the floor. "We'll go to my quarters and have a drink. By the time we're finished we should be able to get down to the holding cells and your people. If there is anything I can do to help you, I will. The more I think about how Saul has made so many decisions for me, the more I think — the last entertainment of one's life should be something of their own choosing. If I anger him, maybe he'll put *me* in the arena."

"Not if I have anything to say about it."

The words hung in the air between them for a moment, and then Mara turned and led the way back to her quarters. Moments later they disappeared inside.

About an hour later, the two made their way back down the same hall, but turned off toward the arena. Sheppard had changed out of his uniform at Mara's insistence. Neither of them believed Saul would buy that he'd converted so quickly, but it was important to appear to play along, just the same. Anything they could do that bought them time was worth the attempt.

He wore loose fitting pants of a soft, dark material, and a pullover shirt. The shirt was slightly large — he had insisted on wearing his equipment beneath it. When they stepped into the hallway, Mara giggled and hung on his arm like a love struck schoolgirl, and Sheppard played along. He drew her close so she leaned on his shoulder, and the two wove a bit as they walked to give the impression they'd had too much to drink.

They turned into the downward sloping passageway and followed the path the others had been led down earlier. There were a few other citizens lingering in the passageway, laughing and talking, and laying early bets on the night's combat.

"The large one with the long hair," one man said, "will put up a fight. He has the look of a warrior."

"What would you know Danin?" the woman standing beside him said, laughing derisively. "You haven't seen a real warrior in so long you wouldn't know one if you saw him."

"I know plenty," Danin replied. "It's in his eyes. And I've seen Alden Zane, the same as you have. There are plenty of warriors on Admah."

Sheppard and Mara passed through the others as quickly as they could. Mara was forced to stop several times to introduce him to friends and acquaintances. One tall, dark haired man tipped his glass at Sheppard and nodded.

"I'm disappointed," he said. "I had the feeling that you'd be in the arena tonight, and I was looking forward to it. Several of my friends and I have decided that, despite the fact you are not as large as some of your companions, if given the opportunity you'd acquit yourself well."

"It didn't seem the best use of my time," Sheppard replied. "They probably have room for you though. Maybe we should see if they have armor in your size?"

The man frowned. He was about to say something more, but Mara burst out laughing and fell across Sheppard's shoulder.

"I can see it now," she said. "We can all go in there, wave our drinks at whatever adversary they send after us, and ask it how it likes the odds on the next fight. If we are truly lucky, we will wave one of the weapons at it, and it will charge, impaling itself and ending the fight in victory!"

They all stared at her, and then the dark haired man grinned. "I think you have started your celebration sooner than usual," he said. "I hope the two of you will join us tonight?"

The woman who stood at his side was tall, thin, and had the most utterly bored expression on her face Sheppard had ever seen. Her clothing clung to her, and she was a very attractive woman, but every bit of passion had drained from her — maybe years in the past. She didn't even pretend to pay attention to the conversation. Instead she stared off down the passageway toward the arena.

"Looks like that would be a bundle of laughs," Sheppard said.

Mara pulled him away and started down the passageway again. The man stared after them, but the woman never acknowledged they'd been there at all.

"Friendly folks," Sheppard observed.

"The only thing they care about is the entertainment," Mara said. "They barely speak to one another, and she never speaks to anyone else. I have the feeling that, as far as they are concerned, tonight is too long to wait for it all to come to an end. It's possible that the world will end, and she'll never notice. She has been gone for years."

They reached the room at the bottom of the passageway, and Mara turned him to the right.

"We need to examine *all* of the combatants," she said. "Going straight to your people will draw attention, and if he locks you up with the others, you won't have much chance of freeing them later."

Sheppard nodded. He scanned the room and the various doors, then turned and stared at the huge arena entrance. They turned and started down the line of doors slowly. Mara pressed a button by the first door. It slid open — beams of energy criss-crossed the open frame, but they could see into the interior clearly.

"This is Balleth," Mara said.

The man in the cell stood nearly seven feet tall. He wore leather boots, a dark, coarse tunic, and leather bands around his biceps. His hair was dark, and his eyes were darker. He glared out at them defiantly, but didn't speak. He stood as if he were used to being studied and examined. He had obviously been in this position before.

"He's undefeated in six combats, two with adversaries," Mara said. "He's a crowd favorite."

"Friendly too," Sheppard observed.

Mara closed the door, and they continued around the room. They saw a heavily muscled woman with wild eyes who paced her cell like a caged cat. There was a short, squat man with arms the size of tree trunks who held a huge axe in one hand. Then there was the blonde warrior from the previous night's battle, Alden Zane, who nodded at them as they passed. Finally, they reached the door to the cell where Rodney and the others were being held.

As the door slid open they all turned, staring at Sheppard. They stood very still, as if in shock, and after a moment he took a sip from the drink he carried and frowned. "What?"

"Good to see you've been killing yourself out there trying to get us free," Rodney said. "I'd hate to think you'd been drinking and… entertaining yourself."

Sheppard smiled and stepped closer. "We have a better chance of getting you out with me on this side of the force field. What did you learn?"

He stepped back then, as if examining something, and swirled his drink. Mara strolled out of the cell, keeping a casual lookout for guards. Her absence also gave them a degree of privacy.

Rodney kept one eye on her as, in a low voice, he said, "The signal has been sent to Atlantis…at least I hope it has. We have about an eight hour window before the surface temperature gets too hot to make it to the gate. I've got the coordinates to another planet — not Atlantis, but a place that has never had a gate opened to or from Admah. If they got the message, they have the coordinates too. They should be waiting for us. The thing is, unless we can get the shield down in the upper city, we're not going anywhere."

"John," Mara called, her voice light yet holding just enough warning to make him turn.

Saul was approaching from across the room. He smiled thinly, but there was no hint of amusement or good humor in the expression.

Glancing back at McKay, Sheppard murmured, "Leave the shield to me."

Saul looked like a snake attempting to fool its prey with a broken smile. "Somehow I knew I'd find the two of you here eventually,"

"I come here before every entertainment," Mara said with a shrug. If she was nervous, it didn't show. "Why would today be any different? This is shaping up to be the finest entertainment in many years."

"You didn't stop to talk to the others," Saul pointed out.

"Were you watching me?"

"Hey, I tried to talk to that first guy," Sheppard cut in. "He wasn't in a very chatty mood."

"You don't have to play games with me, Colonel," Saul said. "If I believed you were any threat to me, or to the security of the entertainment, I'd have locked you up with the others from the start. I know you are checking on your people, and I suspect you still have some strange idea that you'll escape. You are mistaken. You are very close to the end of your existence — we all are — and it's going to be a glorious ending. You can embrace it, or try to run from it, but the outcome will be the same. You could even be proud to be a part of the end of it all…the battles tonight will be spectacular."

"You're such a cheerful guy," Sheppard said. "I noticed that about you right away. Others tell me you have a serious side, but I have to tell you — I don't see it."

"You are a very amusing man, Colonel," Saul said.

"We'll see how amused you are when tonight's entertainment starts. One of your people will be the lead-off entertainment."

Saul left, before Sheppard or anyone else could speak.

"How long before that battle?" Sheppard gripped Mara's arm.

She shook free. "An hour — two at the most," she said. "The early battles are less well attended — usually — but this is different. He'll start as early as he can, and he'll keep it all running until there are no more warriors or adversaries left."

"I suppose that means it's me," Rodney said. He stood straight, but his face was pale.

"I don't know," Mara admitted. "There has been a lot of talk. The two favorites among the citizens are you," she pointed at Ronon, "and you," she indicated Teyla. "The two of you look like fighters, and that's what they are all coming to see. No one wants to see a slaughter — at least not unless there's been a good fight first."

"But neither of them will be able to operate the weapons," Rodney said.

"Saul doesn't care. He'll be counting on whatever skills you have in battle to make a good show, and if the weapons fail to work, that will only add to the amusement."

Frustrated, Sheppard scrubbed a hand through his hair. "What can we do?"

"I don't know," Mara sighed. "But we can't talk about it here. I don't even think my quarters are safe. I have an idea, but we'll need to get going now. If we can get in there before they realize we're missing, I'll see what we can find out."

"Fair enough," Sheppard said. He turned to the others. "I'll be back for you, one way or the other. If we have to, we'll fight our way out of here, but we're going to be at that gate before this place fries. Understood?"

They all nodded.

"Good," Sheppard said. "I'll try to be back before the first fight. If I'm not — delay in any way you can."

Then, drawing Mara tight against his hip, he turned away and headed on around the last few cells, pretending to examine the night's prospects.

CHAPTER TWENTY-THREE

ALMOST AS SOON AS Sheppard and Mara were out of sight, Saul returned to the circular chamber. He was accompanied by a small army of guards. He walked straight to the cell where the team was being held and pressed the button, opening it up so that only the energy beams contained the prisoners. He examined them for a long moment, and then began to speak.

"I wish we'd had time to run all of you through our training, but it can't be helped. Gravity has put some-what of a crimp in my ability to alter schedules, so I'm afraid the time has come," he said. "If we are going to get through all the planned levels of the night's grand enter-tainment, we have to start soon."

He gazed at each of them in turn. "The only question that remains is, who shall I choose?"

Unable to contain a sudden burst of rage, Ronon charged at Saul. He struck the beams of force containing them with incredible force. The air crackled with energy, and he cried out. The force of the collision knocked him back, dazed, and he dropped to one knee, shaking his head, stunned.

"You really should save your energy for the arena," Saul said drily. "All of you will get your chance." He glanced down at Ronon. "You will be one of the last. There has been much speculation about you — a lot of money has changed hands."

"Money?" Rodney spluttered. "Who cares about money? We're all going to die!"

"As I would have expected from one so caught up in the science of things," Saul said, "you have missed the point entirely."

He gestured to one of the guards, and the man deactivated the energy beams. "That one," Saul said, pointing directly at Teyla.

"Wait a minute," Rodney said, stepping between Teyla and the advancing guards. "You don't want her. I know, I know, she looks tough and athletic, but really — she hasn't got what it takes for your arena. She's a teddy bear, and besides — Saul has lied to you. This lady," he pointed back at Teyla, "can't even turn on your weapons. She won't last five minutes in there. You should take me."

Teyla stared at Rodney. All of them did. Ronon stood, still groggy.

"I know who I want, and in what order, Dr. McKay," Saul said. "I'm also aware of Colonel Sheppard's claim that only the two of you contain the genetic makeup to use our weapons. I find it odd, though, that he's not here. I find it unlikely that, if he was the only one who could enter that arena and survive, that he'd walk away and leave all of you to take his place. He seems a more courageous and honorable leader than that. Unless there's something else you'd like to tell me?"

Rodney's mouth opened, and then it closed. He didn't move out of the way, but neither did he speak. The guards pushed their way into the room and brushed him aside. Ronon staggered toward them, but he was quickly overwhelmed. The guards grabbed Teyla by the arm, but she shook them off. With an angry glare, she followed them out of the room, never once looking back. Ronon lept after her but was tossed backward and the beams of energy returned, cutting them off from the outer room and any hope of helping their comrade.

"Don't worry," Saul said. "You'll all have the opportunity to follow her progress. We wouldn't just separate you and leave you waiting and wondering about her fate." He smiled. "We'll be starting soon."

Then the door closed and cut them all off from the rest of the city. Ronon smashed his fist into it in frustration.

Once Sheppard and Mara cleared the passageways leading to the arena, she led him back through the main hall where they'd first met. It was silent, a giant empty cavern. Without the lights and dancers and music, it felt like an amphitheater after a concert or the fairgrounds an hour before the roustabouts knocked it down and carted it to the next town.

"There are cameras and security circuits everywhere," she said. "I've never had any reason to give it more than passing thought, but now I see how it is that Saul always seems to know exactly what's going on. I don't believe his people can monitor everything at once, though. If they are watching for us in my room, somewhere else should be safe, for a while."

She led him across the chamber, and he recognized the passageway they entered on the far side. "The observatory."

Mara nodded. "It's one of the last places anyone in Admah would go during Saul's entertainments. Why visit the beauty of the universe when all the excitement you need is waiting for you inside? Or maybe they just don't want to be reminded how false all of it really is by comparison to something — infinite. It will buy us a few moments."

She led him up the stairs for the second time, and again they came out into the room with a ceiling of stars. For just a moment the two of them stood, staring up into that vast, open expanse.

"I needed to get you away from the cell where your people are held," Mara said. "If there is any chance at all to break them out of there, it has to be after the entertainment has begun, and it has to happen from outside the cell. There have been attempted break-outs before, and Saul has tightened his hold on the cells themselves. Even your Dr. McKay will have a hard time getting around that.

"From out here, though, we have a chance. Security will be busy with the combatants and the crowds, and Saul's attention will be focused on making certain his plans are not altered or spoiled. Particularly tonight, with everything he's been telling the people on the line, he will be in fine form."

"What's your plan?" Sheppard said. "Do you have access to the computer system?"

"Everyone has access, but we won't need that," she replied with a laugh. "There is a panel right by their door that opens the cells. But you'll need surprise on your side to pull it off — you'll need to act when the entertainment is in full swing and the guards are distracted."

Suddenly a soft, trilling sound invaded the room. Lights on the wall blinked, and Mara frowned. "It's begun!" She stepped over to the lights and touched a button, causing a screen to drop down from the ceiling. "Saul has started the entertainment."

The screen flickered, and then the arena came into sharp focus. They watched as Saul, on his platform above the ring, began his address to the crowd.

"Ladies and gentlemen," he cried. "This is the night you've all been waiting for. Some of you have waited several lifetimes. I will do all within my power to see that your wait has not been in vain. There is a grand finale approaching, a last brilliant flash to lead us to whatever comes next, but it starts here, and it starts now. From this moment, until the last, I will be here. We will continue the entertainment that has escorted and led us through the years until the heavens decree it final and complete. I beg your attention."

"What is he planning?"

"I don't know…" Mara replied.

As her words faded away, Saul continued.

"As you all know, fate has dropped an unexpected bounty in our laps in these final hours. It has been many years since anyone of interest arrived through our gate. I can only take it as a sign that now, on the eve of our finest moment, fate has brought us some of the worthiest combatants to ever grace our arena. For your entertainment — fighting here for the very first time — I bring you the outsider known as…Teyla."

"Oh no," Sheppard said. He started back toward the door.

"Wait," Mara said. "See who, or what, she is fighting. Maybe she can win. If so, she'll be taken back to the cell. If you just go running back there, you won't save anyone."

On the screen, the first of the doors in the arena opened. Teyla stepped into view. She held a very long, very ornate sword in both hands. She swung it experimentally, and while she lacked the finesse of the blond barbarian from the previous night's entertainment, she showed a natural grace and skill with the weapon. It seemed that the sword, whatever other powers it might possess, was also a well-balanced blade. At least that much was positive.

Then Saul began to speak again.

"For many years we have been searching for a good match for our very first Woard. One by one, the challengers have fallen. I had thought that Alden Zane would be the one — that we would match those two finally, tonight, but now...now I have decided on another. Maybe this will be the night this adversary's streak will end. Perhaps this will be the battle that kills a legend. He's fierce. He's inhuman. I present to you, the First Woard! Let the battle begin."

"My God," Mara said. Her hand rose to her lips so quickly it nearly muffled her words.

The larger gates opened and a huge, misshapen hulk shambled into view. It vaguely resembled the Woard that had fought the night before, but it was huge. The creature turned its head from side to side, as if it had trouble focusing on the room. Sheppard thought it was possible that the thing had some genetic defect placing its eyes too far apart — that its system wasn't equipped for its own immense size.

"This is bad," Mara said. "The first Woard has never been defeated. It's never even been damaged."

"That sword," Sheppard said, "is it supposed to do something special?"

"Of course," Mara said. "Without some sort of weapons advantage, sending someone in against that creature would be like sending an animal to slaughter."

"I was afraid you'd say that," Sheppard replied. "There was a point where I thought maybe Saul really was in this for the sport of it, but he knows Teyla can't use that blade, and he sent her in there anyway. Come on!"

He turned and ran down the stairs, turning back into the passageway. Mara followed, having trouble matching his pace. They made it to the large, central chamber, but there — waiting for them — was a group of guards.

"Let us pass," Mara cried. "How dare you try to bar our way?"

"Saul has asked that you view this first battle in his company," one guard said.

"What if we have other plans?" With a suggestive leer, Sheppard slipped his arm around Mara's back and pulled her close.

"He insists. It's going to be very special."

Sheppard turned to Mara, who met his gaze levelly. "Then of course we will accompany you," she said. "It will be our pleasure."

The guard nodded and Mara grabbed Sheppard tightly, dragging him along toward the arena.

"I can't watch this and do nothing," he hissed.

"You have more than one person with you," Mara replied, keeping her voice very low. "If you want them all to be killed, cause a problem now. Otherwise, come with me. We will get away from Saul as quickly as possible, and when we do, I promise you I will help. If you fight him at this point, he'll know for certain that you are going to cause trouble and he'll simply lock you away, or throw you in the arena."

Sheppard still hesitated. Then the logic of her words struck him, and he nodded, hurrying along at her side and hoping they would not arrive too late to at least witness what was about to happen.

CHAPTER TWENTY-FOUR

SHEPPARD AND MARA WERE ESCORTED into a large, plush chamber overlooking the arena. At the front of the room, a door opened out onto a balcony and from there it was possible to step onto the moveable platform from which Saul made his announcements and played Ringmaster.

"You have to stop this," Sheppard said without preamble. The door slid closed behind them.

Saul turned to him, amused. For once, the amusement seemed genuine. "Why would I do that? This may prove the finest battle we've ever witnessed. In all the years we've been holding these entertainments, the excitement has never been higher."

"She doesn't have the gene," Sheppard grated. "I told you that. Only Rodney and I can use your weapons. You've sent Teyla to her death."

"She would die with or without the weapon's special powers," Saul shrugged. "That is why I chose one without the gene for the battle. The first Woard is not going to fall to a single opponent, man or woman, no matter how tough they might be. Even if she wields an almost magical weapon, this is a one-sided contest. It's a shame she chose not to watch the entertainment at my side, but we all make our own choices, don't we? The entertainment is not about who wins and who loses, but in how well the two fight. How long do you think your Teyla will last?"

"You're insane."

Sheppard started toward Saul, but Mara grabbed his arm and held on like an anchor.

"There's nothing you can do," she said. Her voice was calm, but there was a tremor in it.

Before Sheppard could respond, there was a horrible scream of rage and they spun toward the arena. Sheppard ran to the glass windows separating him from Teyla and the creature below. The Woard had sensed the presence of its opponent and leaped with unexpected speed to where Teyla hoisted the sword, and waited.

"My God," Sheppard said. "That thing is fast."

"You have no idea, Colonel. I have waited a very long time for this…and now, it begins."

In the cell where Rodney and the others were being held, a video panel had opened on the wall. Behind a thick plate of glass, a video screen flickered to life and they had a clear view of the arena. On screen, the Woard leaped.

"Oh man," Rodney said, staring at the screen.

Cumby looked away. "She's going to be slaughtered."

Ronon slammed into the door, trying to force it to open or crack.

"You're going to injure yourself," Cumby said softly.

"He's right," Rodney said. "There's nothing you can do. If they choose you next, do you want to go in there with a broken arm, or do you want to fight?"

Ronon's eyes blazed, but he didn't speak. He turned to the screen on the wall.

Teyla had slipped the initial charge, taking advantage or her superior speed and agility. She swung the sword in a glittering arc that drove it into the Woard's side.

The blade sliced in beneath the creature's arm, drawing first blood. The Woard swung back at his attacker, but Teyla was quick. Anticipating the counterattack, she ducked. Her adversary's huge arm slashed the air above her head and she leaped up, jabbing with the sword. It entered through the ribs and cut deep a second time. The Woard screamed in pain and anger and staggered back, retreating.

Teyla took advantage of the opening. She dragged her blade free of the creature's torso and changed tactics. She slashed down, swinging the blade at the Woard's ankle. It tried to back away, but she caught it cleanly, severing the tendon behind its lower calf. With a screech, the creature dropped sideways, half its support cut away.

"Yes!" Ronon cried, fists clenched.

On the screen the Woard rolled away from Teyla toward the wall, clutching at its ruined ankle. It could not rise to its feet, but it was still considerably larger and stronger, and it was not hobbled by rational thought or conscience. If anything, despite the pain and confusion, it had grown angrier.

"That creature is only injured," Cumby said. "Teyla should be careful."

As if in response to her words, the Woard, having lain still for a moment, whirled very suddenly. It flung its arm out and down, and despite her quickness, Teyla caught a glancing blow that spun her away and nearly tore the sword from her grip. The Woard didn't hesitate. It couldn't get back to its feet, so it spun and crawled rapidly across the arena, directly at Teyla, who recovered quickly from the blow she'd been dealt and leapt into the air.

That leap saved her life. She cleared the Woard's arm as

it swung for her and drove down with the blade. It entered at the top of the creature's shoulder and dug far down through flesh and bone into the soft organs beneath. The Woard screamed again. Teyla dug her feet in and pulled on the blade, but it wouldn't release. She tried again, but the creature shuddered, and then bucked up off the floor, sending its attacker flying. The sword remained embedded just below the thing's neck.

"Oh no!" Cumby cried.

There were no other weapons in sight, nothing else Teyla could use to defend herself. She sprinted across the arena. The Woard tried to lunge after her, but the sword had apparently embedded itself in a tendon, or a nerve. It moved slowly, partially paralyzed and roaring in pain and fury.

"She hurt it," Cumby cried. "She hurt it bad. How long can she stay clear?"

"There's nowhere to go," Ronon said. "She has to get the sword back."

Teyla, as if she'd heard Ronon's words, started a slow circle of the beast. It crawled toward where she'd been moments before, single-minded and blinded by pain. Teyla took advantage of this, slipped around beside the creature, and with a running leap clawed her way suddenly up its side. Even with the creature down, the sword's hilt hung tantalizingly, six or seven feet off the ground. She made the first couple of feet easily, and lunged, stretching out to catch the blade.

The crowd were on their feet, screaming for her to get it, to finish the Woard. The sound seemed to energize the beast. It sensed Teyla's presence at the last second. As her hand clutched the hilt of the sword, the creature swung up and back, drawing its elbow in close and catching Teyla solidly in the back. She cried out as she was driven over the Woard's back and into the wall.

The sword came free, but she couldn't hold on. It clattered to the arena floor as Teyla toppled over and fell beside it. The Woard had used up most of its remaining strength with that blow. Blood flowed freely from the wound at its neck. It scrabbled about almost blindly, searching for its tormentor. Teyla shook her head and fought for the breath that had been knocked from her in the fall. She glanced over and saw the sword. She rolled toward it, gripped the hilt and turned back.

The Woard lifted itself up on one arm and turned. The two combatants came face to face. Teyla was a little shaky, but she held the blade out and stood her ground. The Woard saw her. It tried another roar, but the sound was feeble — a shadow of its former strength and rage. It half rose, and it seemed the effort would be too much for it. Teyla looked ready to drop the blade and walk away, but in that second of hesitation the Woard lunged.

Every bit of its remaining life went into that final attack. Teyla staggered back. She held the blade high, and the Woard's weight drove it down over the cold, hard steel. The creature's momentum took it forward, and it fell heavily atop Teyla, who was lost from sight.

"No!" Rodney cried out.

In that moment, the image on the screen dimmed, and grew dark. The panel in the wall closed, and they were left to stare at one another in shock as the crowd's cheer erupted in the arena above.

CHAPTER TWENTY-FIVE

SHEPPARD SPUN on Saul, grabbed him before he could back away, and shoved him against the wall. "You did this! Her blood is on your hands!"

The door opened and a guard stepped through, his weapon raised. Saul waved him away. Sheppard glanced at the guard, as if daring him to try something, and then released Saul with a shove that smacked his head soundly on the wall before he turned and strode to the window. Both hands pressed to the cool glass, he stared down at the arena. All around it, people were on their feet, cheering and throwing things at the battlefield. Preparations were being made to move the dead Woard but Sheppard couldn't watch. He didn't want to see Teyla's crushed body when they moved the beast, so he turned away, eyes and fists clamping tightly and his body shaking.

"I don't know what sort of sick pleasure you got out of making me stand here and watch that," Sheppard growled from between gritted teeth. "Did you just do it so you could tell me I'm next, or am I free to go?"

"By all means," Saul answered, sweeping one hand in the general direction of the door. "It will take awhile to clean up the mess and ready the next combatant. I assume the two of you will want to see how it turns out…"

Sheppard risked a glance at Saul, noted the self-satisfied grin and the hungry gleam in his eye. More than anything in the world, he wanted to kill the man where he stood. He thought briefly of taking a shot — seeing if he could slam Saul's body through the glass and send it crashing to the arena below. Maybe he could work the weapons.

Instead, he grabbed Mara's arm roughly and pulled her toward the door. "Come on...before I do something Saul might regret."

Saul laughed at this, and Sheppard hurried his steps, trying not to see the huge body of the Woard toppling onto Teyla's prone form. Trying not to think about the fact he'd lost a team member, and a friend, in this crazy pit of lunatics. Trying not to snap when the rest of the team needed him most.

Mara stumbled after him, trying to keep up. As the door slid shut on Saul, they heard him chuckle.

"Slow down, please," Mara begged, still struggling to keep up. "Where are we going?"

"I need to have a look at your computer system."

"You can't. Saul will know if we log on — it isn't allowed."

He turned on her, stopping her with a twist of her arm. She cried out.

"Look," he said, thinking on his feet, "if I have any hope of stopping this insanity and keeping my friends alive, I have to know the weapons. I have to know what they are, how they can be used, and exactly what their powers are. To do that, I have to study them. Now, take me to a computer console. If Saul finds out, he finds out. We're flying into a sun — what difference could it possibly make? We don't have much time."

Mara stood motionless, breathing heavily and mulling over his request. "You're right. It's the least I can do.

There isn't anything else you could access that would matter…"

Sheppard shook his head and sighed. "Rodney's the computer jockey, not me. I'm not familiar with your system and I wouldn't have any idea how to access anything else."

"There are consoles in the medical clinic that are unmonitored. I can sign in and you'll find what you need there." She pulled her arm free and rubbed the reddened spot where Sheppard had been gripping it. "This way."

They wound through hallway after hallway, taking a lift at one point to access the lower levels. Apparently a number of extra labs had been converted to medical facilities. Considering their chief form of entertainment, and the genetic research necessary to create the adversaries, it was no real surprise. Sheppard briefly wondered how many people were hauled off to be cremated, or buried, or whatever they did with the fallen, and how many actually survived to fight again.

They finally reached a set of double doors on one of the lower levels. The lights in the hallway were dim and, for the moment at least, they appeared to be alone. Mara stopped in front of the doors and turned to face him.

"I'm sorry about this but I really have no other choice."

"What are you…?"

Without warning she punched him hard in the face, landing a solid blow to his jaw. She had wrapped her fist in her metal belt and it left an imprint on her knuckles when she hit him. Sheppard's lip was cut and bleeding, and his jaw was already swollen.

"What did you do that for?" He winced from the pain

and touched one thumb to his lower lip. It came back bloody.

"I need an excuse to take you in there. I'm not exactly a regular visitor in the medical wards. I can't just go in there, sit you down in front of a console, and log in. But if you need medical attention…"

"I guess not," Sheppard said. He spit into his hand, wiped it on his pants leg, and frowned. "That hurt! Maybe *you* should have been in the entertainment instead of those gladiators."

Mara smiled, shook her head, and pulled open the doors to the medical ward. She stepped inside, holding onto Sheppard's arm as she went. She leaned in close and whispered to him. "You should, as you say, sell it."

Sheppard moaned and reeled a bit, closing one eye for effect.

A young man of about thirty stepped into the room to greet them. His face fell immediately and he shook his head. "Woard?"

"Heavens no!" Mara laughed. "A Woard would have just killed him. This was done by a Valhund."

"Take him into one of the exam rooms. I'm finishing up a cast, but I can see him in a few minutes."

"Thank you."

Mara turned quickly and dragged Sheppard down the hall to one of the examining rooms. She shut the door behind them and turned the lock, then moved quickly to the computer monitor.

"We won't have much time, but I can hold him off for awhile." She said. "He probably wishes he was up with the rest, watching the Entertainment. I'm frankly surprised to see anyone down here at all."

A few keystrokes and she was logged in.

"Won't Saul know it's you?"

"I didn't log in as myself," she explained. "I've spent time with my share of others here over the years. I'm very observant, and I'm not without secrets of my own. Here. You will find what you need in this file. I'll listen for the doctor."

Sheppard sat down and began reading through the file as quickly as possible. It contained diagrams, graphic images, and even demonstration videos for each of the Ancient weapons. The information was fascinating, and any other time he'd have loved to spend some time studying it, but time was something he was just about out of.

He checked to make sure that Mara was still distracted at the door, and then he quickly scanned the system files for the shield controls. Rodney might be the computer jock, but Sheppard was no slouch — he just didn't advertise it so loudly. As it turned out, the code Mara had provided gave him high level access. Higher, perhaps, than she knew — there were advantages, he guessed, in sleeping with the enemy. Metaphorically speaking, of course.

As he worked, he glanced at Mara now and then and smiled. She wouldn't be happy if she knew what he was really doing and she might be inclined to stop him. He wasn't sure how far to trust her, and decided this wasn't the time to test his limits. Luckily, she was distracted by the various sounds emanating from the hallway.

She kept her ear pressed to the door. "Are you finding what you need?"

"Yes. Almost done."

The shield controls weren't encrypted, and he supposed there'd be no reason for that kind of security — who would want to covertly take them down from inside a city that had spent millennia hiding from the galaxy? However, he did notice a set of alarm protocols set to alert Saul when the shield had been deactivated — in case, he supposed, he was having too much fun to notice. It only took a couple of keystrokes to toggle the alarms off and silently drop the shield. It was a risk, but calculated and minimal. With the surface temperature rising and the Entertainment in full swing, he doubted anyone was topside to notice the shield drop. Or, frankly, to care.

Satisfied, he logged out of the shield controls and returned to the weapons page. He went over them once more, so he'd know enough to make it seem as if he'd studied them, and then logged off the terminal. He rose and crossed to the door. The shield was down, the message had been sent to Atlantis; all he had to do now was bust his team out of jail and get the hell out of Dodge before the moon's surface started to cook. Piece of cake.

"I have everything I need," he whispered, tapping Mara on the shoulder.

She started a bit, and then smiled. "Good. Let's get out of here before the doctor comes back." She turned the lock on the door and nearly pulled it open before thinking better of it. "Wait!"

She hurried to a nearby cabinet and flung the door open, studying the contents for good measure. On the top shelf was a small box and she grabbed it, pulling from it a rather large bandage. She peeled the backing from it and slapped it onto Sheppard's jaw with a smile.

"Ow! Hey!" He recoiled from the blow. "What'd you do that for?"

"Effect. Come on! Let's get out of here." She pulled open

the door and stood aside.

"I think you just like hurting me." He stepped through the door and turned toward the hallway.

They were nearly to the outer door of the medical facility when the doctor stepped into the room. "I thought your friend needed medical attention."

"Oh, he did," Mara chirped. "I took care of it." She spun Sheppard around and pointed to the bandage. "See? Good as new."

The doctor frowned and nodded. "I see," he said. Then he glanced around the room almost dejectedly. "I supposed, at this point, it really doesn't matter."

"You should go to the arena and watch," Mara said. "The First Woard was killed. This is no place to meet the grand finale, and really, who is going to come here for medical aid this night? Or ever?"

"You're right," the man said. He dropped the clipboard he was carrying and turned to the door, hurrying away.

Sheppard smiled weakly and shrugged, then stepped into the hall after him.

"Good thinking," he said.

"I meant what I said," Mara shrugged. "No one should reach the end of their life alone, and there's no reason for him to be here. Let's get moving."

They hurried back up toward the main levels, taking a series of side passages on the off chance that Saul was paying attention to them and planned to stop them. They encountered no one. With the exception of the arena, Admah was silent.

CHAPTER TWENTY-SIX

ZELENKA SAT HUNCHED over his console, his fingers operating the controls delicately. On the monitor, the signal he'd discovered danced in and out of a larger sine wave pattern. Meticulously, he removed one frequency at a time, checking it against the earlier signals that had not contained the static. He needed to use the original as a filter, remove everything that was *not* the static and leave behind only the new, odd signal.

As time passed, he intensified his concentration. He didn't know how he knew but somehow he did — Rodney was behind this. That stray bit of frequency shift held some sort of message, or a clue how to help, and Zelenka was determined to figure out what it was. He wouldn't have admitted it if challenged, but half the reason he was so determined was that he didn't want anyone saying Rodney had sent him a message he wasn't capable of deciphering.

He turned a final knob very slowly. The signal wavered, and then the background carrier disappeared.

"Yes!" he said.

He pulled back quickly, saved the signal, and transferred it to another screen. His fingers trembled as he started to play the signal through. The screen immediately filled with a short burst of text, followed by numbers. Zelenka read, memorized, and then transferred the message to Woolsey's terminal. Before the transfer was complete, he'd turned away and was on the move.

Woolsey looked up as Zelenka burst through his door, hair wilder than normal and eyes wide.

"Did you see?"

"See what? You could have —"

"We don't have time," Zelenka interrupted.

Woolsey sat back, confused. "We don't have time for what?"

"On your terminal. I've sent you a file," Zelenka said. "Rodney found a way to get through. He sent us a message and coordinates. We have to start."

Frowning, Woolsey turned to his terminal. He found the message Zelenka had sent, opened it, and read quickly. He didn't pause to memorize.

"Mobilize the backup team. Get extra security up to join them. We don't know what might be waiting on the other side of that gate."

"Yes sir," Zelenka turned and disappeared.

Woolsey sat a moment, watching the empty doorway, and then turned to his console. He keyed communications system and waited a moment.

"Yes sir?" a voice reported immediately.

"Have you had any luck reaching the *Daedelus*?"

"Yes sir. They have received your message and they have altered course. They have informed us that it is unlikely they will be able to reach Admah before it is destroyed, but they are making all possible speed for the attempt."

"Thank you." Woolsey said, disconnecting the communicator and rising slowly.

Straightening the papers on his desk, he stepped out of

his office and into the passageway beyond. He picked up speed as he made his way toward the control room, and by the time he reached the elevator and the final hatch his expression was resolute. There would be very little time for consultation or discussion. He was going to have to direct the coming operation, and whatever the outcome he was going to have to take responsibility. He knew the regulations, and he knew the laws and codes behind them. When he'd first come to Atlantis, he'd believed this to be more than adequate — the perfect qualification for command.

At that moment, however, stepping into the control room and finding himself the focus of all those on the backup team, those at the control consoles, and those who had gathered to lend their support, he understood what Colonel Sheppard must feel every time he led his team through the Stargate. The responsibility was total.

Woolsey moved quickly and with as much confidence as he could muster to the DHD, where Zelenka and a couple of lab assistants were gathered. "Do you have the coordinates?"

"Yes," Zelenka said. "We don't have much information on the world on the far side. Rodney's message said he can't be certain it will support life, but it must have supported some type of life at one point, or there wouldn't be a gate. He gave no more detail and there's no time to send a MALP…"

Woolsey cut him off. "Is the team ready?"

"Yes sir."

"Then let's get this operation underway." Woolsey turned to where the team waited, their equipment packed and ready and their eyes bright.

"Normally, I would be the last person to send you blind into a new world," he said. "But today we have no choice. Major Lorne?"

Lorne stepped forward with a crisp salute. "Sir."

"Take up a secure position around the gate and wait," Woolsey said. "You'll be on your own until Colonel Sheppard dials in from Admah."

"Understood, sir." Lorne replied. "We'll bring them back."

Woolsey nodded. "I know you will, Major. Good luck." He turned to Zelenka. "Ready?"

"Ready sir."

Zelenka began to dial. The symbols lit and came to life, one character at a time, and after a moment the space in the circle grew brighter, and the gate surged open. The event horizon shivered, and then settled.

The team stood for just a moment, watching it, and then they moved forward, one after the other, plunging into the wormhole and disappearing from sight. When the last of them had passed through and the gate had closed, Zelenka turned to Woolsey. The two men held one another's gaze for a long moment, then turned in opposite directions and walked away."

CHAPTER TWENTY-SEVEN

RONON SAT IN ONE CORNER of the holding cell, his legs propped up and eyes closed, pretending to sleep. The steady click of computer keys lulled him, but he heard something beneath that; something farther away and growing louder. His muscles tensed and his eyes slid open just as the doors did.

Three of Saul's guards stood in the opening, brandishing their weapons. "You! Come with us!"

The guard pointed directly at Rodney. Rodney looked behind him, to each side, then back to the guard. "Me?"

"You are the one that Saul wants. It's your time. Let's go."

The guard took one slow step forward and Rodney was on his feet. He managed to keep the laptop concealed behind him, and Cumby, who'd been sitting beside him, moved as if to grab Rodney and stop him. When the guards were momentarily distracted, he slid the laptop behind his back.

"You don't want me," Rodney said. "I'm no fighter. I couldn't fight my way out of a paper bag. Ask any of them."

Ronon stood up and crossed the room in three quick steps. He stood toe to toe with the guard, staring daggers at him. Another half a step, and their chests would have bumped. The guard brought his weapon up and trained it directly on Ronon's face.

"He's right," Ronon said. "You want entertainment, and that means you want me. This one won't last five minutes. He'll be dead before the doors even close on him. I can take anything you throw at me."

The guard said nothing in response, only glared into Ronon's steely eyes.

"Take me instead." Cumby stepped forward and inserted himself into the tiny space between Ronon and the guard, pressing them apart. "What you really want, what your entertainment needs, is me. What better entertainment than someone who can use brains instead of brawn? Colonel Sheppard lied before — I have the gene, and I can use your weapons. I'm smaller than he is," he nodded at Ronon, "but I can fight."

The guard let his gaze trickle over Cumby; he smirked, but said nothing.

"You won't be disappointed, I assure you."

"Forget them. He fights like a girl," Ronon said. He turned toward Rodney, "And he'll faint like a girl."

"Hey!" Rodney said. Then, as if thinking about what he was doing, he added, "He's right, of course. I'd probably just pass out. He's the warrior. He's the one you want."

"Come on," Ronon laughed. "Wouldn't you rather see me take on that beast? I know I would."

"Enough!" The guard pushed Ronon aside and stepped around to where Rodney stood, seizing him by the arm. His partner flanked him and they held Rodney between them. "What I want doesn't matter. I have orders to bring this one to the arena. Now, step aside before we put you out of your misery."

"Hey! Wait!" Rodney's heels scuffed along the floor as the guards dragged him toward the doors. "Can't we at least talk about this?"

Ronon moved to follow, but Cumby grabbed his arm. He couldn't have restrained the bigger man, but the last guard had his weapon trained on Ronon and he didn't look like he would hesitate to use it. Ronon shook free, but not before Rodney had been dragged into the outer room.

The doors shut on the three of them and Rodney's whining voice grew muffled and more distant.

"He's going to be killed out there. He won't stand a chance," Cumby said.

Ronon's jaw tensed and he began to pace. "We should have done more. We should have stopped them."

"Yeah, sure we should, because that worked so well last time," Cumby said dryly. "They would have just shot you, and you'd be no good to anyone."

"I know, but to just let him be taken like that?"

He dropped heavily onto the stout chair in the far corner of the room and turned away. Cumby held his silence.

"Hey! How's about slowing down a bit, huh?" Rodney said. "Sheesh! By the time we get wherever we're going, I'll be too exhausted to fight."

He alternately dragged his heels to gain time, and struggled to keep up with the two larger guards as they hauled him in and out of elevators, down corridors, and finally into the staging area. He heard the roar of the crowd all around him, muffled a bit by walls but nonetheless disconcerting. He felt disoriented, and things around him passed in a haze. His nerves were badly frayed. He needed to concentrate, but he was terrified, and that sense of dread grew each moment he drew closer to — what? He had no idea what sort of creature he would be fighting. His knees began to shake.

First, he was relieved of his jacket and shoes, and then redressed in armor. It was made of a very light metal and shone like silver, even in the dim light. There were crystals embedded in the surface, forming a pattern. He'd never seen it, but he recognized it as the work of the Ancients. As he waited, he chattered to himself nervously, eyes darting around, trying to get some glimpse of something that would tell him what he was up against.

"It's okay. Everything's going to be okay. You're a smart guy. You'll find a way out of this. Sheppard won't just leave you out here to die. He never does. Besides, you prepared for this. You're ready."

Guards and trainers jerked him around, thrusting him this way and that, shoving things at him and barking orders.

"Maybe the weapons will give me some idea what creature I'm fighting. Don't panic, Rodney. You'll get through this. You always do." And then, "Hey! Watch it! I bruise easily. Don't I at least get a chance to practice?"

"Stop complaining. Your friend was right about you," the guard growled.

"Oh yeah? Well, you may have giant mutant creatures, but I have a secret weapon." Rodney smiled and nodded, tapped his head. "Besides, I don't see any of you jumping into that arena."

Ronon leaped up from his seat in the corner when the view screen opened. Cumby was on his feet already, leaning against the wall by the door. He turned his head and frowned. "That was fast. Didn't they even take the time to show him how the weapons work?"

"Apparently not," Cumby said, stepping over to the screen. He rubbed his arms to ward off the chill that had suddenly stolen his voice.

There was nothing in the center of the arena save for a mechanical horse, which stood motionless for want of a rider. The crowd in the balconies above stomped their feet and cheered, hungry for the massacre that was about to take place. They obviously knew something about what was to come, and they knew that horse.

The camera drew in tight on the doors as they slid open. For several long beats, nothing at all happened. Then a figure appeared, dressed in armor and apparently shoved into view. Once he was free of the door, a lance sailed through the air, landing at his feet with a clunk and kicking up dust where it fell. He stumbled several times, the armor clanking and jingling as he did so.

"Is that Rodney? Or the other guy?"

Ronon frowned and tried to find something that would tell him who was in that armor. The uncoordinated stumbling soon gave it away.

"That's Rodney," Cumby said.

"Sure looks like it," Ronon agreed. "And what's up with the horse?"

In the arena, Rodney was having his own problems.

"You can't do this!" he screamed. The sound echoed inside his helmet and he took several clanking steps toward the doors through which he had just passed.

"Hey! Open up! This isn't even a fair fight. I have no idea how these weapons…"

Suddenly, the doors at the opposite side of the arena slid open. A wall-shaking roar filled the arena, inspiring the crowd to scream even louder. They were whipped into a frenzy now, calling for the fight to begin.

Rodney turned, pressed his back against the wall and stared, eyes wide. "Swell! Just swell! They send me a monster and all I have to fight with is this toothpick." He glanced down at the lance and frowned, then shook his head.

Whatever was beyond that door, whatever the thing was that he was supposed to fight, it was loud enough to rattle his brain inside the helmet, and heavy enough that the ground shook with each step. Rodney was rooted where he stood, staring into the open portal and waiting for his fate. His knees shook and his mouth had gone dry. All about him, the crowd screamed, jeered, and cheered, but he heard nothing but the loud pounding of his heart and the roar of his blood in his ears. He tried to think. He tried to make sense of the symbols on the armor, and to figure out what might be special about the lance, but he couldn't calm his nerves.

The beast poked its head through the door, body sliding through after it. It was huge and covered in bright green scales. Rodney's wide eyes took it all in and all he could mutter was, "Holy — "

" — crap!" Ronon groaned. "It's a dragon. He has to fight a freaking dragon."

"Poor Rodney!" Cumby exclaimed, shaking his head

in disbelief. "He doesn't stand a chance."

"You got that right." Ronon said. "That thing is *huge*."

"Great. Just great. I get cast in my first Arthurian role, and they send Merlin in to be Lancelot."

Somehow the sight of the creature released him from his paralysis and he hefted the lance clumsily. The tip was heavy and it dipped to the ground. He lifted it, just for a moment, and then it dropped again.

The dragon still stood in its entrance, and Rodney realized it had not been fully freed yet. Saul was waiting for something — biding his time. Not far from where Rodney stood, the mechanical horse waited, poised but motionless. For all Rodney knew, it would remain so forever. Still, the weapons were designed to even the odds, and the horse was half of what had been provided to him.

"Well, why not?" he said. His heart was hammering, and he kept talking just to try and prevent his mind from sliding over the edge. "I mean, how much worse could it be? When in Rome and all that." He paused. "Wait! Were there dragons in Rome? What am I saying? There weren't dragons anywhere! Dragons don't exist. At least, they don't exist on Earth. They exist here, of course because I'm standing right in front…"

The dragon let loose another fierce roar. It shook its head, trying to free itself of whatever bonds still held it, and its eyes flashed with an animal intelligence.

Rodney screamed. It was a low sound, rising slowly in pitch, and quavering. Like a shot, he lunged for the horse, struggling as he ran to keep the tip of the lance from hitting the ground and tripping him up. Never mind that he had never ridden a horse before; he was about to get a crash course. He knew very little of horseback riding, and all that he *did* know he'd learned from watching movies. He remembered, for some odd reason, that he should mount from the left. He paused for a moment to ponder whether that was the left as you approached from the front or the back. A second roar from the dragon told Rodney that it didn't matter. It was a mechanical horse and it wasn't moving.

He rested the lance against the horse's side and rolled quickly up onto the thing's back. It wasn't very large, as horses go, but it was big enough that Rodney could sit on it comfortably without feeling like he would slide off. With no small effort, he hoisted the lance's tip upward until it was level, and then shoved the shaft under one arm.

"Just like all those Errol Flynn movies," he muttered.

He expected the lance to do something, anything, when he held it. After all, they had said these were Ancient weapons, activated only by one who has the gene. Rodney had the gene and still there was no sign of life from the lance. Had they sabotaged it somehow? Or had they merely lied to him? Or maybe —

"Of course!"

He braced the lance against the horse's head and shook off his glove. The moment his bare hand slid onto the grip, the lance hummed to life, glowing blue and pulsing. Very suddenly, it was as light as a feather.

Across the arena, the dragon snorted and pawed the ground restlessly. It was anxious for a taste of flesh. One great foot left the ground and thudded back down, then the other. The dragon was ready for him, hungry. He knew that whoever or whatever still held it in check wouldn't be doing so for very long.

Rodney shuddered. His heart felt as though it might drive its way right through his chest. He shook off the other gauntlet and gripped the reins with his free hand. The horse hummed to life, its eyes lighting up with a mechanical click and its back shifting slightly as some sort of inner hydraulics compensated for Rodney's weight. There were dents and dings all over its body, obviously from previous battles. At the edges of each metal panel was a fringe of corrosion. Rodney worried about its ability to move, about his own ability to command it.

"The tin man had nothing on you!" he exclaimed with a heavy sigh.

Through the small slit in his helmet, Rodney surveyed the crowd. They were on their feet and yelling, some shaking their fists and drinks in the air. To his left was Saul's glass-fronted box and Rodney saw a figure inside, pressed tightly to the glass. He couldn't tell who it was. Saul, probably, but there was no way to be sure. At the side of the box the monocular gaze of a camera followed him and, inside the helmet, he managed a little smile, though no one else could see it. Then he saluted, raising and dropping his lance in what he thought to be a farewell gesture to his friends watching from their cell. He imagined they were saluting back.

With a scream of rage, the dragon was freed. It lunged into the chamber, winding right and left, flowing out of the hole like a giant serpent and heading straight for Rodney.

With a yelp, Rodney turned the horse and managed to get it to move forward, away from the dragon. He turned just in time to see the beast leap toward him, eyes blazing and a low growl emanating from its wide throat.

CHAPTER TWENTY-EIGHT

THE DRAGON ROARED AGAIN, and Rodney's salute turned into a wild lunge to the side. His reaction time wasn't great, but the horse, somehow, sensed the danger, and moved. Rodney clutched at the reins and leaned forward, trying to stay seated. The dragon's breath was hot.

"Don't tell me," Rodney groaned.

Flames shot from the creature's mouth. It wasn't like in the old movies. The flame was bluish in tint, not bright, and focused. It was closer to the fire of a gas torch than a bonfire. Some chemical reaction in the beast's organs created fumes that were lethal and flammable.

Rodney didn't have time to think about it. The horse spun, and almost of its own accord the lance rose level with the dragon's chest. The horse dove forward. Rodney cried out, half in surprise and fear, half in exhilaration. The lance bit flesh and the creature reared up and back, screaming its own pain and rage.

There was no time to think, only to act. He pulled the lance free and his mount, which now reacted almost like an extra limb, darted to the far end of the arena. He lifted the lance straight up and pivoted. The dragon had dropped low to the ground. Blood oozed from a large cut in its upper thigh, but its body was serpentine. It flowed along the floor, rolled and compensated for the injured limb.

Rodney tilted his head, and the visor of the helmet he wore dropped over his eyes. He tried to fumble it back up, but before he could, something amazing happened. The inside of the visor lit up like a control panel. He saw the dragon clearly, but more — he knew things about it. He saw its weaknesses and felt its power as if he were part of the creature itself. Somehow the helmet had integrated his mind, the horse, and the lance. He'd become a single entity, a weapon with one purpose, and that purpose slid across the floor toward him; blue shimmering flame licked at its chin and it stared at him through eyes as large as basketballs.

Rodney felt a strange sense of calm settle over him. He sat easily in the saddle, the tip of his lance at a slight angle toward the floor. He tugged the reins to the left, just slightly, and the horse began an odd, mincing side-step. There were three places to wound the creature that could stop it. He needed to hit at least two of them to bring it down. The wound to its leg, while painful, would barely slow it, and now that it was injured, it would feel cornered. That would render it more dangerous and less predictable.

"Come to poppa," Rodney whispered.

He felt stronger than he'd ever felt before. He knew he should be terrified, but the longer he stayed connected with the armor, horse, and lance, the more self-awareness and courage he gained. Sure, the thing he was faced off against was huge, breathed fire, and could snap him in half with a single bite, but he still felt as if he had the advantage. The weapons he'd been given were specifically geared toward defeating this very creature. He even knew, though he wasn't sure exactly how, that this was far from the first such dragon to enter the arena. He also knew that most of them had been slain in their first battle, and how those deaths had occurred. It was programmed into the helmet's interface. He knew that the dragon he faced was the big daddy of them all, but he had a road-map of how it's brethren had been killed.

The dragon charged. Rodney directed his mount to the side, turned, and then lunged. The lance pierced the dragon behind the neck, just above the shoulder. He pressed it deep, and he knew he'd struck his target cleanly. The dragon reeled up and back, lashing out with its tail. The horse backpedaled and spun, but the tail still struck hard. Rodney and the horse slid across the arena toward the far wall.

This is it he told himself. This is what it all comes to. Then he felt a churning motion, and he realized that, impossibly, the mechanical horse was gaining traction against the skid. They stopped just short of the wall, and he was in motion again. There was nothing he could do but concentrate on the battle and ride it out. Even if he'd wanted to lift the visor, or to turn the horse and run, that wasn't part of the weapons' programming. The fight was on, and no matter what Rodney thought, or what he might want, it was going to reach its conclusion. Unable to stop himself, he cried out. Surprisingly, it sounded like a battle cry.

The horse plunged ahead, the dragon reared, and the crowd came to their feet with a roar of approval.

Sheppard and Mara burst into the main chamber, glancing in both directions, but no one was in sight. It didn't seem that Saul intended to concern himself further with them, but it would be a mistake to underestimate him.

There was a screen on the wall, and it caught Sheppard's eye. It hung over the bar where they'd first had drinks and it showed the arena clearly. Sheppard stepped up to the bar and stared.

On the screen, a dragon slid across the floor clumsily. It had been wounded, but it still looked dangerous. Across the arena, a warrior sat astride an odd looking horse. He wore a visor, and he carried a lance that flickered with energy. Something about the way the man sat the horse caught Sheppard's attention, something familiar. Then the warrior gave out a battle cry and the horse lunged, and in that instant, Sheppard knew.

"Oh no."

"What?" Mara stepped up beside him. "What is it?"

""Not what," Sheppard said, "who. It's Rodney. That's Rodney in there, fighting a dragon, and Saul took him because I told him Rodney could use the weapons."

"He's not dying," Mara said. "Look. He's wounded the beast twice. Maybe you have underestimated him."

"It wouldn't be the first time," Sheppard said.

He watched the screen a moment longer, and then dragged his gaze from it and grabbed her by the arm.

"You have to take me down to that cell. I have to get my people out of there."

He saw the doubt and resistance in her expression and stepped closer, suddenly wrapping her in his arms. He held her there tightly and met her gaze.

"This whole city is about to plunge into a sun, and I'm not ready. I'm not ready to die, and I'm thinking that — if we had a little more time together — we'd find out we aren't done with one another, either. There may not be any way off this planet, but if we can get my people out and get to the star drives, maybe we can change the city's course. Maybe, if we can get past Saul, we can bring this place back to the days you remember — to something worth being part of. The truth is, there's nothing to lose. What is he going to do if he catches us, or stops us? Kill us a few hours early? Send us to the arena? This is better than the entertainments that place provides, because the stakes are real."

Mara watched him for a moment, sizing him up and testing his words for truth. Then, all at once, her expression softened.

"You're right. Saul has been running my life quite long enough. We'll get your people, and we'll see what can be done. Then…who knows?"

Sheppard smiled and squeezed her arm, then let her go.

They turned and ran down the corridor toward the holding cells. There was no one in the passageway. Even the guards were watching the battle in the arena. No one wanted to miss the action, and there was no reason to watch prisoners who were locked up securely.

The two entered the large circular chamber, and it, too, was empty. They ran straight to the cell where Ronon, Teyla, and Cumby were still locked up. Mara worked the control panel quickly. At first, nothing happened.

"Come on," Sheppard said. "What's wrong?"

"My access code," Mara said. "It's been locked out."

"Great," Sheppard replied. "Just great."

"Don't worry," she laughed. "I know other codes."

She keyed in a sequence of symbols, and the door slid

open. Sheppard slipped quickly inside. Ronon, and Cumby were hunched over the view screen. They glanced up in shock, but even the sudden opening of the door couldn't drag their attention from Rodney and the dragon for long.

"Come on," Sheppard barked. "We're no good to Rodney or anyone else if we all end up locked in here. Let's move."

"He's wounded it twice," Ronon said. "Never would have guessed."

Sheppard and Mara slipped up beside them. Just as they did, Rodney and his mount lunged yet again. The lance bit deep, and the dragon reared up. It screamed, but there was more than pain in the sound. It was shrill and final, and even as the creature toppled backward, it was obvious it would never rise again.

"I don't believe it!" Sheppard breathed.

But even as it died, it whipped its monstrous tail in a vicious arc. The roar of the crowd dropped to stunned silence as Rodney turned and saw it move — too late. The tail caught him dead on. It lifted him and the horse from the arena floor and drove them into the wall. The force of the blow was so great that the wall crumbled. Rodney, the tail, and the horse disappeared through the rubble. Dust rose, and the dragon lay still.

"No!" Cumby choked.

On the screen, Saul's face appeared. "The dragon is dead," he said, his voice grave but his eyes dancing with excitement. "Unfortunately, the brave warrior who defeated it has also passed on. When we have finished removing the rubble, the next battle will begin. Colonel Sheppard, wherever you are in the city, you have my condolences. You have lost a brave man."

With a curse, Ronon slammed his fist into the wall and Sheppard dropped his eyes to the floor, breathing hard. He couldn't believe it, couldn't process this twisted reality.

Teyla was gone. Rodney was gone. His team was shattered.

Eyes squeezed shut he dragged in a breath, then another, struggling for self-control. But he couldn't grieve here, he didn't have that luxury. Their lives were measured in hours now and he had to get them home. With effort, he looked up into the bleak faces of Ronon and Cumby. This had to end.

"Come on," he said, and didn't recognize the dead voice that spoke. "We're getting outa here. Now."

"No. We should go back," Ronon said. "We can't leave them here."

Sheppard met his gaze and saw in Ronon's hooded eyes the same rage he felt, constricting his chest like a steel band. It was hard to draw breath against it, hard to focus on anything beyond it. "We have to go," he said, grinding out the words. "There's nothing we can do for them now."

"We can kill Saul," Ronon growled.

"He's going to die anyway. And so will we, if we don't leave. Now."

"Does it matter? Some things are more important than survival."

Sheppard looked away, back at the screen. He could see the creature being dragged away and with a sickening jolt saw the gleam of Rodney's armor laying twisted in the rubble. "Vengeance?" he said, tasting the word in the bile that rose at the back of his throat. He looked at Ronon. "Do you think that's what Teyla would have wanted? Or Rodney?"

Ronon didn't answer, but behind him Cumby scratched a hand across his dirt-streaked face. "Ronon's right," he said. "We can't just leave them here. What if they're not dead?"

And for a moment he was back in the Afghan desert, Holland bleeding out in the sand and not a damn thing he could do about it. He looked away. "Doesn't matter," he said. "We can't go back for them, there's no time."

"But—"

"There's no time!" he snapped. "We're leaving, now. And that's an order, soldier."

Cumby stared at him and then Ronon said, "Sheppard's right. If we go back, we all die."

"Let's go," Sheppard said, heading for the door.

"To the star drive?" Mara said, tentative amid their grief and anger.

"No. To the gate. We're getting out of here."

"But you can't go back to your city," she said, confused. "Why would you go to the gate? I thought—"

He spun around. "Look, the only one of us who could have changed the course of this city was Rodney. And he's dead. So, we have one chance to get out of here — Rodney gave us the coordinates to a world that's not locked out of the system and with a bit of luck our people will be waiting there for us." He paused, bitter from his loss but trying not to take it out on Mara. "Come with us."

"But I thought we were going to try and save Admah first. My home, my friends, they're all going to die and—"

"And my friends are already dead!" he barked, and

just saying it made it too true, too real. He took a breath, tamped down his rage. Later. There'd be time for that later. With effort, he kept his voice even. "Look, Teyla and Rodney were my friends," he said. "They died because of this madness and there's not a damn thing I can do about that. It's too late for them, and it's too late for the city. Rodney was Admah's last hope, and now he's gone." He rubbed a hand across his face. "I'm sorry, we can't help your people. But you? That's another story. You can come with us. You can help *us.*"

Mara stared, eyes wide with fear but her face resolved. "I understand," she said. "I'll come with you. There's nothing left for me here."

"Then let's go," Ronon said. His voice was even, but just beneath the surface it trembled with barely controlled rage.

"Mara, show us how to get to the surface," Sheppard said. "We'll handle it from there."

She nodded and together they slipped out into the passage, heading toward the main room and the halls beyond. On the screens all around, Saul began announcing the next battle. The crowd roared and the games continued unabated.

CHAPTER TWENTY-NINE

LORNE STEPPED INTO a pocket of lush jungle. The gate itself was clear, as was a circle about ten meters around it on all sides. Beyond this, plants and vines encroached, threatening to overrun the clearing and block off the rest of the world they'd entered.

"Move into the brush on the right," Lorne directed. "Let's get set up. We don't know how long we'll be waiting here, and I don't want any surprises. As soon as we get the equipment up and going, send a report back to Woolsey. Verdino, Gravel, you're with me."

"Where are we going, sir?" Corporal Gravel asked.

She was a short, slender woman with long dark hair. She carried her weapon easily. Lorne had chosen this team himself, and he'd chosen Gravel for her intuition and an almost cat-like grace in battle.

"We're going to check the perimeter," Lorne said. "We won't go far, but I don't like the idea of not getting a look around. The way this place is overgrown suggests that there hasn't been anyone around here for some time. Looks can be deceiving."

"They could have let the jungle grow up just to camouflage the gate," Verdino said.

"Exactly," Lorne agreed. "Let's move. We'll keep in touch. See you all shortly. Meanwhile, keep your eyes open, get us entrenched, and let's get ready to welcome Colonel Sheppard and his team back in style."

The three plunged into the jungle, leaving the rest of the team to establish the base. They moved easily. Lorne took point, Gravel swept her gaze and weapon over the jungle to either side of the trail, and Verdino watched their rear, careful not to let anything or anyone slip around behind and cut them off from the gate.

Lorne passed through a particularly thick bank of ferns, and the undergrowth grew suddenly sparser. The ground sloped upward steeply. He raised a hand to slow the others and climbed the slope carefully. Insects buzzed around his face, but he ignored them. There was a sound in the distance, a droning hum that rose slowly.

"I've got a bad feeling," Lorne muttered, as he crept to the top of the ridge and peered over into the valley beyond. His feeling was right. In the distance, a Wraith Hive ship rested while all around it darts flew in and out. There was movement on the ground as well — it was obviously a community built around the ship.

Lorne watched for a few moments. He noted the roads and trails around the ship, specifically one that led in the direction of the gate. No one moved along it at that moment, but it was obviously intended to lead to the Stargate. Lorne slid slowly down the hill and gestured for the others to retreat. He held his silence until they were back beneath the cover of the trees and vines.

"We have a problem," he said. "A big problem."

He quickly informed Gravel and Verdino on the situation. Gravel reached for her radio but Lorne grabbed her hand and stopped her.

"We go back under radio silence. We also have to find a way to minimize reports to Atlantis. Anything we say could be detected or picked up by the Wraith. Opening and closing that gate is going to tip them off for sure, if it hasn't already. If they find out we're here, we won't be able to hold out for long."

"They must know the gate just activated," Verdino frowned.

"Probably, but it's possible they have regular traffic of their own. We're going on the assumption they haven't noticed us, and we're going to lie as low as possible. We have to hold out long enough for Sheppard's team to come through. We aren't here to engage the enemy."

"That's a good thing," Gravel said. "We're good, but…"

Lorne shook his head and laughed. "Yeah, not that good. We'll get back to the others before they dial Atlantis to check in. Last thing we want is a firefight. We're here to bring people home safe, not offer up more casualties."

They made their way quickly back through the jungle.

"The trail I saw would come in from the far side of the gate," Lorne said, keeping his voice low. "We were just lucky choosing to move off to the right. We have to make use of the cover they've grown to hide the gate. If we use it to our advantage, we might be able to lay low long enough to remain undetected until Colonel Sheppard comes through."

They hurried back through the jungle toward the gate. Verdino, still bringing up the rear, kept a careful watch on the jungle, and on the sky above, but there were no sign of Wraith, or darts.

On the hive ship, a Wraith warrior stood, staring up at the cliff where Lorne had lain only moments before.

A flicker of light had caught his eye, and he was trying to focus across the distance and determine the source. There was nothing to see, but he glanced in the direction of the gate and frowned.

He turned and strode into the ship. He made his way through to the control room and stepped up to the main console.

His subordinate looked up from his work. "What is wrong?"

"I saw something out near the Stargate. It is probably nothing, but I want to check the logs."

The screen lit up and his fingers danced over the controls easily. He stopped and stared at the screen for a moment, then spun quickly away.

"I want a patrol in the area of the Stargate immediately," he said. "Send two darts."

Moments later, the small ships shot out from the side of the hive ship and rolled, banking toward the gate.

"Who are you?" the Wraith mused softly. "And where did you come from?"

His answer was silence as he watched the darts disappear low over the jungle growth in the distance.

They heard the darts before they saw them.

"Get down," Lorne called. "Stay low and whatever you do, maintain radio silence."

The Wraith craft roared over the gate, one banking off to either side. They began maneuvering in a zigzag pattern over the trees and growth, searching for any sign of intruders. The team hunkered down and pressed back into the trunks of trees and beneath hanging vines. The darts came over again, and again, but eventually they shot off into the distance in the direction they'd come.

"We're going to have to pull back further from the gate," Lorne said softly. "If they're checking the area, then someone has figured out that the gate was opened. They may not know for sure that anyone came through, but they'll be watching, and they'll be patrolling. We have to be vigilant, quiet, and patient."

Verdino glanced in the direction of the darts. "What if they attack?"

"We could pull back to Atlantis," Lorne said. "Probably. We ought to be able to activate the gate and get through it, but what then? If we retreat and Sheppard manages to get off that death trap moon and through the gate, he'll just be walking into *another* death trap."

"Just asking," Verdino grinned. "I vote we fight."

"I vote we try to stay out of sight and avoid trouble," Gravel cut in. "We should be able to lay low for a few hours. If Rodney's message is accurate, and Zelenka got it right, we shouldn't have to be here too long."

They all nodded, and then settled in. None of them was thinking about retreat, or safety. All of them, at one point or another, had worked with Colonel Sheppard, or Teyla, or even Ronon. They had come on this mission to bring that team home; that was what they'd do.

The eerie quiet of the jungle and the alien sky overhead had taken on an ominous aspect; they knew the Wraith were nearby. All they could do was to wait.

CHAPTER THIRTY

RODNEY SHOOK HIS HEAD, and immediately regretted it. He tried to sit up, and the room around him wavered. His head felt heavy…then his memory cleared, and he realized he was still wearing the helmet. The visor had popped open from the impact. He turned. There was still a break in the wall between him and the arena, but it flickered with an odd translucent light. Some kind of shield had been erected, and from the sound of the cheers and screams from the other side of that shield, the show had continued.

Moving more slowly, he rose. Nothing was broken, but that was no surprise. He reached under the armor and fingered the small device he wore around his neck. It was intact and Rodney grinned.

The room was dark. There were few lights, and in the shadowy interior he saw the detritus of battle scattered over the floor and piled against the walls. Racks of weapons lined one wall: swords, pistols, blades of all shape and size, as well as bows, crossbows, exo-skeletal suits, and armor. The variety was impressive, but it was obvious that in recent times whoever was in charge of maintenance and cleanliness had found a better use for their time.

Now the floor was also piled with the dead. The fallen creatures from the arena had been dragged in and left, some piled atop one another, the larger ones lying and stiffening on their own. Rodney saw, a few yards away, the carcass of the dragon. He stared at it for a long moment, trying to wrap his mind around the idea that he'd killed it.

The horse lay on one side a few feet away. It didn't seem to have been harmed, but it was as silent and still as it had been the moment he first laid eyes on it. The lance lay nearby as well.

"Well," Rodney said to no one in particular. "This is just swell." He kicked at the handle of the lance and it skittered across the floor.

Rodney started a quick exploration of the room. He knew there had to be computer access and he knew he was going to have to find it and get into it quickly, or any chance of catching up to the others — assuming they'd gotten loose and were on their way to the gate — would be lost. He fumbled along the wall, cursing the dim light.

He worked his way around the carcass of the dragon, looking for anything that would add more light to the room. When he neared the racks of weapons, he almost laughed aloud. There was a control console tucked in beside the door, probably used for inventory of the weapons or diagnostics. The screen was lit and open. The dead dragon had prevented him from seeing it glowing in the semi-darkness. Whoever had last used it, they had no fear of anyone in this room accessing the system.

Rodney hurried over and sat down. The first thing he did was check the arena. If one of the others was out there, he knew he'd have to find a way to help them before he moved on. He noticed that it was getting warmer in the room. His brow was coated in sweat, and he felt his shirt matting to his back.

He tapped at the keys, found the video feed, and

brought up the arena. He saw two large creatures that resembled very large wolves squaring off with a woman. Only it wasn't exactly a woman. She had two heads, and at least four arms, two of which held spears. Her eyes flashed, and she was actually smiling.

"Well," Rodney said. "Good luck to you then."

He closed the screen and began digging into the computer system in search of the DHD control system. He needed to know if the others had already opened the gate; without his equipment or his laptop, he didn't know how long he'd been out. He found what he was looking for, tapped in codes from memory, and found his way to the gate.

It had not been accessed from the Admah side in a very long time. He was either going to be early, on time, or the only one who made it to the gate. Next he tapped into the security systems and found video feeds into the various holding cells outside the arena. He didn't know the number of the one they'd been kept in, so he flipped through them one at a time. Most were empty. In a few, warriors of various stripes awaited. Each time he came to one of the cells, he opened it. He didn't know if it would do any of them any good, but he thought evening the odds with Saul and his followers certainly couldn't hurt.

After only a few moments he had opened all the cells, but one stood conspicuously open before he reached it. He hoped that meant the others had made it out, but at the same time, it added urgency to his own plight. He had to get out of this room and soon. If they came in with whoever lost the current battle, he'd be discovered. He needed to get out and up to the gate before he ended up trapped and fried with the good citizens of Admah.

He accessed the map of the city, found the arena, and quickly located the chamber he was in. There were only two exits. One led into the arena, and the other was directly across from that door, making it directly behind him. Rodney thought for a moment. As soon as he opened it, he was going to be setting off alarms. That was almost a certainty. Whether, in the heat of their entertainment, anyone would be monitoring for such a breach of security, or would do anything if they saw it, was a different question altogether. In the end, he settled for unlocking the doorway so that when he was ready to access it, it would open.

He sat at the terminal a few moments longer. There was nothing more to be gained from it, but somehow he was reluctant to give up what might be his last access to a computer. It was difficult to turn away and rely on himself — his physical abilities, strength, and possibly his ability to fight, to win the day. He'd saved the day a thousand times, but he'd used his mind. This time it was going to be of little or no use, and it left him feeling naked.

Finally he pushed away from the console and stood up. He found himself facing the weapons rack, and there, directly in front of him, was the sword he'd seen Teyla use.

Teyla…

The sight of the weapon triggered a flood of pain, and he staggered under the weight of it. She was gone. Teyla was *dead*.

He hadn't had a moment to think about it, the terror of his own battle blotting out everything else — his mind had simply shunted the horrible truth to one side while he fought for his life. But now he felt it — felt the dark edges of it, at least. When he got out of Admah — if he got out — he knew it was going to hit like a hammer blow.

Teyla was gone.

He swallowed hard against rising grief and blinked his watery eyes. Right now, he had to focus. Distraction meant death, and he hadn't killed a dragon just to be flambéed alive instead. He returned his attention to the sword. Teyla's sword. The blade was long, and he saw the symbols of the Ancients on the hilt and scabbard. Without being entirely sure why he did, he grabbed it and belted it around his waist. It was heavy, but somehow it felt good to have it there.

A sudden sound caught his attention and he froze. He looked around self-consciously, as if someone might have been watching him don the weapon, but there was no one to be seen. Then he heard the sound again. It was a groan of pain, and it came from somewhere on the far side of the dragon's corpse.

"Great," Rodney said. "Just great."

He glanced at the door across the room. A few quick paces and he could access it, move into the passage beyond, and be on his way. He stared at it longingly, and then he turned toward the sound with a sigh.

"Who's there?" he called. "Who is that?"

The sound grew louder, but no more coherent. Rodney drew the sword, found the controls that brought it to life, and stepped around the dragon. On the far side he saw the huge carcass of the first Woard, but the sound did not come from the creature. Stepping around its body, he found his answer.

Teyla lay pinned beneath the weight of the beast she'd slain. She was alive! They'd been dragged from the arena in just about the position they'd fallen, but by some miracle Teyla hadn't been crushed.

"Teyla…" He kneeled and touched her shoulder, vision blurring with sudden relief and a wide grin tugging at his lips. "Teyla, wake up."

Her eyes cleared and she stared up. "Rodney?"

"Yeah, it's me. Are you okay?"

Teyla stared down at where her right leg was pinned beneath the Woard. "I have been better." She paused. "I cannot move, but with that creature on my leg I cannot tell how badly I am hurt. There is some pain."

Rodney tried briefly to lift the Woard off of her leg, but there was no way. It didn't move an inch. He stood and drew the sword.

"This is probably going to be messy," he said, "but we don't have a lot of time. Lie very still."

Rodney brought the blade to life and Teyla stared.

"I wish it had done that for me."

"You and me both," Rodney said.

He laid the edge of the blade against the skin of the Woard and began slicing carefully. Bit by bit he cut it away from Teyla, dragging the flesh off her in bloody chunks.

"God," Rodney said. "This thing is *disgusting*."

"Try being trapped beneath it."

"No thanks."

Rodney made a last cut, sheathed the sword again, and reached down. He grabbed Teyla under her arms and pulled, dragging her a few feet away from the beast.

"Oh!" Teyla hissed.

Rodney stopped. "Sorry."

Teyla clenched her jaw. "It is definitely broken."

Rodney glanced again at the door.

"We have a very short time to get out of this room, down a long passageway, up several levels and out the front gates to the catch up with Sheppard. Once they open that gate and go through — and it closes — it can't be opened again to the same location. Can you walk?"

"No. I am sorry, Rodney. You will have to leave me here, I cannot walk."

Rodney's mind went into overdrive. He knew he couldn't leave Teyla, but he also knew they didn't have much time. He glanced back toward the dragon, and there, canted on its side, rested the horse.

"Hold on," he said.

He ran to the fallen creature, grabbed it, and tried to lift. It didn't budge. He looked around for something to use as a lever and he saw the lance. He grabbed it, dragged it closer, and jammed it under the horse. He tried to pry it up, nothing happened.

Then his mind started to click. He was still wearing the helmet — it rested easily on his head and he'd hardly noticed it was there — flipped the visor down, and seized the lance by the pommel. It activated. Power rippled up and down the length of it and he jammed it under the horse again. He pictured the creature up on its feet, closed his eyes, and pushed. When he opened his eyes, the horse stood before him, still as a statue. It appeared to be staring at him, but he knew it wasn't.

He spun back to Teyla. Working quickly, he found two short sticks — probably some sort of fighting staves — and bound them into a splint on her injured leg with strips of cloth he tore from a ruined banner on the floor. Teyla grunted in pain, but gritted her teeth and kept from crying out.

"You're going to have to help me," he said. "I'm going to keep this lance active — it gives me more strength, but we have to get you up and onto that horse. I'm going to climb on behind you, and we'll ride it out of here. You ready?"

"I think you have lost your mind," Teyla said.

"Good," Rodney replied. "Then you and I are about on the same wavelength. Come on."

He planted the lance, held out his hand, and gripped Teyla's arm. She gritted her teeth against the pain, crying out once, but managed to get her good leg beneath her, leaning on the lance.

"Okay," Rodney said.

He slipped closer and got his shoulder under Teyla's arm. Together they limped and hopped over to the horse.

"That was the easy part," Rodney said.

Teyla stared at the creature.

"Rodney, are you sure?"

"I thought the same thing a while ago," Rodney answered. "The dragon got me past that."

Teyla stared at the beast, and then turned back to Rodney. He grinned.

"I am very impressed, Rodney. I believe Colonel Sheppard would say, 'I underestimated you'."

"I get that a lot," Rodney said. "Now climb aboard. We have to get going."

Teyla nodded. The two of them heaved, and somehow, miraculously, she ended up in front of the saddle.

Before anything could go wrong, Rodney swung up behind her and activated their mount. It hummed to life flawlessly, despite the rough treatment it had suffered, and Rodney dropped the visor into place.

Teyla leaned over the horse's neck, and Rodney reached over her for the reins.

"Let's do this," he said.

The horse started forward, and as they reached the exit, the doors swung wide. With a cry, Rodney drove the mechanical steed into the passageway and on up toward the main chamber. No one barred their path.

CHAPTER THIRTY-ONE

THE TEMPERATURE IN THE ARENA had grown uncomfortably warm. The heat rose a few degrees every fifteen minutes or so, and the people in the stands had begun to feel the effects. The musky scent of sweat filled the arena and small fights had begun to break out in the audience — the reality of their fate growing sharper as the temperature climbed. Cold drinks no longer stayed cold for longer than a few minutes, and though — for the moment — they were holding their own, Admah's environmental controls were working overtime. Normally they hummed quietly and only kicked into higher gear occasionally. Now the fans ran constantly, recirculating the air through increasingly inadequate cooling systems.

A maintenance crew worked at preparing the arena for the next bout, but their movements were slow and labored. They were slow to cart off the carcass of the fallen wolves, and the woman with the extra arms held them at bay for some time, refusing to give up her spot in the center of the arena. The crowd grew restless. Catcalls and cries for action reverberated from the walls. The cooling systems were pumping at full capacity but the air that sputtered and whistled through the vent system was just marginally cooler than the air in the arena. It was only a matter of time until it failed, and the heat became unbearable.

Outside the arena, Sheppard and his team moved quickly through the passageway to the main room. They met no resistance, and there were no audible alarms to report their escape. As they moved, the heat worked on them quickly. After only a short distance they were coated in sweat. When they'd last walked those halls the air had been cool and pleasant, but it was beginning to feel stagnant and humid. All of the wonders and luxuries of Admah were failing, and though it was still bearable, it was obvious that it would not be for long.

The hallway emptied into the main room and the team was greeted by a cooler gust of air. Drinks and pitchers still sat on the tables all over the room, and music played through the speakers in the walls. It was surreal, with the world about to end and the music still playing. "This way," Sheppard said, leading them on.

"Wait." Ronon had stopped and was staring off toward another door.

Sheppard tried to wipe the sweat from his face. "What?"

"It's only a little ways to the rooms where they held us. Our weapons are there, and the rest of our gear."

"If they didn't take them away," Cumby said. "It's getting pretty hot in here — we should just go."

Ronon frowned. He knew Cumby was right, but he couldn't stand the thought of losing his weapon. He glanced down at his belt where his gun was conspicuously absent. "I'm going to check, you go on ahead."

"We aren't splitting up," Sheppard said. "Let's make this quick."

Cumby looked unconvinced, and watched over his shoulder as they hurried down the side passage to where they'd been imprisoned. It was only a short way, but the heat, and uncertainty of their escape plan made it sound like a really bad idea. They reached the door, and Mara quickly opened it for them. Their things were right where the guards had tossed them. Ronon grabbed his gun and strapped it on. Sheppard slipped into his gear, leaving everything heavy behind. Cumby grabbed his equipment belt, but he looked as if he'd just as soon be without the extra weight.

"Now," Sheppard said. "If no one has any other little errands they'd like to run, I think we should get out of here. It's getting pretty hot."

"If we want to leave the city, we have to get out into the gardens," Mara said. "There's no shade. There's no water. It's going to be hot."

As they passed the bar in the main chamber, Sheppard paused to liberate several bottles of water. He tossed one to Ronon, and another to Cumby, and they tucked them away.

"This way." Mara pointed down a hall to the left.

Sheppard nodded and swallowed a huge gulp of water. "Let's move."

The echo of raised voices emanated from the long hall behind them. The words were indiscernible but the intent was clear. Saul had discovered their absence, and he was sending pursuit. Sheppard put a finger to his lips and motioned for them to hurry. They slipped out of the main room into the corridor beyond and back down the hall. Overhead, the lights guttered and went out for several beats, then came on again. Admah was dying.

They were halfway to the elevator when a group of guards burst into the hall behind them, and they were forced to turn and fight.

"You aren't going anywhere," the first guard called.

"There isn't anywhere to go. Come back to the arena and fight — it's a good way to meet eternity."

"We're getting out of here," Sheppard replied. "If any of you people had any sense you'd be following us, not chasing us. You feel how hot it is now? It isn't going to be instantaneous. You're going to slow roast, like meat on a spit."

"It's a glorious death."

"Yeah, I've heard all that. Good for you. You're missing your final entertainment, and we're not coming back. I guess you have some choices to make."

The men advanced, and Ronon, tired of all the talk, drew and fired in one smooth motion. The first man fell, and those behind him ducked up against the wall. Someone returned fire, his shot striking the wall about a foot from Mara's head. She screamed and ducked behind Ronon and Sheppard.

Joining Ronon, Sheppard sprayed short bursts into the passage, driving their pursuers back into the main hall.

"Go!" he yelled.

They turned and rushed up the stairs, but the heat made the climb difficult. Cumby started to lag behind, and Ronon grabbed him by the arm and dragged him forward.

"Keep moving," Ronon growled.

"I don't know if I can…"

"Then you'll die here," Ronon said.

Cumby didn't reply, but he also didn't slow down. Ronon kept his grip on the smaller man's shoulder and propelled him up the stairs. Mara held her own, staying close to Sheppard's side, and below they heard Saul's guards gathering. Ronon shoved Cumby up the stairs and spun. He fired twice, and the guards dove for safety. Moments later, the group reached the next level, turned, and bolted down the passageway. One more set of stairs, and they'd reach the surface.

"They don't seem to be following," Cumby said, glancing over his shoulder.

"They probably lost interest," Sheppard said. "Whether they catch us or not, what is Saul going to do? What does it matter? I think it's finally sinking in that they're all going to die, and it wasn't even their choice."

They continued on at a slightly slower pace, letting Cumby catch his wind.

"Here's the elevator," Mara said. "It's faster than the stairs."

Sheppard glanced up at the flickering lights and shook his head. "We can't trust it. The power could go at any time. The closer the city comes to that sun, the fewer systems will remain on line."

He moved forward to the stairs leading to the surface and started up. Mara followed, and Ronon brought up the rear, urging Cumby on as the climb grew longer and harder. The closer they got to the surface, the higher the temperature rose.

"We don't have much time," Sheppard said. "It has to be over a hundred degrees already."

"It will be worse outside," Mara said. "The city gives us protection from the sun."

"Thanks for the cheerful thoughts," Cumby grumbled. He stumbled up the last few steps and bent over, hands on his thighs and breathing heavily.

"Come on," Ronon said. "You can rest when we get back. I'll buy you a beer."

Cumby scowled at the big man.

They passed through the main control center, where Rodney had first accessed the city's systems. After the opulence below, the stark and abandoned looking spaces seemed alien and impossible. It was easy to see how the illusion had fooled the Wraith for so many years. It was also depressing. They stumbled out into the gardens and down the path. The heat slammed into them like a hammer blow as they made their way down the steps. The air was heavy and dry, and everything was far too bright. There was no sign of pursuit and after only a little ways in the overwhelming heat it was all they could do to focus on the ground ahead, and keep their feet in motion.

"It's not too much farther," Sheppard said.

He passed around the bottles of water he'd grabbed. They all drank some, and it helped a little. There wasn't much shade between the city and the gate. Grim faced and fighting their discomfort, they moved on.

Behind them, cries rose again, but they ignored the sound. They needed their strength to reach the gate, and whoever was behind them would fare no better. What it had come down to was a race, and they needed desperately to win.

CHAPTER THIRTY-TWO

THE TEMPERATURE HAD CLIMBED steadily as they moved closer to the surface but here, at the mercy of a huge and blazing sun, the temperature was a good thirty degrees higher than it had been down in the arena. Their bodies had adjusted to the slow increase in temperature but the blast that had struck them when they moved into the open was nearly unbearable.

They paused in the shade of one of the only trees beyond the garden, wishing desperately that it still had leaves, or more branches. They gulped the water as if they'd never see another drop. It seemed to pass right through them, gone as sweat as soon as the water was drunk. Sheppard drew in a deep breath and looked at Mara.

She swiped at her forehead with one arm. Her face was streaked with dirt and sweat and her lips were cracked from the heat, but still she was pretty. "It's not much further," she sighed. "Perhaps another quarter of a mile."

"I know." Sheppard nodded in the direction of the gate, but the last thing he wanted to do was leave the shade of that tree. "Let's get this over with."

Ronon took Cumby's arm again and helped him lever himself away from the tree. Ronon was used to hardship but this was nearly more than even he could bear. He was a big man, and the heat hit him hard.

They moved as quickly as possible across those hot, open spaces, headed for the city gates. They loomed in the distance, seemingly miles away. The water was going fast and the heat was increasing at an alarming rate. Even Sheppard began to doubt whether they would make it.

Mara stumbled and Sheppard grabbed her arm.

"Thank you." Her smile was weak and forced.

"Are you okay?"

She checked his face, saw genuine concern there. "As okay as I can be." She paused for a moment. "You didn't have to pretend, you know."

"Pretend what?" Sheppard feigned ignorance, but the conversation he had dreaded was upon him. They no longer needed Mara, but to have to face her with the truth of his deception was painful.

"You pretended that there was a special connection between the two of us, but all along we both knew you just needed me to get your people out of Admah." When no response was forthcoming from Sheppard, she pressed on. "Don't be ashamed. I understand. You're a good man and a good leader. You would have done anything to save your people. Even a love-sick and very bored woman like me can see that."

"I didn't want to hurt you. I honestly want you to come with us — to save yourself from this. You can't stay here."

She looked away, not answering him. "Your people would die for you, you know that? I can see it in their faces. As far as you are willing to go to protect them, they are willing to go just as far. That's loyalty."

"We've been together a long time. Been through a lot."

She nodded. "And I've been through a lot with my people, too." She jerked her head in the direction of the decrepit city. "They're all I've ever known, for what that's worth. Even Saul hasn't always been so…difficult."

They had reached the gates, two giant wrought iron structures which hung listlessly from the ends of the wall. Waves of heat washed over and around them, making the air swim for a moment with unrealized vapor. Ronon reached out one hand to shove the gate open a bit farther, a gesture as much of frustration as anything. Sheppard was about to tell him to stop when the sound of sizzling flesh filled the air.

"It's hot," Sheppard muttered to no one in particular.

"You think?" Ronon scowled and blew on his hand. It didn't help.

Ronon drew back, steadied himself, and kicked the gate hard. It swung open a few feet, leaving the shallow imprint of the wrought iron on the bottom of Ronon's boot. It made him feel better.

"It was already open," Cumby commented. "It's been open a very long time."

"Whatever," Ronon said.

They passed through the gates quickly, taking care not to touch any part of them. Mara paused before passing that border. She turned and stared back at the city, frowning.

"What is it?" Sheppard said, taking her arm.

"Nothing." She pulled away from him and walked on through the ruined gates.

"I really am sorry."

She studied him, his face streaked with dust and sweat, too red from the sun, and she sighed. "I know." And then she was through the gates, slipping into the group and away from Sheppard.

He went through last. It bothered him that he'd had

to lie to Mara and if there had been any other way, he wouldn't have done it. But he'd pay her back — he'd save her from this fiery death.

Before them lay a long stretch of open field, unfettered by trees or ground cover of any kind. Sheppard blinked hard, trying to force the sweat from his eyes.

"I can see the gate," Ronon offered, pointing into the distance.

Waves of heat roiled over the dead field and in the distance, the gate stood watch. Sheppard nodded and headed off in that direction. Dead grass lashed at their legs and crunched beneath their feet. There were no bugs to fly up into their faces and the sky was completely devoid of clouds. Whatever birds might have dominated the sky had long since died. In that barren, sun-baked landscape, Sheppard and his team were the only living things.

As they approached the gate, Sheppard stepped up to the DHD to activate it. Mara was close on his heels and she wavered where she stood. The sun beat down relentlessly, scorching the tops of their heads and making them all dizzy, despite the fact they'd pulled out jackets and other gear for shade.

"Hang on," Sheppard said, starting to dial, "we'll be out of here soon."

"You are in quite the hurry, Colonel Sheppard." Saul, looking half-dead from heat and fatigue, emerged from behind the gate. Behind him straggled a handful of guards, equally ragged from the heat. But they were armed and Sheppard didn't discount them for a moment. "Did they promise to take you with them?" Saul asked Mara. "Is that why you helped them? Did he tell you that he loved you?" Saul's face was a study in crimson, lost somewhere between crazy anger and pain.

Mara risked a look at Sheppard. The sight of his pained face tugged at her heart and she turned back to Saul. "I helped them because it was the right thing to do."

"Being loyal to your people isn't the right thing to do? You've spent your whole life with us and yet you betray your city in the end? Is that the right thing to do?"

She didn't know what to say. She stood, swooning in the heat, her arms limp at her sides.

Sheppard stepped between them, planting his feet firmly and fighting the urge to sit down. "Your type of loyalty leaves a lot to be desired. You force them to a certain death and you call that loyalty? They are loyal to you, you betray them. In any case, forcing us to be a part of it all? How is that 'the right thing'?"

"Not death, Colonel. Ascension. I'm leading them to a better place, a better plane of existence."

Sheppard turned on Mara, took her by the shoulders. "You don't believe that. You know what ascension meant to your ancestors. This isn't that — this is suicide. This is giving up. You don't have to die like this. You can come with us. You don't have to stay."

"Have you ever believed in something so strongly that you'd give your life for it?" Mara's eyes burned but no tears would come.

"Of course."

"That's how I feel, in a way. I feel like I've given my life already, and now it's time to let it go. I've spent my life here, with Saul and the others. Together, we've spent our entire lives betting. We bet on everything. Games, chance, life, death...it's all a gamble. Gambling is the only thing we know. But at the end of it all, the one thing that drives us is the biggest gamble of all — that there's some sort of meaning in what we do. I think we lost that bet. I know there's no ascension in this death, but for me — for us — ascension is a belief and a dream that died long ago. I believe we're going to have to settle for peace."

He shook her a bit. It was enough to steal her breath in the heat. "But not now. Not this way!"

"Maybe Saul is right. Maybe this is the right time and the right way. The gambit is over. There's nothing left for us. Our way of life was empty even before Saul steered us toward the sun."

"Listen to her, Colonel. She speaks the truth." Saul still looked tortured by the heat but beneath all that, there was a touch of arrogance, self-righteous indignation.

"Come with us." Sheppard's eyes pleaded with her. "There's a better life on the other side of that gate. A whole world. I can show you records of your people, the truth — the real truth. You just have to give me the chance to do it."

"There's a better life on the other side of death, as well," she said. "At least it won't be more of this."

Sheppard searched her face but could find no shred of hope there. He nodded and let go of her. Mara stepped down to where Saul stood and let him put one sweat-slickened arm around her shoulders.

"Be well, John Sheppard. And remember me."

Sheppard nodded, heaved a last, painful sigh. "Cumby," he said, "dial us up." She watched them go, one by one, to the safety of that other world. Ronon stepped through first, then Cumby. Sheppard went last, risking one last, agonized glance over his shoulder and pausing just before stepping through the gate. Then he lifted his hand to his head—a salute, she realized. But not for her; his gaze was fixed on the city—the final resting place of his fallen friends. "Dr. Rodney McKay, Teyla Emmagan," he said. "We won't forget you."

And then his eyes narrowed, peering into the distance, and his hand fell to his side. "What the hell...?"

CHAPTER THIRTY-THREE

LORNE AND HIS TEAM waited. The gate stood idle but the Wraith were not. Someone on that hive ship knew the team was there, and anything that even smelled odd was going to be checked out thoroughly. Lorne had only one objective: defend the gate at all costs, and watch for the moment Sheppard's team stepped through. They had no idea what they were crossing into, and it would be up to Lorne to provide cover fire.

He tried to occupy his mind by counting the times Sheppard had saved his life. He wouldn't let the Colonel down — couldn't let him down. Lorne just prayed that Sheppard would show up soon, hopefully before the Wraith.

The team was firmly ensconced in a small stand of trees just east of the gate. While the gate was clearly visible, it was some forty meters away. Standing out in the open was suicide. They could better defend the gate from the safety of the woods and, besides the cover, it offered shade. There was no way to know exactly how long they'd be there, and it was best to be prepared.

Lorne heard a small noise, sort of a hum and a whine. He stood very still and listened; he knew the sound only too well.

"Cover," he barked. "Wraith incoming."

The dart dropped in over the tops of the trees, closely followed by a second. They cruised by very low, and Lorne knew they'd be scanning for intruders. They were well hidden, but all it would take was a small break in the foliage overhead to give away their position.

"Stay down!" he hissed. He brought his gun up and held it ready, keeping a close watch on the trees, and listening for the next pass.

A patrol of Wraith warriors in their odd helmets broke from the trees, and at that moment the two darts returned, soaring overhead and providing cover as the ground forces rushed forward. One of them must have seen something, because he waved the others forward and signaled to the darts. The darts banked and returned, sailing up over the trees and bearing down on the team. Their cover was blown.

Lorne fired.

The darts were a good hundred feet away. On a good day it was a nearly impossible shot, but he took it and somehow he managed to clip the left stabilizer. The craft wavered, engines screaming, and then careened off over their heads. The damage wasn't enough to take it down, but it bought them some time. It turned in a wide, looping curve that brought it back on target.

Gravel and Verdino knelt back to back and opened up on the remaining dart, the others busy holding off Wraith ground troops. There were only scouts so far, and they were holding back. Lorne concentrated. He took aim again, focusing on the first dart. The Wraith ship fired back; the shots glanced off of the trees behind them and sent a hail of bark into the air.

The dart swept overhead again and another round rained down on them. The air filled with the acrid scent of burning foliage and melting sand. Lorne fired again.

He squeezed off two carefully aimed bursts, and the front stabilizer spun off through the air and the pilot lost control. The dart spun and crashed in the woods behind them. Lorne smiled grimly and turned toward the second ship.

Behind him, someone screamed. One of his men, a grizzled veteran named Simon, had been hit. He was rolling around on the ground and holding his shoulder. Smoke drifted up from his partially melted shirt and his face was a study in agony. Another man rushed in, grabbed him under his good arm and hauled him to the relative safety of the deeper woods.

The remaining dart whipped around and bore down on the group, spinning into position to pin them between its line of fire and the encroaching ground troops.

Lorne waved his arms furiously, firing as he spoke. "Fall back! Fall back! Take deeper cover."

They backpedaled into the woods, still firing. There were more darts now, and behind them a small fire had ignited, devouring the dead leaves and spiraling smoke up into the air.

Lorne's headset crackled, and he flinched. He hadn't been watching the time. Reports were scheduled every twenty minutes. Woolsey must have opened the gate to get a signal through. The commander's voice came across, a bit shrill.

"What in God's name is going on over there?"

Lorne thought about ignoring the call. He knew Woolsey was likely to order them back, but he wasn't ready to give up on Sheppard. He fired another burst.

"We're under attack, sir. I know we're scheduled for a report, but you need to close that gate. We're under fire from Wraith darts. There's a hive ship about a mile from here."

"You aren't equipped or manned to do battle on that scale. Get your team back to the gate. That's an order, Major."

Lorne fired off a few well-placed shots but they had no effect other than to cause the probe to momentarily veer off course. "With all due respect, Sir, there's no way. We're currently cut off from the gate, and even if we weren't, we haven't spotted Colonel Sheppard's team."

"It won't do Sheppard and the others any good if you die before they come through the gate."

"It won't do them any good if we tuck our tails and run — they'll be walking into an ambush. And Colonel Sheppard can't come through if you don't close the gate."

Behind him, someone else screamed.

The one remaining dart was firing on them from overhead. It had blasted a hole through the trees and was firing straight through it. From where it hovered, none of the men would get a clear shot. Lorne stepped out of the woods, standing in the open and planting his feet firmly in the grass. He knew he was risking being taken by the dart's culling beam, but he needed a shot.

He fired a single shot at the dart, and it zipped past, wheeling to turn on him. The Wraith pilot dropped a bit lower. Its culling beam activated, and it swooped straight at them. Lorne wasted no time. He blasted the thing with it everything he had. Someone stepped up beside him and also opened fire. It was Gravel. She stood her ground unflinchingly, and despite the danger of the moment, Lorne grinned.

The dart withstood their fire for a few seconds and showed no sign of damage. Lorne and Gravel continued firing, and eventually the constant barrage of shots chipped away at the craft's outer plating, opening a hole in its inner housing. Something leaked from the hole and the dart started to shift sideways as it passed, zigging and zagging closer to Lorne's position. The pilot could have turned away and tried to make it back to the hive ship, but instead he drove straight at Lorne, still firing.

The dart's final shot struck the ground at Lorne's feet, and he staggered back, grabbing Gravel by the arm and pulling her to safety. As he backed away, he continued to fire from his hip. He watched as the dart spun out of control. Apparently the pilot was finally attempting to flee the scene and escape to the safety of the hive ship. Then very suddenly the nose dipped, the ship whirled like a top and crashed into several treetops. About forty meters away, it hit the ground and exploded.

A cheer rose from the embattled team and Lorne sprinted to where the two injured men rested against the trees.

Verdino and Gravel helped the injured men back through the trees, concealing his position as well as possible. The rest of the team covered them, scanning the jungle for any lingering Wraith. The gate stood dormant.

"Okay, Sheppard," he muttered. "Any time now. Any time."

Woolsey sat and stared at his console in frustration; he hated waiting. He hated not knowing what was going on. He hated that there was nothing more he could do to help.

A young man tapped him on the shoulder, and he spun. "What is it?"

"Mr. Woolsey, the *Daedelus* is hailing us."

"Patch them through," he said, grateful for the distraction. "Colonel Caldwell, I have to tell you — I could really use some good news."

"I'm afraid I don't have good news, Woolsey. We can't reach Admah in time. I'm afraid there's nothing we can do."

Woolsey bit into his lip and slumped further. "Damn!" He paused for a moment, thinking. "Is there any way you can reach M3T-842? We have a team there waiting for Sheppard and his people to come through the gate. They might need some backup."

Caldwell's voice was muffled as he spoke to his people. "We're close," he said. "And we're on our way. Caldwell out."

Woolsey shut down the console and stood up again. At least help was on the way for Lorne and his team.

"If that gate opens, send for me immediately," he said. Then stiffly, as if he'd been through a fight, he walked from the room.

CHAPTER THIRTY-FOUR

RODNEY CLUNG to the reins, doing his best to help support Teyla, who was weak and having trouble remaining upright with one injured leg. The mechanical horse flew up the stairs as if it was climbing a gentle grassy slope. There was no hesitation, and there was no drop in speed, despite the steep incline and the tricky footing. All pursuit fell away behind them, and he knew if he could just keep them both mounted long enough to reach the upper level there was no way those coming up from behind could catch them

He also noticed that it was hot. Very hot. The adrenalin of the initial charge was giving way to a queasy, sweaty haze that fogged his vision and slicked his hands. It was more difficult to grip the reins and his strength grew less with every passing moment. He wished he'd taken the time to find a drink, but back in the chamber, just off the arena, the heat hadn't been as obvious. It had been warmer, but now they were approaching the surface of Admah. Nothing stood between them and the approaching sun but a steadily thinning atmosphere.

The horse climbed the final few steps and leveled out.

"Oh thank God," Rodney said.

He turned the horse toward the control room and the gardens beyond. The colorful posters on the wall that had fascinated the team on their way in mocked him.

He watched them as he passed, but they blurred into a surreal wash of colors and shadows. He turned past the control room and wondered if there was anything he was forgetting, something he should do to the computer system, but by the time the thoughts were fully formed they'd already moved past and into the great hall leading to the gardens and the gates of the city.

Rodney watched it all and frowned. Something was different, something important. Then he laughed, and the laugh became a dry, rasping cough, as he realized the only thing that was different was that he was sitting astride a horse. It all looked smaller somehow. He tried to pull himself together. The stairs leading down into the gardens would probably prove more difficult to manage than those they'd already climbed, and they were approaching fast.

He tried to sit up straighter. He wished he'd taken off the helmet. It was adding its weight to the heat. Sweat dripped from it down his neck and over his face. He felt as if every ounce of liquid was being steamed from his body. He expected to see the steam rising any moment, and to feel his flesh baking. He was staring at his arm in fascination when they reached the top of the steps. Without warning or hesitation the horse dove down the steps.

Rodney screamed. The visor of the helmet, jarred by the sudden motion, dropped over his face, and the armor of the Ancients came to life once more. He felt a sudden energy — and he managed to squeeze the horse with his knees, though he had no idea how he'd known to do it. Teyla started to slip, but Rodney gripped her and found that he could lift her easily back into position.

There was no time to wonder at the seeming magic of the Ancient creature he rode. He turned its head toward the gate and kicked his heels, hoping that it was a universal symbol for go like a bat out of hell. His mount reacted, whether to the nudge from his knees, or the thought from his mind. He knew it didn't matter. He had new strength, and there was a chance they'd make it to the gate. From there, he'd take his chances. If the others were gone, and the gate was closed, he'd open another one to somewhere, anywhere, and he'd dive through it. He might die wherever he ended up, but he would not die sitting by helplessly as he plunged into a sun.

He held Teyla in place on the neck of the horse easily. Somehow her extra weight no longer mattered. His vision was sharper. They slipped through the broken gate and onto the fields beyond, breaking into a full gallop, and Rodney actually threw back his head and cried out with the sudden rush of power. The faster the horse ran, the stronger he became. The land was rough; Rodney remembered it from their trip in. Though it flew by quickly, he was aware of every variance in the pitch of the ground, or shift in the terrain. It was strange, but he had the odd sensation that the horse was feeding on the freedom, the chance to run.

In the distance, he could just make out the clearing where the gate stood. There was motion there, and for a fleeting moment he thought it might be the team. He tried to call out, but despite the energy the visor and the armor were giving him, he couldn't bring his parched lips to part and emit sound. In that moment he became aware of just how precarious his situation was. He was empowered by the armor and the visor, but if it failed, or if it was knocked free somehow, he wouldn't move another inch.

"Swell," he whispered.

They charged toward the gate, and though he still hoped he'd find the others there, some instinct drove his hand to the handle of his lance and he pulled it from its sheath. As he drew nearer he saw a small crowd gathered before him in a semi-circle. Some held weapons, and two — standing behind them — merely watched, wide-eyed, as he approached.

The gate shimmered, the wormhole open, and Colonel Sheppard stood with one arm rammed into the event horizon — holding the gate open — watching in amazement. The two nearest the DHD came into focus, and Rodney realized it was Saul — and Mara. The others were guards. They held their weapons loosely, obviously feeling the heat and barely able to remain upright.

"Stop him!" Saul croaked, staggering backward and flinging Mara from him. Rodney saw with horror that he was headed for Sheppard. It looked as if he intended to force the Colonel through and close the gate. If he reached it — if he managed to overpower Sheppard in some mad burst of strength — it was over. Rodney reacted without thought.

He raised the lance and a bolt of energy shot from the end of it. It caught Saul in the back and sent the man reeling. He lurched toward Sheppard, who waited for him and thrust him aside at the last moment, keeping his arm inside the event horizon. The others, seeing the fire shoot from the lance, dove for cover. Rodney lowered his head, held tight to Teyla, and with a last burst of speed cut through the parting guards and dove into the heart of the Stargate. Sheppard stepped as far as he could to one side, then, when Rodney was safely through, he followed.

CHAPTER THIRTY-FIVE

WOOLSEY WAS JARRED FROM his thoughts by his radio. He jerked up, not sure what had been said, only that there had been a sound.

"What is it?"

"The *Daedalus*, sir," came the excited voice. "Colonel Caldwell."

"Patch him through," Woolsey said, sitting upright.

"Mr. Woolsey?" Caldwell's voice crackled over the speaker.

"This is Woolsey," he said. "Where are you?"

"We're in position, sir. We've scanned '842 and located your people. From the numbers, it looks like Colonel Sheppard's team has joined them."

"Why haven't they opened the gate?" Woolsey said, stomach knotting. "Why are they still there, if Sheppard is back?"

"My best guess?" Caldwell said, half a question. "They can't get to the DHD."

"Can you help?"

"I'll do what I can," Caldwell said. "We're keeping a low profile — don't want to alert that Hive ship to our presence. As far as I can see, they've only sent darts and ground troops to the gate. They don't know what the threat is, and they aren't committing fully until they do. That buys me a little time. I'm going to go in and give them some cover fire, but I won't have long — as soon as

I start firing, the Wraith will know I'm there. I have to get out before they can send any serious pursuit."

"Understood," Woolsey replied. "Can't you transport them out?"

"I don't know. We'll be moving fast, and under fire — it would be crap shoot. If I can't get them out safely they'll have to use the gate."

"Very well. Do what you can, Colonel. Woolsey out."

He sat and stared into the distance for a moment, then contacted the control room.

"Stand by to receive both teams," he said. "Have medical on alert."

He sat and waited, staring at the wall. There was nothing else he could do, nothing but sit and wait. The matter was in other hands — in capable hands, no doubt, but that didn't ease his tension. He felt powerless, just sitting there in the calm halls of Atlantis while other men and women fought and, perhaps, died. This, he realized, was the true burden of command; he wondered if he would ever get used to its weight…

"Bring them home, Colonel," he said with a sigh. "Just bring them all home."

CHAPTER THIRTY-SIX

THE SKY WAS BRIGHT, SO BRIGHT it was painful to look at it for more than a second. Saul ignored the pain. He lay back in Mara's arms, staring and gasping for breath. There had been clouds in the sky once, but they were gone, burned away by the heat. Nothing stood between the surface of their moon and the searing heat of the sun. Saul coughed. It turned into a fit that seemed as if it might consume all that remained of his breath, and to make it worse, he began to laugh.

Mara shook him gently.

"Stop it! You need your strength."

"For what?" Saul coughed out. "Oh, I had plans, didn't I? The grand finale. Do you think they are still holding the entertainments in Admah? Do you think they have let out all the gladiators to roam the halls and find what pleasure they can in their final moments? Perhaps they are just fainting in their seats, giving way to the heat, or seeking one last cold drink. The party never ends, in Admah…"

"It has ended," Mara said softly. "I think maybe it ended a long time ago. We've been parodying what we once were — going through the motions and losing ourselves in whatever sensation presents itself, but there is nothing new. Nothing has been new for so long I can't even remember when the boredom first set in."

"You were always quicker than the others," Saul said.

"You have seen things sooner, understood them better. And I? I have been the one who was blind. I had this vision, this final moment of glory that would make all of it worthwhile and usher us toward a higher realm."

Deep, heaving coughs cut off his speech, and he doubled up in pain. Mara held him tighter, clutching him to her sweaty body and laying her head on his shoulder. Eventually the coughing passed. Saul laid very still, and Mara thought for a moment that he might be finished. Then he regained control, and continued.

"I wish that they had never come, Colonel Sheppard and his team. I wish that they had gone to any of a thousand worlds they might have enjoyed and left us to the façade of our brilliance. I had it worked out so carefully. It was going to be so…splendid."

"It was never going to be splendid," Mara chided him. "It was going to end. That is what we have all been seeking, even if we weren't willing to admit it. There is nothing left on the road we chose so long ago. When our brethren took the higher road — the road to ascension, we chose to descend and see just how far down we could go. Over the past few days, the answer to that became too obvious, and we reacted poorly. We should have let them go. Maybe we should have gone with them, or turned the city away and traveled."

"There was a time when that was still possible," Saul said. "I can remember thinking about it — dreaming about it — standing in the conservatory and watching the stars and wondering why we did what we did day after day and night after night."

"We did it for you," Mara said. "You know that, and you knew that. We did it because you convinced us that it was the right thing to do. We believed in you when we knew deep inside that we should believe in ourselves and seeking our own fulfillment. It was the easy way—the entertaining way."

"It was entertaining, wasn't it?" Saul said.

"It certainly had its moments."

Saul coughed again, and this time blood trickled from the edge of his mouth. He fought through the pain.

"It's ironic," he said.

"What?"

"This…" He tried to wave his arm, but it nearly sent him into another fit, and he grew still. "I wanted so much to see that last moment—to ride Admah into the next level of existence—to feel the heat wash over me and melt me and make me one with all the molecules of the universe. I planned it, I dreamed of it, and in the end…it was my inability to let go of the material world that cost me my own dream. If I'd just seen Sheppard and the others on their way—just kept my eyes firmly on the future. If I'd just understood how much it meant to me…"

He stiffened then and with a rasping gasp sagged against her. He was gone. Mara stroked his hair and watched his still face for a moment, then gently eased him off her lap and onto the parched ground. She stood, and found the effort almost more than she could bear. Turning, she saw that the guards who had accompanied them still waited. They leaned on trees or lay sprawled on the ground. The heat bore down and through them all.

"Let's try to make it back to the city," Mara said. "It won't be much comfort, but it will be some. If Saul will miss the finale, it doesn't mean that we all should."

She began walking back toward the city. One of the

guards, a tall young man with dark hair, stepped up beside her and offered his arm for support. She took it gratefully and, leaning on one another, they staggered back toward Admah. Behind them, the others struggled along as well as they could. They moved very slowly, and the city seemed to be miles distant. The air wavered with heat.

Very distantly, Mara was aware of the heat of the ground burning up through her shoes to the soles of her feet, and that her clothing clung to her, matted with sweat. She wished she'd brought water, knew it wouldn't help, and kept on putting one foot in front of the other.

"Do you think," she asked the guard through thick, parched lips, "that the bar will be open?"

They both laughed, and it nearly did them in. Then, without another word, they continued on toward the city.

CHAPTER THIRTY-SEVEN

THE GATE WAS SURROUNDED on all sides by Wraith ground troops. Sheppard was about to order Cumby and Ronon back into the jungle for cover, when a sudden blast of energy vaporized one of the Wraith darts. In the center of the clearing, impossibly, the horse of the Ancient's reared. Rodney sat astride it and, across the beast's neck, Teyla clung for dear life.

"What the hell?" Cumby said. "Rodney?"

The lance fired again, sending a rippling blast of energy across a line of advancing Wraith ground troops."

"I don't believe it," Ronon said. He stood and ran forward, drawing his weapon and flanking Rodney's charge.

"There's equipment here," Cumby called out, "but I don't see a team."

"Get your weapon and stay out the line of fire." He ducked behind the scant shelter of the gate and toggled his radio. "This is Colonel Sheppard. Does anyone copy?"

The radio squawked. "Colonel Sheppard, this is Lorne. Sir, it's good to hear your voice."

"Where are you?" Sheppard shouted as a dart screamed overhead.

"Not far from the gate, Colonel, but we can't get close enough to dial Atlantis. We're pinned down — there's too many of them."

Sheppard glanced over to where Rodney swung the

lance of the Ancients from side to side, skewering Wraith warriors and sending bursts of power into their ranks, driving them into retreat. Beside him, using the horse as a shield, Ronon backed him up.

"Get back to the gate, we've got you covered," Sheppard said. "But you aren't going to believe how unless you see it."

"On my way."

Rodney barely had time to think. He'd fired at the dart instinctively, but now that he'd had a moment to take in his surroundings, he saw the surrounding forest was alive with Wraith. Above them, more darts appeared. He knew Sheppard must be behind him, and Ronon had stepped up at his side. When there was a temporary break, he turned. Teyla was weakening, and she'd started to slump off the side of the horse. Rodney grabbed her easily in one armor-strengthened arm and lowered her to the ground. He turned, and saw Sheppard rushing up from behind.

Rodney turned back to the battle without another glance. The helmet had brought his mind to life in ways he was unaccustomed to…he was aware of threats almost before they occurred, and the armor reacted with incredible speed. It was almost as if he was only along for the ride.

There were two darts closing in. Rodney spurred the Ancient horse and it veered to one side, drawing fire away from where Teyla had fallen. He raised the lance, aimed, and a bolt of energy slammed into one of the two darts. It dove off to one side, and he spun sending a bolt at the second, even as his mount spurred forward to avoid incoming fire.

He vaguely heard Sheppard behind him, ordering others

to move up and provide cover, but he was one with the helmet, and the horse, and the lance moved almost of its own accord. He fired again and again, lunging from side to side to avoid incoming fire. The Wraith on the ground began to converge. He took a last shot at one of the darts. It struck home and the craft wobbled, made a hideous screeching sound, and slammed in through the trees overhead, disappearing into another explosion of flame.

Rodney ditched the lance. He drew the great sword and spun, driving his mount along the front rank of Wraith. He slashed right, and then left, and then drove his blade deep through the armor of a third Wraith soldier. A fourth came at him from the left, and he tried to pivot back. Before he could make it, Ronon stepped in. The big man fired, and the Wraith reeled back. Rodney caught the gleam of battle in Ronon's eyes, and he smiled, though no one could see it beneath the helmet.

He felt it. His normal reaction to a situation like this was nothing but a very strong urge toward self-preservation, but now — with the visor guiding him and the Ancient weapons giving him strength and speed — he felt invincible.

Lorne came up suddenly on the other side and with him two others. Rodney thought one of them was named Gravel, but he couldn't quite recall. They advanced on the retreating Wraith with a vengeance, keeping in a tight group.

Cumby turned and stared at the approaching Wraith. He saw the others battling for their lives, and stared incredulously at Rodney, who led the attack. Then he turned, and nodded to himself. It was his turn to make a contribution. He hunkered down low to make as small a target as possible, and he ran toward the DHD. He didn't look at the battle again. Either he'd make it, or he wouldn't. He'd never actually dialed an address for a gate, but he'd seen it done dozens of times and for him that amounted to owning the skill. He knew the address for Atlantis. He knew the addresses of every gate that had been opened since he'd been part of the Atlantis crew, and several others he'd chanced across in the course of his work.

He had no experience in battle and was terrified, but he kept moving. Somehow, seeing Rodney and Teyla again, when he'd thought they were dead, opened an unexpected reserve deep inside him. He wanted to be part of it. He wanted to do something that mattered, and this was his chance. He wanted to open that gate.

A blast from one of the Wraith weapons shot past him and he ducked, but he didn't look up to see where it had come from. He kept his head down, and he ran for the DHD. When he finally turned and put his hands on it, he saw that Sheppard wasn't far behind him. The colonel was dragging Teyla's limp body, dodging blasts as well as possible.

Cumby hunched over the DHD, closed his eyes and concentrated. He saw the symbols in their proper order, opened his eyes, and began to press buttons. He tried not to pay attention to the firefight just beyond the gate. He ignored the fact the charge was being led by a medieval knight on a mechanical horse. The symbols on the gate began to illuminate, and his fingers flew over the Ancient glyphs.

"Hurry!" Sheppard called.

Cumby pressed the final glyph. The gate lit up, the

glowing space inside the giant ring pressed out as if something was rushing through from within, then snapped back and settled.

Lorne barked a command, and Ronon, Gravel, Verdino and the others began to slowly backpedal toward the gate. Within moments, Rodney found himself alone in front. He tried to order the horse to retreat, but apparently it was programmed for one thing, and one thing only. To do battle. There were still enemies faced off against him, and the visor sighted in on them, one after another. He slashed out with the sword again, dropping a Wraith warrior, and then sheathed it, reaching once more for the lance.

The whine of incoming darts filled the air and the stallion reared. Rodney leaned into it, gripped with his knees, and leveled the lance at the tree line. Two darts soared up into sight, and he fired. He hit the first one directly and it spun out of control, but the second returned fire. The blast struck the front of the horse and it reared again, this time too fast and too hard. As it went up and over, Rodney spun, aimed, and fired. He caught the rear of the dart as it passed overhead and it burst into flames, canted crazily to the right and dove into the trees. It met the ground with a scream of tortured metal. Rodney let go of the lance and tried to hold his balance, but it was no use. The horse was not meant for the angle it had reached, and it toppled. He dove clear, crashed to the ground, and bounced hard.

"Get through the gate!" Sheppard cried. He ran to where Rodney had fallen, reaching out to grab him by the arm. He stopped, stunned, when Rodney bounced to his feet, brushed himself off, and turned.

The Wraith realized that the advantage had shifted and surged forward. Rodney glanced up and saw that they were only yards away.

Then there was a sudden roar of engines, and the front line of Wraith were nearly cut in half by a sudden blast from above. Cover fire drove the advancing Wraith quickly into the woods.

Sheppard screamed, "Rodney! Run! The gate!"

Rodney nodded, and the two sprinted after the others. Ronon and Lorne stood, one to each side of the gate, offering covering fire. The others had gone through. Behind them, the Wraith were still in retreat, firing randomly after Sheppard and Rodney.

"Go!" Sheppard cried to the others. "Get through and close the gate!"

He dove, and Rodney dove beside him. Ronon and Lorne let loose a final burst of fire and spun through after them.

As they passed through, the gate shimmered and closed.

The room was as silent as a tomb for about ten seconds, and then everyone seemed to talk at once. Rodney stood, and Sheppard stared at him. His jacket had come open, and a small device glowed on his chest. Sheppard recognized it immediately. It was the small personal force-field Rodney had nearly trapped himself in shortly after reporting to Atlantis. He'd wondered what happened to the thing.

"When were you planning on mentioning you were wearing that?" Irritated, he pushed Rodney so hard he fell over backward — and bounced right back to his feet with a grin. Sheppard shook his head, not amused. "We thought you were dead, Rodney. We nearly left you behind."

"Sorry, the time never seemed quite right," McKay said. "I just figured that it might come in handy." He grinned, and then deactivated the device. "You never can tell."

Sheppard let out a breath and turned away, just in time to see the medical team lifting Teyla onto a gurney. She was conscious and, despite her pain, she smiled at him. "We made it."

"Yeah." He stepped over and put his hand on her arm, feeling her solid and real beneath his touch. Thank God. A sudden rush of emotion caught him by surprise, choking him, and he had to clear his throat a couple of times before he could say anymore. "I thought…"

"I know," she said, covering his hand with her own. "I am sorry to have given you cause for concern."

"Concern?" He half laughed, a bark of giddy emotion. "Yeah, 'concern' is exactly what it was." Then he squeezed her arm again and jammed his hands into his pockets; after the relief came the guilt. "Listen, I'm sorry. I should have gone back for you. I shouldn't have left without — "

"Had you done so," she said, her voice strong despite her injuries, "we would not have survived."

He looked at her from beneath his brow. "You don't know — "

"Rodney could not have carried us all on his horse," she said with a smile. "And without it, we could not have reached the gate in time. Of that, I am certain."

"Still…"

"You did what was right, John," she said. "And what I would have done, had the situation been reversed."

For a moment he held her gaze and there was honesty there, like there always was with Teyla. She wouldn't lie to him, not about this or anything else. And then she was wheeled away and he watched her until she was out of sight.

He turned to Woolsey, who stood to one side looking uncomfortable, and offered a tired salute. "Thank you," he said. "Thanks for getting us home. And if you get a chance, thank Caldwell for that cover fire. He cut it pretty close, but Rodney and I wouldn't have gotten out without his help."

"Of course," Woolsey said, awkward as he often was, but sincere nonetheless. "And thank you, Colonel, for bringing them back."

Sheppard smiled. "Any time, sir," he said. "Any time."

CHAPTER THIRTY-EIGHT

BOTH TEAMS had gathered around the conference table for the debriefing. Woolsey sat at the head of the table. As usual, he had papers and a folder before him, and he shuffled through them as he gathered his thoughts. Teyla's leg was in a cast, and several others appeared a bit the worse for wear. Still, they were back, and they were safe.

"So," Woolsey said, glancing up at last. "This Saul has been imprisoning travelers in his city for a very long time. I find myself wondering how many of those creatures in the entertainment started life as simple visitors — how much blood was spilled."

"For what it's worth," Sheppard said, "I saw no indication that they modified actual living beings. The 'adversary's' seem to have been created from genetic material, blended from Wraith and races we've never even encountered."

"That dragon, for one," Rodney said. "I mean, who grows something like that?"

Woolsey stared at Rodney for a moment, and Rodney fell silent, looking a bit sheepish. "Well," he said, "it was big."

"Yes, Rodney," Sheppard cut in. "We were all proud of the way you stood up to the dragon, and that charge out of the gate, I won't forget that any time soon. But you *were* wearing a force field that literally removed you from any real danger."

"You mean other than being left behind to be burned to a crisp by a sun? Or maybe you're talking about how I got Teyla out of there? Sort of like Lancelot and Guinevere, wasn't it? None of that was too risky; I mean, on a scale of one to ten…"

Ronon laughed. "You did a good job. You killed a dragon. Isn't that enough?"

Rodney tilted his head to the side, as if caught halfway between two thoughts, clamped his lips together, and nodded. "I think that will be…fine."

"If we could get back to the debriefing?" Woolsey said, clearing his throat. "We gained little from this excursion, other than information."

"We have the lance," Rodney said quickly, "and the visor. We're analyzing them to see if any of the weapons technology can be adapted. I think we might be near some real breakthroughs."

"That's fine," Woolsey said, "but we have storerooms full of artifacts and an entire Ancient database we've only begun to delve into. The last thing we needed was more to investigate."

"But…" Rodney started.

Woolsey held up his hand. "Be that as it may," he said, "I am going to consider this mission a success. We actually learned some things about the interface of the gates and the DHD, and thanks to Mr. Cumby, we have identified at least one warning message that — previously," he glanced at Rodney pointedly, "we have overlooked."

"I think we learned something about the Ancestors, as well," Teyla said. "We've encountered them at their finest, and we've encountered them when they were so detached that nothing mattered but their ascension. These were very—human. They were flawed, and selfish, violent and in love with their own warped form of entertainment. They were far from perfect, despite their age, and the knowledge they've accumulated over the centuries. No matter how well a civilization starts out...its ending is determined by the culture that is shared."

"They aren't Gods," Sheppard said. "They are beings, just like we are. They've been around a lot longer, they've learned things we haven't, but they're as prone to mistakes and flaws as any of us. Some of them found their way—others found..."

The door opened, and a young man stepped into the room.

"Sir, you asked me to call you when it was time."

Woolsey nodded. He stood slowly. "If you will all join me in the control room?"

The others glanced at one another, then rose slowly and filed out. Woolsey came last. He still carried his papers, but he no longer pretended to be worrying about reports or paperwork.

As he entered the room, Woolsey said, "Go ahead, Colonel Caldwell, put it on screen."

The screen flickered to life and the image of the city of Admah came into focus, relayed back to them via the long-range sensors of the *Daedalus*. The surface of the moon rippled with heat haze. The light from the star, very close, licked at the walls of the city and the air shimmered. Smoke rolled over the stones.

"It won't be long now," Woolsey said.

"Do you think anyone in there could still be alive?" Cumby said. "I mean, the city was built by the Ancients. Surely they have ways to seal themselves off—shields or some sort of —"

"Nothing is going to save them," Sheppard said. "They might still be alive, and they might even remain alive a little bit longer, but nothing survives that. Saul knew what he was doing when he chose his final act."

"He never got to see it," Rodney said.

They all turned to him.

"He was at the gate when I passed through. I fired at him with the lance. I don't know if it killed him, but I'm sure he never made it back to the city. I think I also damaged the gate. It was closing when we leaped through. They really were trapped."

"Nothing you could have done would have changed that," Woolsey said. "They would have kept you there too if they could. They would have kept all of you. "

Rodney nodded, but he turned back to the screen. They all watched as Admah and its moon reached the point of no return. The surface began to glow and then to crumble. Its descent toward the center of the sun sped up, and as they watched it began to melt, slowly at first, and then running like lava, until finally, in a flash of fire that filled the screen, it disappeared forever.

Sheppard stood very still. He thought of Mara, and remembered the last few moments they'd spent — the look in her eyes as she turned away and returned to Saul.

"Goodbye," he said. "If there's a better place, I hope you find it."

The screen went dark. No one spoke as they turned and disappeared into the city. The gate stood large and empty, and Woolsey stared into that giant eye as if it had secrets he could read. Finally, he shook his head and walked away. As if noticing it for the first time, he turned to the paperwork in his hand. Somehow he thought he'd better get it finished soon. There was no telling when the next disaster might strike and he knew he had to be ready.

SNEAK PREVIEW
STARGATE ATLANTIS: HOMECOMING

Book one of the Legacy series

by Jo Graham & Melissa Scott

AZURE STREAKS FLASHED AND DANCED, blue shifted stars shapeless blurs in the speed of her passage. Atlantis cruised through hyperspace with the majesty of Earth's old ocean liners, her size impossible to guess in the infinity of space. Her towering spires and thousands of rooms were nothing compared to the vast distances around her. Atlantis glided through hyperspace, her massive engines firing white behind her, shields protecting fragile buildings and occupants from the vacuum.

Behind, the Milky Way galaxy spun like a giant pinwheel, millions of brilliant stars stabbing points of light in the darkness. Atlantis traversed the enormous distance between galaxies, hundreds of thousands of light years vanishing swifter than thought. Even with her enormous hyperdrive, the journey was the work of many days.

It was nine days, Dr. McKay had predicted, from Earth to Lantea, Atlantis' original home in the Pegasus Galaxy, deserted these two and a half years since they had fled from the Replicator attack. Of all the places their enemies might seek them, they were least likely to look where they were certain Atlantis wasn't.

Of course, no one person could stay in the command chair that controlled the city's flight for nine days, not even lost in the piloting trance that the Ancient interfaces fostered. Not even John Sheppard could do that. Lt. Colonel Sheppard had come to Atlantis five and a half years ago at the beginning of the expedition, and the city had come to life at his touch. The City of the Ancients awoke, long-dormant systems coming on slowly when someone with the ATA gene, a descendant of the original builders, came through the Stargate. Atlantis had been left waiting. Though it had waited ten thousand years, humans had returned.

But even Sheppard could not spend nine days in the chair. The Ancients would have designated three pilots, each watching in eight hour shifts, but the humans from Earth did not have that luxury. Sheppard was First Pilot, and Dr. Carson Beckett, a medical doctor originally from Scotland, was Second. Twelve hour shifts were grueling, but at least allowed both men time to eat and sleep.

Five days of the journey gone, 20:00 hours, and Dr. Beckett was in the chair. His eyes were closed, his forehead creased in a faint frown, his arms relaxed on the arms of the chair, his fingers resting lightly on the interfaces. Nearly six years of practice had made him a competent, if reluctant, pilot. And so it was Dr. Beckett who noticed it first.

It was one tiny detail, one anomaly in a datastream of thousands of points, all fed through the chair's controls and interpreted by the neural interfaces that fed data straight into Beckett's body, as though all of Atlantis' enormous bulk was nothing more than the extension of himself.

It felt like...a wobble. Just a very faint wobble, as when driving an auto along the highway you wonder if one of the tires is just a little off. It might be that, or it might be the surface of the road. Nothing is wrong on the dashboard, so you listen but don't hear anything, and just when you've convinced yourself you imagined it entirely, there it is again. A wobble. A very small movement that is wrong.

Perhaps, Beckett thought, if you were borrowing a friend's car you wouldn't notice it at all. You'd just think that was how it was. But when it's your own car, lovingly cared for and maintained every 5,000 km, you know something is not quite right. Perhaps one tire is a little low. Perhaps you've dinted the rim just a tad, and the balance is not entirely even. It's probably not important. But if you're the kind of man who keeps your car that way, you know. You notice.

Beneath the blue lights of the control room, Beckett's eyes opened. The young technician monitoring the power output looked around, surprised. It was very quiet, watching someone fly Atlantis.

His tongue flicked over his lips, moistening them, reminding himself of his own physical body, and then he spoke into the headset he wore. "Control, this is Beckett. I've got a wobble."

There was a long moment of silence, then his radio crackled. "Say it again. You've got a what?"

"A wobble," Beckett said. "I don't know a better word for it."

"A wobble." The voice was that of Dr. Radek Zelenka, the Czech scientist who was, with Dr. McKay, one of the foremost experts on Ancient technology. Certainly he was one of the foremost experts on Atlantis, having spent most of the last five and a half years repairing her systems.

"It doesn't feel right," Beckett said. "I don't know how to put it better, Radek. It feels like a tire about to go off."

"Atlantis does not have tires, Carson," Zelenka replied.

"I know it doesn't." Beckett looked up toward the ceiling, as though he could see Zelenka in the gateroom many stories above, no doubt bent worriedly over a console, his glasses askew. "That's what it feels like. That's how my mind interprets it."

"He says we have a wobble. Like a flat tire." Zelenka was talking to someone else. "I do not know. That is what Carson says."

"A wobble?" That was McKay, the Canadian Chief of Science. "What's a wobble, Carson?"

"It feels wrong," Beckett said. "I don't know how to explain the bloody thing! It feels like there's something wrong."

"I am seeing nothing with propulsion," Zelenka said. Beckett could see how he would say it, his hands roving over the control board, data reflected in his glasses. "Everything is well within the normal operating parameters."

"I think I would interpret a propulsion problem as an engine light," Beckett said slowly.

"And a tire is what?" McKay would be putting his head to the side impatiently. "Do you think you can give me engineering, not voodoo? Your vague analogy is next to worthless."

Lying back in the chair, Beckett rolled his eyes. Five and a half years he'd put up with Rodney bullying him over this damned interface. "Something to do with the hyperdrive?" he ventured.

"The hyperdrive. That's very informative. The hyperdrive is a major system, Carson. It has literally tens of thousands of components."

"I don't know any more than that, all right?" Beckett snapped. "If you want a second opinion, get Sheppard down here and have him take a go at it."

"He has only been off duty for two hours," Zelenka said, presumably to McKay. "He is probably still in the mess hall. I can call him." McKay must have nodded, because his next words were not addressed to Beckett. "Colonel Sheppard to the command chair room. Sheppard to the command chair room."

He should love being pulled away from his dinner after a twelve hour shift. Beckett felt vaguely guilty about that. He sat up a bare ten minutes later as Sheppard barreled into the room, an open bottle of soft drink in his hand, his dark hair ruffled.

"What's the problem?" Sheppard said. He couldn't be too worried if he'd brought along his drink. Soft drinks were rare in Atlantis, since they had to be brought from Earth, and though they'd laid in a limited supply it could be expected to run out soon. Sheppard was unwilling to abandon his short of murder and mayhem.

Beckett smiled ruefully. For all their differences of background and skills, he had developed a considerable respect for Sheppard in their years of working together, a respect he thought was mutual. "Sorry to take you from your dinner. I've got an anomaly I can't pin down." He sat up, letting the chair come upright, the sticky interfaces disengaging from his fingertips. "It feels like a wobble. You know. When you've got a tire about to go."

Sheppard frowned and put his drink down on the edge

of the platform. "Ok. Let's have a look," he said with the air of a man about to look under a friend's hood.

Beckett stood up, catching himself for a moment on the arm of the chair. It always felt very strange to settle back into his mere physical body after some time in the interface.

Sheppard slid into the chair and leaned back, his eyes closing as the interfaces engaged, the chair lighting around him as power flowed, a profound expression of peace on his face. Beckett knew better than to interrupt. Sheppard's fingers twitched lightly in the interface, then stilled. He would be diving into it now, the pathways of the city's circuits and cables mirroring the neural pathways of his mind. Done right, impulses flowed like thoughts, data streaming effortlessly into easy interpretations. Beckett usually did not find it quite that simple. Practice and diligence had made him a competent pilot for the city, but he had never quite gotten the knack of thinking in three dimensions, of visualizing so many moving points completely. He wasn't a pilot. He was a medical doctor who through some trick of genetics had the particular piece of code that the city responded to. Sheppard was in his twentieth year in the Air Force, a man whose natural talents ran this way, honed by years of experience in high speed aircraft. He could get a lot more out of the interface than Beckett could.

It was nearly fifteen minutes before Sheppard surfaced, his eyes opening and the chair tilting halfway up. His glance fell on Beckett, but he spoke into his headset. "Control, this is Sheppard. We've got an anomaly in the number four induction array."

"The east pier," Zelenka said. "*Zatraceně!* Will we ever get that piece of trash fixed?"

"Carson's the one who tore it up fighting with the hive ship," McKay said. "And I thought we had it. I ran a stress test on it the night before we left."

"Well, you must have missed something," Zelenka said. "Because here we go with it again."

"It doesn't look like it's that bad," Sheppard said, cupping the headset and straightening up completely in the chair. "It's a wobble, like Carson said. It's not a flat. It's just a variance in output."

"A crashingly small one," McKay said. "I've got the power log in front of me now. Five one hundredths of one percent."

"After running at full power for five days?" Zelenka was probably leaning over McKay's shoulder, looking at the numbers. "No wonder you didn't catch it. That is nothing. We cannot expect every system to run at optimal for days on end. It would not show up in a stress test."

"Give me the summary." That was a new voice, Richard Woolsey, Atlantis' commander. "Should we drop out of hyperspace?" He was probably hovering over the two scientists by now.

It was McKay who spoke, of course. "And do what? We're between the Milky Way and the Pegasus Galaxy, right in the middle of a whole lot of nothing. I'm not seeing any kind of damaged component that we can repair, or quite frankly anything that amounts to a problem. Carson, it's nice of you to tell us about every little wobble, but this is just that. A little, tiny wobble."

Sheppard looked at Beckett and shrugged. "That now we know about. So we can keep an eye on it. It's just exactly like a tire. You may not need to run and do something about a little dent in the rim, but you keep an eye on it."

Beckett unhunched his shoulders, putting his hands in his pockets.

"Yes, well. We will keep an eye on it," McKay said. "But I think we can all take a deep breath and put this away."

Sheppard stood up, flexing his hands as he withdrew them from the interface.

"I'm sorry to put you to trouble," Beckett said. "I hope your dinner's not cold."

"It's ok." Sheppard picked his drink up off the floor. "Better safe than sorry. And we should keep an eye on that. You have a little wobble in your tire one minute, and the next thing you know you have a blowout doing eighty."

"And that would be bad," Beckett said, imagining what the analogy to a high speed blowout might be piloting a giant Ancient city through hyperspace between galaxies. It would put a pileup on the M25 to shame.

"Damn straight," Sheppard said, taking a drink of his soda. "See you at 06:00, Carson."

"This turn and turn again is getting old," Beckett said. "What I'd give for another pilot!"

"We couldn't exactly bring O'Neill with us under the circumstances," Sheppard said.

"Four more days," Beckett said. "Over the hump." He slid back into the chair, feeling the interfaces clinging to his fingertips in preparation. "See you in the morning." He closed his eyes, sinking into Atlantis' embrace.

Nearly seven days of the journey gone, 02:47 hours. The control room was quiet, only the gentle counterpoint of machine noises breaking the silence. By their purely arbitrary designation, it was the middle of the night. Airman First Class Salawi, a new third shift controller, put her coffee carefully on the rubberized mat that Dr. McKay had specially constructed for Atlantis' sloping control boards. At the station above on the upper tier, Dr. Zelenka had the watch, his glasses on the end of his nose as he scrolled through something on his laptop.

Salawi sighed. Three hours and a bit more of her shift. Somehow, she had thought keeping watch on a massive alien city on its way to another planet would be a little more exciting. She had been doing it for a week now, and nothing interesting had happened yet. She glanced down at her screen again, the data streaming almost too fast to make sense of it.

And then her board went crazy.

"Dr. Zelenka!"

He careened around the corner at an alarming rate, nearly throwing himself into her lap in his haste to get to the board, all the while letting forth a stream of invective in a language she didn't understand. "Move, now. There." She slipped out of her seat, catching her coffee before it landed on him as he ran his hands over the unfamiliar alien keys.

"I don't know what happened," Salawi said. "I didn't do anything!"

"I know you did not," he gave her a swift sideways look, a half nod that was reassurance. "This is something in the hyperdrive induction array."

"What the hell just happened?" His radio squawked, Scots accent obvious even over Zelenka's headset.

"I do not know, Carson." Zelenka's hands were flying, pulling up one incomprehensible menu after another. "I am trying to find that out." He spared a glance for the Airman at the gate board. "Get Dr. McKay up here. And

Colonel Sheppard too." He leaned back, looking along the board to Dr. Kusanagi at the far end as the overhead lights flickered. Another incomprehensible expletive. "Miko, get the power variance under control! We are having a serious problem."

"I'm losing systems," Beckett said over the radio from the chair room stories below. "I've just lost the lateral sublight thrusters. The sublight engines have lost power."

"What does that mean?" Salawi asked.

"It means Dr. Kusanagi had better stop the power fluctuations," Zelenka said grimly.

"I have not got it!" Kusanagi called from the other end. "I have rerouted the priority to the shield, but I cannot stop the power drain. We are using power too fast!"

"If the shield goes..." Nobody answered her. Salawi could guess what that meant. The fragile glass windows of the control room were not meant to take hard vacuum. If the shield failed they would blow out in an explosive decompression that would fling them into space. The question would be whether they would be torn apart before or after they asphyxiated.

"It is the hyperspace corridor," Zelenka said. "Why are you doing this!"

"The power usage is increasing exponentially," Kusanagi called. "It's pulling from all available systems."

Zelenka cupped the mouthpiece of the headset. "Carson, shut it down! Bring us out of hyperspace now!"

"We're not..."

"Bring us out now!" Zelenka shouted. "I do not have time to argue with you!"

The city shook. No, shuddered was more the word.

Salawi had felt something like this before, in an earth-quake, the terrifying bone-deep movement at the core. The lights flickered and died, the screens of the laptops blanking though the Ancient displays were steady. The city heaved, throwing her to one knee beside the board, lukewarm coffee splashing over her hands.

Outside, the blue of hyperspace faded, blue to black, the pinprick lights of a million wheeling stars.

"Jesus Christ," Beckett said over the radio. "What the bloody hell was that?"

Zelenka held on to the edge of the board and shoved his glasses back up his nose with one finger. "We are spinning. Carson, can you level us out?"

"Not without the lateral thrusters!" Beckett said indignantly. "I've got no power to any propulsion systems. Get me some power and I'll see what I can do."

Zelenka's hands skimmed the board. "I am doing. I am doing."

Colonel Sheppard came charging up the steps from the lower doors, in uniform pants over a faded t shirt that proclaimed him a patron of Johnson's Garage, his hair askew. "What happened?" he demanded.

"We have a problem in the hyperdrive induction array," Zelenka said, not even looking up from his screen. "It started pulling power from other systems. Kusanagi rerouted priority emergency power to the shield so we did not lose that. I had Carson drop us out of hyperspace."

"Where are we?" Sheppard asked.

"That is the least of our troubles at the moment." Zelenka spared him a sideways glance, and Sheppard swallowed.

Dr. McKay bounded up the stairs two at a time in

what appeared to be flannel pyjama pants with a uniform jacket over them. "What did you do?"

"The number four induction array went crazy," Zelenka said. "Carson's little wobble, remember?" He looked at McKay over the top of his glasses. "As much as I can tell, it started opening a wider and wider hyperspace corridor, and drawing sufficient power to do so from all available systems."

"Did you…" McKay began.

"I had Carson drop us out of hyperspace. All the propulsion systems are offline."

Salawi moved out of the way so that McKay could crowd into the board. "Did you…"

"Yes, of course I did."

"Would somebody like to tell me what that means?" Sheppard asked, scrubbing his hand over his unshaven chin.

McKay shoved Zelenka over, his hands on the Ancient keys.

Zelenka looked round at Sheppard. "When a ship opens a hyperspace window, the window occupies real space. It has a location and a size. The larger the ship, the larger the window it needs to open. This is intuitive, yes? The Daedalus does not require as large a window as a hive ship, nor a hive ship as this city. And the size of the window determines the power requirements. A big window requires exponentially more power than a small window. Daedalus could not open a window for Atlantis. She would not have enough power to do so." He spread his hands. "It looks like the induction array malfunctioned and began expanding our hyperspace window as though the city were much larger than it is. To do so, it pulled power out of all other major systems to sustain an enormous hyperspace envelope."

"That's not the only thing it pulled power out of," McKay said grimly. "The ZPMs are at 20%. It's eaten our power."

Teyla Emmagen folded her hands on the conference table in front of her, tilting her head toward Rodney as he spoke.

"We've restored power to all vital systems, but that's not going to do it for us. The shield draws massive amounts of power, and it's not optional. So rather than have the kind of involuntary rolling shutdown we had before, we're shutting down systems manually."

"Water filtration, for example," Radek said from the other end of Woolsey's conference table. "We have ten days supply already clean. We can resume filtration when it's necessary."

"And of course power to unoccupied parts of the city," Rodney said. "But I cannot stress enough that this is not going to help much."

"So we're all going to die." John leaned back in his chair. "What's the bad news?"

"No," Rodney said shortly. "We are not all going to die. At least I hope not."

At the head of the table, Richard Woolsey looked as though his head were hurting. "Is there enough power for the hyperdrive?"

"Yes," Rodney said.

"No," Radek said.

They exchanged a glance. "There is technically enough power," Rodney said. "But it doesn't matter. The overload has destroyed the induction array command crystal, one of those beautiful Ancient parts that we have no idea how to make. We've learned how to repattern some of the less complex crystals, the ordinary ones used in many systems, but the command crystal for the hyperdrive is much more complicated. We would need to pull it and replace it, and as we have no idea how to synthesize even an ordinary one…"

"The answer is no," Radek said.

"I was coming to that," Rodney said.

Teyla thought Woolsey looked as though he wished to kill them both. It seemed like time to sum up. "So the hyperdrive is inoperable, and will be for the forseeable future?"

Rodney pointed a forefinger at her and gave her a smile. "Got it in one."

"No rolling shutdowns?" John asked, letting his chair spring forward again and resting his elbows on the table. Teyla remembered all too clearly the last time Atlantis had been lost in space, power depleted by the Replicator weapon that had nearly killed Elizabeth Weir. She was quite certain that he remembered far too clearly as well.

"Not at this point," Radek assured him.

"So where are we?" Woolsey asked, a question directed to John rather than the scientists. Atlantis' command chair gave a far clearer picture of their navigational situation than any other.

"Just inside the Pegasus Galaxy," John said, tilting his head to the side. "A couple of hours earlier and we'd be in real trouble. As it is, there are three systems in reasonable sublight range, none of them with Stargates and only one of them in Atlantis' database. It's a binary system."

"No inhabitable planets," Rodney said. "They're all too close to one or another primary."

Woolsey twitched. "And the other two?"

"We are analyzing data now," Radek said. "The odds are reasonable that one of them will have a suitable planet."

"And if they don't?" Woolsey asked.

Rodney's face was eloquent. "They'd better. We can't get anywhere else. May I stress that we are right on the fringe of the Pegasus Galaxy? The stars are not exactly thick out here."

"If they do have an inhabitable planet, why did the Ancients not build a Stargate there?" Teyla asked.

"Perhaps they did and it was lost," Radek said.

"And the Daedalus is thirteen days out," John said. "Minimum."

"We can last that long," Rodney said. "Assuming we can communicate our position."

"Then let's get to it," Woolsey said, rising to his feet.

Teyla lagged behind, falling into step with him as the conference room emptied. "We were in far worse condition last time," she said reassuringly.

Woolsey gave her a grim look. "You aren't wishing you'd stayed on Earth?"

"That was not an option under the circumstances," Teyla said.

Coming home...
October 2010

STARGATE UNIVERSE: AIR

by James Swallow
Price: £6.99 UK | $7.95 US
ISBN-13: 978-1-905586-46-2
Publication date: November 2009

Series number: SGU-01

Without food, supplies, or a way home, Colonel Everett Young finds himself in charge of a mission that has gone wrong before it has even begun. Stranded and alone on the far side of the universe, the mismatched team of scientists, technicians, and military personnel have only one objective: staying alive.

As personalities clash and desperation takes hold, salvation lies in the hands of Dr. Nicholas Rush, the man responsible for their plight, a man with an agenda of his own…

Stargate Universe is the gritty new spin-off of the hit TV shows Stargate SG-1 and Stargate Atlantis. Working from the original screenplay, award-winning author James Swallow has combined the three pilot episodes into this thrilling full-length novel which includes deleted scenes and dialog, making it a must-read for all Stargate fans.

A new danger lurks in the Pegasus Galaxy

STARGATE ATLANTIS

HOMECOMING
Book one of the LEGACY SERIES

Jo Graham & Melissa Scott

Based on the hit television series created by
Brad Wright & Robert C. Cooper

Series number: SGA-16

STARGATE ATLANTIS: HOMECOMING

Book one in the new LEGACY SERIES

by Jo Graham & Melissa Scott
Price: £6.99 UK | $7.95 US
ISBN-10: 1-905586-50-7
ISBN-13: 978-1-905586-50-9
Publication date: October 2010

Atlantis has returned to Earth, its team has disbursed and are beginning new lives far from the dangers of the Pegasus galaxy. They think the adventure is over.

They're wrong.

With the help of General Jack O'Neill, Atlantis rises once more – and the former members of the expedition must decide whether to return with her to Pegasus, or to remain safely on Earth in the new lives they enjoy...

Picking up where the show's final season ended, Stargate Atlantis Homecoming is the first in the exciting new Stargate Atlantis Legacy series. These all new adventures take the Atlantis team back to the Pegasus galaxy where a terrible new enemy has emerged, an enemy that threatens their lives, their friendships – and the future of Earth itself.

STARGATE ATLANTIS: DEATH GAME

by Jo Graham
Price: £6.99 UK | $7.95 US
ISBN-10: 1-905586-47-7
ISBN-13: 978-1-905586-47-9
Publication date: September 2010

Colonel John Sheppard knows it's going to be a bad day when he wakes up in a downed Jumper with a head wound and no memory of how he got there.

Things don't get any better.

Concussed, far from the Stargate, and with his only remaining team mate, Teyla, injured, Sheppard soon finds himself a prisoner of the local population. And as he gradually pieces the situation together he realises that his team is scattered across a tropical archipelago, unable to communicate with each other or return to the Stargate. And to make matters worse, there's a Wraith cruiser in the skies above…

Meanwhile, Ronon and Doctor Zelenka find themselves in an unlikely partnership as they seek a way off their island and back to the Stargate. And Doctor McKay? He just wants to get the Stargate working…

Order your copy directly from the publisher today by going to www.stargatenovels.com or send a check or money order made payable to "Fandemonium" to:

<u>USA orders:</u> $10.95 ($7.95 + $3.00 P&P).

<u>Rest of world:</u> $13.95 ($7.95 + $6.00 P&P)

Send payment to: Fandemonium Books, PO Box 2178, Decatur, GA 30031-2178 USA.

Or check your local bookshop – available on special order if they are out of stock (quote the ISBN number listed above).

STARGATE ATLANTIS: HUNT AND RUN

Ronon's past catches up with him

STARGATE ATLANTIS™

HUNT AND RUN

Aaron Rosenberg

Based on the hit television series created by Brad Wright and Robert C. Cooper

Series number: SGA-13

by Aaron Rosenberg
Price: £6.99 UK | $7.95 US
ISBN-10: 1-905586-44-2
ISBN-13: 978-1-905586-44-8
Publication date: June 2010

Ronon Dex is a mystery. His past is a closed book and he likes it that way. But when the Atlantis team trigger a trap that leaves them stranded on a hostile world, only Ronon's past can save them — if it doesn't kill them first.

As the gripping tale unfolds, we return to Ronon's earliest days as a Runner and meet the charismatic leader who transformed him into a hunter of Wraith. But grief and rage can change the best of men and it soon becomes clear that those Ronon once considered brothers-in-arms are now on the hunt — and that the Atlantis team are their prey.

Unless Ronon can out hunt the hunters, Colonel Sheppard's team will fall victim to the vengeance of the *V'rdai*.

Order your copy directly from the publisher today by going to www.stargatenovels.com or send a check or money order made payable to "Fandemonium" to:

<u>USA orders</u>: $10.95 ($7.95 + $3.00 P&P).

<u>Rest of world</u>: $13.95 ($7.95 + $6.00 P&P)

Send payment to: Fandemonium Books, PO Box 2178, Decatur, GA 30031-2178 USA.

Or check your local bookshop — available on special order if they are out of stock (quote the ISBN number listed above).

STARGATE ATLANTIS: DEAD END

by Chris Wraight
Price: £6.99 UK | $7.95 US
ISBN-10: 1-905586-22-1
ISBN-13: 978-1-905586-22-6
Publication date: June 2010

Trapped on a planet being swallowed by a killing ice age, Colonel Sheppard and his team are rescued by the Forgotten — a race abandoned by those who once protected them, and condemned to watch their world die.

But when Teyla is abducted by the mysterious 'Banshees', Sheppard and his team risk losing their only chance of getting home in a desperate bid to save Teyla and to lead the Forgotten to a land remembered only in legend.

STARGATE ATLANTIS: ANGELUS

by Peter Evans
Price: £6.99 UK | $7.95 US
ISBN-10: 1-905586-18-3
ISBN-13: 978-1-905586-18-9

With their core directive restored, the Asurans have begun to attack the Wraith on multiple fronts. Under the command of Colonel Ellis, the Apollo is dispatched to observe the battlefront, but Ellis's orders not to intervene are quickly breached when an Ancient ship drops out of hyperspace.

Inside is Angelus, fleeing the destruction of a world he has spent millennia protecting from the Wraith. Charming and likable, Angelus quickly connects with each member of the Atlantis team in a unique way and, more than that, offers them a weapon that could put an end to their war with both the Wraith and the Asurans.

But all is not what it seems, and even Angelus is unaware of his true nature — a nature that threatens the very survival of Atlantis itself...

STARGATE ATLANTIS: NIGHTFALL

A terrifying weapon threatens the Pegasus galaxy

STARGATE ATLANTIS.

NIGHTFALL

James Swallow

Based on the hit television series created by Brad Wright and Robert C. Cooper

Series number: SGA-10

by James Swallow
Price: £6.99 UK | $7.95 US
ISBN-10: 1-905586-14-0
ISBN-13: 978-1-905586-14-1

Deception and lies abound on the peaceful planet of Heruun, protected from the Wraith for generations by their mysterious guardian—the Aegis.

But with the planet falling victim to an incurable wasting sickness, and two of Colonel Sheppard's team going missing, the secrets of the Aegis must be revealed. The shocking truth threatens to tear Herunn society apart, bringing down upon them the scourge of the Wraith. Yet even with a Hive ship poised to attack there is much more at stake than the fate of one small planet.

For the Aegis conceals a threat so catastrophic that Colonel Samantha Carter herself must join Sheppard and his team as they risk everything to eliminate it from the Pegasus galaxy...

STARGATE SG-1: OCEANS OF DUST

by Peter J. Evans
Price: $7.95 US | £6.99 UK
ISBN-10: 1-905586-53-1
ISBN-13: 978-1-905586-53-0
Publication date: March 2011

Something lurks beneath the ancient sands of Egypt. It is the stuff of Jaffa nightmares, its name a whisper in the dark. And it is stirring…

When disaster strikes an Egyptian dig, SG1 are brought in to investigate. But nothing can prepare them for what they find among the ruins. Walking in the dust of a thousand deaths, they discover a creature of unimaginable evil – a creature the insane Goa'uld Neheb-Kau wants to use as a terrible weapon.

With Teal'c and Major Carter in the hands of the enemy, Colonel O'Neill and Daniel Jackson recruit Master Bra'tac to help track the creature across the galaxy in a desperate bid to destroy it before it turns their friends – and the whole galaxy – to dust…

STARGATE SG-1: SUNRISE

by J.F. Crane
Price: $7.95 US | £6.99 UK
ISBN-10: 1-905586-51-5
ISBN-13: 978-1-905586-51-6
Publication date: February 2011

On the abandoned outpost of *Acarsaid Dorch* Doctor Daniel Jackson makes a startling discovery – a discovery that leads SG1 to a world on the brink of destruction.

The Elect rule Ierna, ensuring that their people live in peace and plenty, protected from their planet's merciless sun by a biosphere that surrounds their city. But all is not as it seems and when Daniel is taken captive by the renegade Seachráni, Colonel Jack O'Neill and his team discover another side to Ierna - a people driven to desperation by rising seas, burning beneath a blistering sun.

Inhabiting the building tops of a long-drowned cityscape, the Seachráni and their reluctant leader, Faelan Garrett, reveal the truth about the planet's catastrophic past – and about how Daniel's discovery on *Acarsaid Dorch* could save them all...

Order your copy directly from the publisher today by going to www.stargatenovels.com or send a check or money order made payable to "Fandemonium" to:

<u>USA orders:</u> $10.95 ($7.95 + $3.00 P&P).

<u>Rest of world:</u> $13.95 ($7.95 + $6.00 P&P)

Send payment to: Fandemonium Books, PO Box 2178, Decatur, GA 30031-2178 USA.

Or check your local bookshop – available on special order if they are out of stock (quote the ISBN number listed above).

STARGATE SG-1: FOUR DRAGONS

Jack takes matters into his own hands to save Daniel

STARGATE SG·1

FOUR DRAGONS

Diana Botsford

Based on the hit television series developed by
Brad Wright and Jonathan Glassner

Series number: SG1-16

by **Diana Botsford**
Price: $7.95 US | £6.99 UK
ISBN-10: 1-905586-48-5
ISBN-13: 978-1-905586-48-6
Publication date: August 2010

It was meant to be a soft mission, something to ease Doctor Daniel Jackson back into things after his time among the Ancients – after all, what could possibly go wrong on a simple survey of ancient Chinese ruins? As it turns out, a whole lot.

After accidentally activating a Goa'uld transport ring, Daniel finds himself the prisoner of Lord Yu, the capricious Goa'uld System Lord. Meanwhile, SG1's efforts to rescue their friend are hampered by a representative of the Chinese government with an agenda of his own to follow - and a deep secret to hide.

But Colonel Jack O'Neill is in no mood for delay. He'll go to any lengths to get Daniel back — even if it means ignoring protocol and taking matters into his own hands.

STARGATE SG-1: THE POWER BEHIND THE THRONE

by Steven Savile
Price: $7.95 US | £6.99 UK
ISBN-10: 1-905586-45-0
ISBN-13: 978-1-905586-45-1
Publication date: August 2010

SG-1 are asked by the Tok'ra to rescue a creature known as Mujina.

The last of its species, Mujina is devoid of face or form and draws its substance from the needs of those around it.

The creature is an archetype – a hero for all, a villain for all, depending upon whose influence it falls under.

And the Goa'uld Apophis, understanding the potential for havoc Mujina offers, has set his heart on possessing the creature...

STARGATE SG-1: VALHALLA

by Tim Waggoner
Price: $7.95 US | £6.99 UK
ISBN-10: 1-905586-19-1
ISBN-13: 978-1-905586-19-6

Upon the legendary fields of Valhalla, the spirits of Viking warriors do eternal battle in service to their god, Odin. By night they feast and toast the fallen, but at dawn the dead are restored to fight until the end of times.

When SG-1 find themselves trapped in this endless battle, prisoners of Odin, they must discover the strange truth about Valhalla before it is too late — and then confront the giant, Surtr, a terrible and immortal enemy bent on revenging himself against his god.

In order to defeat Surtr, Carter suggests using a naquadrium power cell Jonas Quinn has developed on his home world, but when she and Colonel O'Neill arrive on Langara they realize their problems have only just begun...

STARGATE SG-1: HYDRA

by Holly Scott & Jaimie Duncan
Price: $7.95 US | $9.95 Canada |
£6.99 UK
ISBN-10: 1-905586-10-8
ISBN-13: 978-1-905586-10-3

Series number: SG1-13

Rumours and accusations are reaching Stargate Command, and nothing is making sense. When SG-1 is met with fear and loathing on a peaceful world, and Master Bra'tac lays allegations of war crimes at their feet, they know they must investigate.

But the investigation leads the team into a deadly assault and it's only when a second Daniel Jackson stumbles through the Stargate, begging for help, that the truth begins to emerge. Because this Daniel Jackson is the product of a rogue NID operation that spans the reaches of the galaxy, and the tale he has to tell is truly shocking.

Facing a cunning and ruthless enemy, SG-1 must confront and triumph over their own capacity for cruelty and violence in order to save the SGC – and themselves...

Order your copy directly from the publisher today by going to www.stargatenovels.com or send a check or money order made payable to "Fandemonium" to:

<u>USA orders:</u> $10.95 ($7.95 + $3.00 P&P).

<u>Rest of world:</u> $13.95 ($7.95 + $6.00 P&P)

Send payment to: Fandemonium Books, PO Box 2178, Decatur, GA 30031-2178 USA.

Or check your local bookshop – available on special order if they are out of stock (quote the ISBN number listed above).

STARGATE
SG·1

STARGATE
ATLANTIS

STARGATE UNIVERSE

Original novels based on the hit TV shows **STARGATE SG-1, STARGATE ATLANTIS** and **STARGATE UNIVERSE**

AVAILABLE NOW
For more information, visit
www.stargatenovels.com